Barbara Pym has been acclaimed as 'the most underrated writer of the century' (Philip Larkin). Pym's substantial reputation evolved through the publication of six novels from 1950 to 1961, then resumed in 1977, after a hiatus of sixteen years, with the publication of *Quartet in Autumn* and three other novels. She died in 1980.

# JANE AND PRUDENCE

# JANE AND PRUDENCE

## BARBARA PYM

A Dutton Obelisk Paperback

DUTTON / NEW YORK

OBELISK/DUTTON
Published by the Penguin Group
Penguin Books USA Inc., 375 Hudson Street, New York, New York 10014, U.S.A.
Penguin Books Ltd, 27 Wrights Lane, London W8 5TZ, England
Penguin Books Australia Ltd, Ringwood, Victoria, Australia
Penguin Books Canada Ltd, 2801 John Street, Markham, Ontario, Canada L3R 1B4
Penguin Books (N.Z.) Ltd, 182–190 Wairau Road, Auckland 10, New Zealand

Penguin Books Ltd, Registered Offices:
Harmondsworth, Middlesex, England

This is an authorized reprint of a hardcover edition published by E. P. Dutton.

First Obelisk paperback printing, June, 1990
10 9 8 7 6 5 4 3 2 1
Library of Congress Catalog Card Number:
90–81367

ISBN 0-525-48570-8

Printed in the United States of America

# JANE AND PRUDENCE

# *Chapter One*

JANE AND Prudence were walking in the college garden before dinner. Their conversation came in excited little bursts, for Oxford is very lovely in midsummer, and the glimpses of grey towers through the trees and the river at their side moved them to reminiscences of earlier days.

'Ah, those delphiniums,' sighed Jane. 'I always used to think Nicholas's eyes were just that colour. But I suppose a middle-aged man – and he is that now, poor darling – can't have delphinium-blue eyes.'

'Those white roses always remind me of Laurence,' said Prudence, continuing on her own line. 'Once I remember him coming to call for me and picking me a white rose – and Miss Birkinshaw saw him from her window! It was like Beauty and the Beast,' she added. 'Not that Laurence was ugly. I always thought him rather attractive.'

'But you were certainly Beauty, Prue,' said Jane warmly. 'Oh, those days of wine and roses! They are *not* long.'

'And to think that we didn't really appreciate wine,' said Prudence. 'How innocent we were then and how happy!'

They walked on without speaking, their silence paying a brief tribute to their lost youth.

Prudence Bates was twenty-nine, an age that is often rather desperate for a woman who has not yet married. Jane Cleveland was forty-one, an age that may bring with it compensations unsuspected by the anxious woman of twenty-nine. If they seemed an unlikely pair to be walking together at a Reunion of Old Students, where the ages of friends seldom have more than a year or two between them, it was because their relationship had been that of tutor and pupil. For two years, when her husband had had a living just outside Oxford, Jane had gone back to her old college to help Miss Birkinshaw with the English students, and it was then that Prudence had become her pupil and remained her friend. Jane had enjoyed those two years, but then they had moved to a suburban parish, and now, she thought, glancing round the table at dinner, here I am back where I started, just another of the many Old Students who have married clergymen. She seemed to see the announcement in the *Chronicle* under *Marriages*, 'Cleveland-Bold', or, rather, 'Bold-Cleveland', for here the women took precedence; it was their world, the husbands existing only in relation to them: 'Jane Mowbray Bold to Herbert Nicholas Cleveland.' And later, after a suitable interval, 'To Jane Cleveland (Bold), a daughter (Flora Mowbray)'.

When she and Nicholas were engaged Jane had taken great pleasure in imagining herself as a clergyman's wife, starting with Trollope and working through the Victorian novelists to the present-day gallant, cheerful wives, who ran large houses and families on far too little money and sometimes wrote articles about it in the *Church Times*. But she had been quickly disillusioned. Nicholas's first curacy had been in a town where she had found very little in common with the elderly and middle-aged women who made up the greater part of the congregation. Jane's outspokenness and her fantastic turn of mind were not appreciated; other qualities which she did not possess and which seemed impossible to acquire were apparently necessary. And then, as the years passed and she realised that Flora was to be her only child, she was again conscious of failure, for her picture of herself as a clergyman's wife had included a large Victorian family like those in the novels of Miss Charlotte M. Yonge.

'At least I have had Flora, even though everybody else here has at least two children,' she said, speaking her thoughts aloud to anybody who happened to be within earshot.

'I haven't,' said Prudence a little coldly, for she was conscious on these occasions of being still unmarried, though women of

8

twenty-nine or thirty or even older still could and did marry judging by other announcements in the *Chronicle*. She wished Jane wouldn't say these things in her rather bright, loud voice, the voice of one used to addressing parish meetings. And why couldn't she have made some effort to change for dinner instead of appearing in the baggy-skirted grey flannel suit she had arrived in? Jane was really quite nice-looking, with her large eyes and short, rough, curly hair, but her clothes were terrible. One could hardly blame people for classing all university women as frumps, thought Prudence, looking down the table at the odd garments and odder wearers of them, the eager, unpainted faces, the wispy hair, the dowdy clothes; and yet most of them had married—that was the strange and disconcerting thing.

Prudence looks lovely this evening, thought Jane, like some-body in a woman's magazine, carefully 'groomed', and wearing a red dress that sets off her pale skin and dark hair. It was odd, really, that she should not yet have married. One wondered if it was really better to have loved and lost than never to have loved at all, when poor Prudence seemed to have lost so many times. For although she had been, and still was, very much admired, she had got into the way of preferring unsatisfactory love affairs to any others, so that it was becoming almost a bad habit. The latest passion did not sound any more suitable than her previous ones. Something to do with her work, Jane believed, for she had hardly liked to ask for details as yet. The details would assuredly come out later that evening, over what used to be cocoa or Ovaltine in one of their bed-sitting-rooms when they were students and would now be rather too many cigarettes without the harmless comfort of the hot drink.

'So you have all married clergymen,' said Miss Birkinshaw in a clear voice from her end of the table. 'You, Maisie, and Jane and Elspeth and Sybil and Prudence . . .'

'No, Miss Birkinshaw,' said Prudence hastily. 'I haven't married at all.'

'Of course, I remember now – you and Eleanor Hitchens and

Mollie Holmes are the only three in your year who didn't marry.'

'You make it sound dreadfully final,' said Jane. 'I'm sure there is hope for them all yet.'

'Well, Eleanor has her work at the Ministry, and Mollie the Settlement and her dogs, and Prudence, her work, too . . .' Miss Birkinshaw's tone seemed to lose a little of its incisiveness, for she could never remember what it was that Prudence was doing at any given moment. She liked her Old Students to be clearly labelled – the clergymen's wives, the other wives, and those who had 'fulfilled' themselves in less obvious ways, with novels or social work or a brilliant career in the Civil Service. Perhaps this last could be applied to Prudence? thought Miss Birkinshaw hopefully.

She might have said, 'and Prudence has her love affairs', thought Jane quickly, for they were surely as much an occupation as anything else.

'Your work must be very interesting, Prudence,' Miss Birkinshaw went on. 'I never like to ask people in your position *exactly* what it is that they do.'

'I'm a sort of personal assistant to Dr. Grampian,' said Prudence. 'It's rather difficult to explain. I look after the humdrum side of his work, seeing books through the press and that kind of thing.'

'It must be wonderful to feel that you have some part, however small, in his work,' said one of the clergymen's wives.

'I dare say you write quite a lot of his books for him,' said another. 'I often think work like that must be ample compensation for not being married,' she added in a patronising tone.

'I don't need compensation,' said Prudence lightly. 'I often think being married would be rather a nuisance. I've got a nice flat and am so used to living on my own I should hardly know what to do with a husband.'

Oh, but a husband was someone to tell one's silly jokes to, to carry suitcases and do the tipping at hotels, thought Jane, with a rush. And although he certainly did these things, Nicholas was a great deal more than that.

'I like to think that some of my pupils are doing academic work,' said Miss Birkinshaw a little regretfully, for so few of them did. Dr. Grampian was some kind of an economist or historian, she believed. He wrote the kind of books that nobody could be expected to read.

'Here we are all gathered round you,' said Jane, 'and none of us has really fulfilled her early promise.' For a moment she almost regretted her own stillborn 'research' – 'the influence of something upon somebody' hadn't Virginia Woolf called it? – to which her early marriage had put an end. She could hardly remember now what the subject of it was to have been – Donne, was it, and his influence on some later, obscurer poet? Or a study of her husband's namesake, the poet John Cleveland? When they had got settled in the new parish to which they were shortly moving she would dig out her notes again. There would be much more time for one's own work in the country.

Miss Birkinshaw was like an old ivory carving, Prudence thought, ageless, immaculate, with lace at her throat. She had been the same to many generations who had studied English Literature under her tuition. Had she ever loved? Impossible to believe that she had not, there must surely have been some rather splendid tragic romance a long time ago – he had been killed or died of typhoid fever, or she, a new woman enthusiastic for learning, had rejected him in favour of Donne, Marvell and Carew.

> Had we but World enough, and Time
> This Coyness Lady were no crime . . .

But there was never world enough nor time and Miss Birkinshaw's great work on the seventeenth-century metaphysical poets was still unfinished, would perhaps never be finished. And Prudence's love for Arthur Grampian, or whatever one called it – perhaps love was too grand a name – just went hope-lessly on while time slipped away. . . .

'Now, Jane, I believe your husband is moving to a new parish,' said Miss Birkinshaw, gathering the threads of the conversation together. 'I saw it in the *Church Times*. You will enjoy being in the country, and then there is the cathedral town so near.'

'Yes, we are going in September. It will all be like a novel by Hugh Walpole,' said Jane eagerly.

'Unfortunately, it is rather a modern cathedral,' said one of the clerical wives, 'and there is one of the canons I do not care for myself.'

'But I've never thought of myself as caring for canons,' said Jane rather wildly.

'One woman's canon might be another woman's . . .' began another clerical wife, but her sentence trailed off unhappily, giving an effect almost of impropriety which was not made any better by Jane saying gaily, 'I can promise you there will be nothing like *that*!'

'It is an attractive little place you are going to,' said Miss Birkinshaw. 'Perhaps it has grown since I last saw it, when it was hardly more than a village.'

'I believe it is quite spoilt now,' said somebody eagerly. 'Those little places near London are hardly what they were.'

'Well, I expect it will be better than the suburbs,' said Jane. 'People will be less narrow and complacent.'

'Your husband will have to go carefully,' said a clerical wife. 'We had great difficulties, I remember, when we moved to our village. The church was not really as *Catholic* as we could have wished, and the villagers were very stubborn about accepting anything new.'

'Oh, we shall not attempt to introduce startling changes,' said Jane. 'There is a nearby church quite newly built where all *that* has been done. The vicar was up here at the same time as my husband.'

'And we are to have your daughter Flora with us, next term,' said Miss Birkinshaw. 'I always like to see the children coming along.'

'Ah, yes; I shall live my own Oxford days over again with her,' sighed Jane.

There was a scraping of chairs and then silence. Miss Jellink, the Principal, had risen. The assembled women bowed their heads for grace. '*Benedicto benedicatur*,' pronounced Miss Jellink in a thoughtful tone, as if considering the words.

There was coffee in the Senior Common Room and then chapel in the little tin-roofed building among the trees at the bottom of the garden. Jane sang heartily, but Prudence was silent beside her. The whole business of religion was meaningless to her, but there was a certain comfort even in the reedy sound of un-trained women's voices raised in an evening hymn. Perhaps it was because it took her back to her college days, when love, even if sometimes unrequited or otherwise unsatisfactory, tended to be so under romantic circumstances, or in the idyllic surroundings of ancient stone walls, rivers, gardens, and even the reading-rooms of the great libraries.

After chapel there was more walking in the gardens until dusk and then much gathering in rooms for gossip and confidences.

Jane ran to her window and looked out at the river and a tower dimly visible through the trees. She had been given the room she had occupied in her third year and the view was full of memories. Here she had seen Nicholas coming along the drive on his bicycle, little dreaming that he was to become a clergyman – though, seeing him standing in the hall with his bicycle clips still on, perhaps she should have realised that he was bound to be a curate one day. She could remember him so vividly, wheeling his bicycle along the drive, with his fearful upward glance at her window, almost as if he were afraid that Miss Jellink and not Jane herself would be looking out.

Prudence had her memories too. Laurence and Henry and Philip, so many of them, for she had had numerous admirers, all coming up the drive, in a great body, it seemed, though in fact they had come singly. If she had married Henry, now a lecturer in English at a provincial university, Prudence thought, or Laurence, something in his father's business in Birmingham, or even Philip, small and spectacled and talking so earnestly and boringly about motor cars . . . but Philip had been killed in North Africa because he knew all about tanks. . . . Tears, which she had never shed for him when he was alive, now came into Prudence's eyes.

'Poor Prue,' said Jane rather heartily, wondering what she could say. Who was she weeping for now? Could it be Dr. Grampian? 'But after all, he *is* married, isn't he? – I mean there is a wife somewhere even if you've never met her. You shouldn't really consider him as a possibility, you know. Unless she were to die, of course, that would be quite all right ' A widower, that was what was needed if such a one could be found. A widower would do splendidly for Prudence.

'I was thinking about poor Philip,' said Prudence rather coldly.

'Poor Philip?' Jane frowned. She could not remember that there had ever been anyone called Philip. 'Which, who . . . ?' she began.

'Oh, you wouldn't remember,' said Prudence lighting another cigarette. 'It just reminded me, looking out at this view, but really I haven't thought about him for years.'

'No, I suppose Adrian Grampian is the one now,' said Jane.

'His name isn't Adrian; it's Arthur.'

'Arthur; yes, of course.' Could one love an Arthur? Jane wondered. Well, all things were possible. She began to think of Arthurs famous in history and romance – the Knights of the Round Table of course sprang to mind immediately, but somehow it wasn't a favourite name in these days; there was a faded Victorian air about it.

'It isn't so much what there *is* between us as what there *isn't*,' Prudence was saying; 'it's the *negative* relationship that's so hurtful, the complete lack of *rapport*, if you see what I mean.'

'It sounds rather restful in a way,' said Jane, doing the best she could, 'to have a negative relationship with somebody. Of course a vicar's wife must have a negative relationship with a good many people, otherwise life would hardly be bearable.'

'But this isn't quite the same thing,' said Prudence patiently. 'You see underneath all this, I feel that there really is something, something *positive.* . . .'

Jane swallowed a yawn, but she was fond of Prudence and was determined to do what she could for her. When they got settled in the new parish she would ask her to stay, not just for a week-end, but for a nice long time. New surroundings and new people would do much for her and there might even be work she could do, satisfying work with her hands, digging, agriculture, something in the open air. But a glance at Prudence's small, useless-looking hands with their long red nails convinced her that this would hardly be suitable. Not agriculture then, but a widower, that was how it would have to be.

## Chapter Two

✠

'I FEEL THAT a crowd of our new parishioners ought to be coming up the drive to welcome us,' said Jane, looking out of the window over the laurel bushes, 'but the road is quite empty.'

'That only happens in the works of your favourite novelist,' said her husband indulgently, for his wife was a great novel reader, perhaps too much so for a vicar's wife. 'It's really better to get settled in before we have to deal with people. I told Lomax to come round after supper, perhaps for coffee.' He looked up at his wife hopefully.

'Oh, there will *be* supper,' said Jane in a firm tone, 'and there may be coffee. I suppose we could give Mr. Lomax tea, though it wouldn't be quite the usual thing. I wonder if we are well-bred enough or eccentric enough to carry off an unusual thing like that, giving tea after a meal rather than coffee? I wouldn't like him to think that we were condescending to him in any way because his church is not as ancient as ours.'

'Of course coffee does tend to keep people awake,' said Nicholas rather inconsequentially.

'Lying awake at night thinking out a sermon,' said Jane; 'that might not be such a bad thing.'

'What are we having for supper?' asked her husband.

'Flora is in the kitchen unpacking some of the china. We could open a tin,' added Jane, as if this were a most unusual procedure, which it most certainly was not. 'Indeed, I think we shall probably have to, but I know we've got some coffee somewhere if only we can find it in time. Will he be bringing Mrs. Lomax with him?'

'No, he is not married as far as I know,' said Nicholas vaguely, 'though it is some time since we've met. Our conversation yesterday was mostly about parish matters. I remember at Oxford he rather tended towards celibacy.'

'I dare say he was a spectacled young man with a bad complexion,' said Jane. 'He may have thought there was not much hope for him, so he became High Church.'

'Well, my dear, there are usually deeper reasons,' said Nicholas, smiling. 'Not all High Church clergymen are plain-looking.'

'Nor all Moderate ones, darling,' said Jane warmly, for her husband's eyes were still blue and he had kept his figure.

They were in the room which was to be Nicholas's study, sitting in the middle of a litter of books which Jane was arranging haphazardly in the shelves.

'These are all theology,' she said, when Nicholas suggested that it might be better if he did them; 'as long as nothing unsuitable-looking appears among these dim bindings I don't see that the arrangement really matters. Nobody could possibly want to read them. You're sure you wouldn't rather have the room upstairs for your study? It looks over the garden and might be quieter.'

'No, I think this room is the best for me. It seems somehow unsuitable for a clergyman's study to be *upstairs*,' said Nicholas, and then, before Jane could enlarge upon the idea with her vivid fancy, he added hastily, 'I shall have my desk in the window – it is sometimes an advantage to be able to see people coming.'

'Then you must have a net curtain across the window,' said Jane, 'otherwise you will lose your advantage if they can see you too. But at the moment it seems as if nobody will ever come to see us. . . .' She looked out over the laurels to the green-painted gate. 'You would think they'd come out of curiosity, if for no nobler reason.' She turned back to arranging the books.

'But there *is* somebody coming,' exclaimed Nicholas in a rather agitated voice. 'A lady, or perhaps a woman, in a straw hat with a bird on it, and she is carrying a bloodstained bundle.'

Jane hurried to the window. 'Why, that's Mrs. Glaze. It must be! She is to do for us. I quite forgot – you know how indifferent I am to domestic arrangements. I hadn't realised she was coming to-night.' She ran out into the hall and flung open the front door before Mrs. Glaze had even mounted the steps.

'Good evening, Mrs. Glaze. How kind of you to come to us on our first evening here!' Jane cried out.

'Well, madam, it was arranged, Mrs. Pritchard said you would want me to.'

'Ah, yes; she and Mr. Pritchard were so kind. . . .'

'*Canon* Pritchard,' Mrs. Glaze corrected her gently, entering the house.

'Yes, of course; he is that now. *Canon* Pritchard, called to a higher sphere.' Jane stood uncertainly in the hall, wondering if perhaps such words were found only on tombstones or in parish magazine obituary notices, and were hardly suitable to be used about their predecessor, who was still very much alive.

'Well, if you will excuse me, madam——' Mrs. Glaze made as if to pass.

'Oh, certainly!' Jane stood aside, for she had hardly yet grasped where the kitchen was and in any case it was a part of the house in which she took little interest. 'I don't know what we are going to have for supper.'

'Don't you worry about that,' said Mrs. Glaze, raising her bloodstained bundle and thrusting it towards Jane. 'I've got some liver for you.'

'How wonderful! How did you manage that?'

'Well, madam, my nephew happens to be a butcher, and one of the sidesmen at the Parish Church too. I warned him when you would be coming and naturally he wanted to see that you had a good supper. He loves his work, madam. He's as happy as a sandboy when the Christmas poultry comes in – looks forward to it all the year round. Of course, he can't take the same pride in it that he used to, not every day, that is – meat has never been at such a low ebb as it is now, what with everything having to go through the Government; it's no wonder the butchers can't go on grinding out the ration, is it madam?'

'No, indeed, one does wonder how they grind it out,' said Jane fervently. 'My husband is so fond of liver. But what about vegetables?'

'Why, in the garden, madam,' said Mrs. Glaze in a surprised tone.

'Of course – "well-stocked garden". We didn't have much of a garden in London,' said Jane apologetically.

By this time they had reached the kitchen, which was at the end of a long stone passage. Flora was just putting away the last of the china. She had not inherited her mother's vagueness and looked very much like her father, tall and slim with blue eyes and dark smooth hair. She was eighteen and looking forward to going up to Oxford in the autumn.

'This is my daughter Flora,' said Jane. 'She's been putting away the china.'

'Well now, isn't that kind,' said Mrs. Glaze; 'that's saved me a lot of work. And I see she's even got the vegetables; I can start getting supper right away. Then you will be ready for Father Lomax when he comes for coffee.'

It was almost soothing that she should know so much about one's life, Jane thought. 'Yes,' she said. 'I do hope he will be able to tell us something about the parish and what we should know about everybody. You see, we are like people coming into the cinema in the middle of a film,' she went on, losing consciousness of her audience. 'We do not know what, if anything, has gone before, or at the best we have a bald and garbled synopsis whispered to us by somebody on his way out; that's Canon Pritchard, of course.'

'Mother,' said Flora a little desperately, 'shall I put out the coffee cups on the silver tray?'

'Yes, darling, by all means.'

'Oh well,' said Mrs. Glaze in an easy tone that promised much, 'I've lived in this parish all my life. If Mr. Meadows, our curate, had been still here, he'd have been a great help to the vicar. But of course he left when Canon Pritchard did. He was married just before he went.'

'Married? Oh, how nice. Was his wife from this village?'

'No, madam. He was engaged when he came to us.' Mrs. Glaze turned her back and busied herself at the sink. A certain flatness in her tone roused Jane from her own thoughts and caused her to look up. Engaged when he came to them. Oh, but that was bad! Bad of the Bishop to send them a curate already engaged. It was a wonder the ladies of the parish hadn't torn him to pieces. A married man would have been preferable to an engaged one, for a curate's wife was often a dim, manageable sort of woman, whereas a fiancée, especially an absent one, has an aura of mystery, even of glamour about her. Who else is there? she wanted to ask. Tell me all about everybody. But she couldn't put it as bluntly as that even though Mrs. Glaze was obviously ready to do her part.

'Has Mr. Lomax a curate?' she asked at last.

'Father Lomax, he calls himself,' corrected Mrs. Glaze; 'but of course he isn't married. There's no woman sets foot in that vicarage, except Mrs. Eade to clean, and the ladies of his parish, of course. No, madam, Father Lomax hasn't got a curate. Not more than twenty or so go to his church. You see, madam, it's the form of service. Romish practices, you know what I mean. Though I must say he's got Mrs. Lyall going there and that's something. But *we've* still got Mr. Edward,' her voice softened and she looked up from her vegetables, a smile on her face, 'and that's as it should be, isn't it, madam?'

'Mr. Edward?' echoed Jane hopefully, for there was much here that she did not understand.

'Yes, Mr. Edward Lyall, our Member of Parliament, such a nice young man. Of course his father was Member before him and his grandfather, oh, we couldn't have anybody but a Lyall as our Member. They've always lived at the Towers as long as anybody can remember and always come to the Parish Church, except this Mrs. Lyall, that is. Some vicar in Kensington, London, got hold of her, madam, ten years ago she started going to Father Lomax's, but Mr. Edward's always come to the Parish Church.'

'Does he read the Lessons sometimes?' asked Jane. 'It seems right for a Member of Parliament to read the Lessons in his constituency.'

'Oh, yes, madam; when he's here he does. But of course there's Mr. Oliver too, he reads the Lessons sometimes, though Mr. Mortlake and his friends, oh, they don't like it, madam, but no doubt you'll be hearing about *that*. And they do say that Mr. Fabian Driver would like to do it. Oh, he'd fancy himself standing up there looking like a lion above the bird, but we haven't come to that *yet*. Have you got a flour-dredger, Miss Flora? I'll just be flouring the liver.'

*Mr. Mortlake and His Friends . . . A Lion above the Bird . . .* but these are the titles of new novels still in their bright paper jackets, thought Jane with delight. And they are here in this parish, all this richness.

'Mother, I think we'd better have supper as soon as we can,' said Flora firmly, 'wasn't Mr. Lomax invited for half-past eight? We don't want him to arrive and find us in the middle of our supper, do we?'

'No, darling, especially as he may not have had liver.'

'He won't have done, madam. I can tell you that,' said Mrs. Glaze. 'Mrs. Eade didn't get any this week – she does all his shopping for him. Of course, my nephew shares out the offal on a fair basis, madam, but everybody can't have it every time. Father Lomax will have had his liver *last* time,' she concluded firmly. 'And he will have it *next* time,' she added on a note of hope.

'Which won't be much consolation to him now,' said Jane, 'so he had better not see us eating it. Like meat offered to idols,' she went on. 'You will remember that St. Paul had no objection to the faithful eating it, but pointed out that it might prove a stumbling block to the weaker brethren – not that Father Lomax would be that, of course.'

'In fact, Mother, the whole comparison is pointless,' said Flora, 'as our liver won't have been offered to idols.'

'No; but people in these days do rather tend to worship meat for its own sake,' said Jane, as they sat down to supper. 'When people go abroad for a holiday they seem to bring back with them such a memory of meat.'

'This certainly looks very good,' said Nicholas, putting on his spectacles to see better what he was about to eat. 'Mrs. Glaze seems to be an excellent cook. Pritchard spoke very highly of her. Of course, I believe they had a resident maid as well.'

'Yes,' said Jane; 'somebody handing the vegetables, holding the dish rather too low. I remember that when we lunched with them. Quite unnecessary, I thought it.'

The Clevelands were still at the supper table when the front door bell rang, and a man's voice was heard in the hall.

Mrs. Glaze appeared at the door.

'I've put him in the drawing-room, madam,' she announced. 'I'll be bringing the coffee directly.'

'I'm afraid our drawing-room can hardly be compared with Mrs. Pritchard's,' said Flora. 'Mr. Lomax is probably noticing that.'

'Oh, but it looks "lived in",' said Jane, 'which is supposed to be a good thing. I thought Mrs. Pritchard's a little *too* well-furnished – those excessively rich velvet curtains and all that Crown Derby in the corner cupboard, it was a little overwhelming.'

'Shall I come in too, Mother?' asked Flora.

'Of course, darling. After all, it's really a social occasion, isn't it?' She stood up and brushed some crumbs from her lap, glancing at her dress in a doubtful way as she did so. 'I really meant to have changed into something more worthy, but perhaps he will understand and make allowances. I don't suppose he is anything of a ladies' man.'

Flora, who had changed her dress and tidied her hair, made no comment. She knew her mother well enough by now to realise that Mr. Lomax's understanding and making allowances really mattered very little to her.

When the drawing-room door was opened, Father Lomax was discovered standing with his back to the fireplace, whose emptiness was not even decently filled in with a screen or vase of leaves or dried grasses.

He was not at all the ascetic type of clergyman, and Flora felt a rush of disappointment at the first sight of him, fair and ruddy-complexioned, with the build of an athlete. She liked men to be dark, but in any case he was old, a contemporary of her father's, and therefore uninteresting and profitless.

'Well, Father Lomax,' said Jane pleasantly as she poured the coffee, 'it is very good of you to come along, especially as I suppose we are rivals, really.'

'Yes, you might say that,' Father Lomax agreed, 'but I expect your husband and I can come to some amicable arrangement not to poach on each other's preserves. After all, we were up at Oxford together, you know. I've been here several years and can probably tell him quite a lot about the parish. We neighbouring clergy get to know things about other parishes – a word or a hint here and there, a casual remark in the public-house, things have a way of getting around.'

'One hopes there isn't really anything to get around,' said Jane, 'or at least not in public-houses.'

'Oh, Lomax means the general way things go,' said Nicholas vaguely. 'Numbers of congregations, personalities and so forth.'

'Ah, personalities,' said Jane; 'that's really what one wants to know about.'

But Father Lomax did not take the hint and began reminiscing with Nicholas about college days in what seemed to Jane a very boring way. He then recalled how Nicholas's father had opposed his ordination and had even called round to see the Principal of their college to register a protest.

'You were never able to bring him round to your way of thinking?' he asked Nicholas.

'No, I'm afraid not. He died without believing in anything, I'm afraid.'

'I suppose old atheists seem less wicked and dangerous than young ones,' said Jane. 'One feels that there is something of the ancient Greeks in them.'

Father Lomax, who evidently thought no such thing, let the subject drop and then somehow he and Nicholas were talking about parish matters, parochial church council meetings, Sunday school teachers and visiting preachers. Jane lay back in her chair lost in thought, wondering about Mr. Mortlake and his friends. Flora got up and quietly refilled the coffee cups, offering a plate of biscuits to Father Lomax. But he refused them with an absent-minded wave of the hand. Meat offered to idols, thought Flora scornfully, taking a biscuit herself and eating it. Then, as nobody seemed to be taking any notice of her, she ate another and another until the clock struck ten, and her mother, oblivious of their guest, stood up, stretching her arms and yawning.

'Young Francis Oliver rather fancies himself at reading the Lessons,' Father Lomax was saying, 'and there may be trouble in that quarter from Mr. Mortlake. I have heard that the atmosphere at the last P.C.C. meeting was very strained.'

'Dear, dear,' said Nicholas, who was a mild, good-tempered person and never saw why any atmosphere should be strained, 'we shall have to try and change that.'

'Both Oliver and Mortlake are extremely stubborn,' said Father Lomax with satisfaction. 'My own Council are very different – I never have any trouble.'

'Well, I don't see why either of them should read the Lessons,' said Nicholas.

'Ah, but during the war, when Canon Pritchard had no curate, the custom grew up.'

'Couldn't Mr. Fabian Drover read the lessons?' asked Jane innocently.

'You mean Driver?' asked Father Lomax. 'Oh, I hardly think *that* would be suitable. He isn't what one would call a church-man, you know. He occasionally goes to Evensong, I believe. He has even been to my church once or twice.'

'People always seem to like Evensong, don't they?' said Jane. 'I mean, it seems more attractive to them than the other services. The old Ancient and Modern hymns especially seem to have an appeal to something very deep in all of us – I don't exactly know what you would call it.'

Neither Nicholas nor Father Lomax had any ready answer to this, and as they had been standing in the open doorway for some time Father Lomax finally edged his way down the steps and disappeared into the darkness.

'A fine, upstanding man, isn't he?' said Nicholas absently. He was evidently thinking that perhaps they might have a round of golf together on Mondays.

# Chapter Three

✕

O N SATURDAY morning Jane crept quietly into the church to have a good look at it. It had been so full of people at the induction service – the Bishop, robed clergy and inquisitive parishioners – that she had hardly been able to form any idea of what it was like, except that it was old. Dear Nicholas, he would no longer have to say to visitors in his gentle, apologetic tones, almost as if it were his own fault, 'I'm afraid our church was built in 1883,' as in the suburban parish they had just left. For here were ancient stones, wall tablets and carved bosses in the roof, and in one corner the great canopied tomb of the Lyall family – a knight and his lady with a little dog at their feet.

Jane moved quietly about the church, reading inscriptions on wall and floor, noticing, without realising its significance, the well-cleaned brass. She was just standing in front of the lectern, almost dazzled by the fine brilliance of the bird's head, when she heard footsteps behind her and the sound of women's voices, talking in rather low, reverent tones, but nonetheless with the authority of those who have the right to talk in church. One voice seemed louder than the other – indeed, when she had listened for a minute or two, Jane decided that the owner of the louder voice was somehow in a superior position to that of the softer one.

'Harvest *Thanksgiving*, we call it,' said the louder voice. 'Harvest *Festival* has a rather different connotation, I feel. There is almost a pagan sound about it.'

'Oh, yes.' The softer voice sounded very demure. 'Festival is altogether more pagan – I could almost see Mr. Mortlake in a leopard skin with vine leaves in his hair.'

'Hush, Jessie,' said the louder voice on a reproving note.

'We must not forget that we are in church. Ah, here are Mrs. Crampton and Mrs. Mayhew. Perhaps we had better start.'

The speakers had now come into view and Jane saw a large woman who gave the impression of being dressed in purple hung about with gold chains, and a smaller younger one in brown with a vase of dead flowers in her hands. They were greeting two middle-aged ladies in tweed suits carrying bunches of dahlias.

An English scene, thought Jane, and a precious thing. Then she realised that it was of course Harvest Festival or Thanksgiving, and the ladies had come to decorate the church. She slipped quietly away behind their backs and found herself in the porch surrounded by fruit, vegetables and flowers.

'Who was that?' asked Miss Doggett, the lady in purple, who was elderly with a commanding manner.

'I think it was the new vicar's wife,' said Jessie Morrow, her companion, in an offhand way. 'It looked like her, I thought.'

'But why was I not told?' Miss Doggett raised her voice. 'What must she have thought of us not even saying good morning?'

Mrs. Crampton and Mrs. Mayhew stood with their dahlias, expressions of dismay on their faces.

'She will surely want to help with the decorating,' said Mrs. Crampton, a tall woman with what is thought to be an English type of face, fresh colouring, blue-grey eyes and rather prominent teeth.

'I wonder she didn't introduce herself,' said Mrs. Mayhew, who looked very much like Mrs. Crampton. 'Mrs. Pritchard wouldn't have been so backward, would she? Of course, I did recognise her myself, but I was so surprised at her walking away like that that I couldn't even say good morning.'

Miss Doggett went out into the porch. 'Why, she is in the churchyard walking about among the tombs,' she exclaimed. 'That long grass must be very wet – I wonder if she is wearing galoshes?'

'Shall I go and see?' asked Miss Morrow seriously.

'Well, you could certainly ask her to come into the church,' said Miss Doggett. 'I mean, indicate to her that we should be very pleased if she would join us. After all, she may have her own ideas about how the Harvest decorations should be arranged.'

Miss Morrow nearly let out a shout of laughter. Even Mrs. Pritchard, the last vicar's wife, who had been a forceful woman, had been unable to depose Miss Doggett from her position as head of the decorators. Mrs. Cleveland, as far as one could see, looked as if she would be neither desirous nor capable of doing any such thing.

Miss Morrow padded through the long grass and tombstones, humming a popular song of the day. She picked her way carefully, for she had a feeling about walking on the older graves, and some were so overgrown that it was difficult to avoid them.

She found Jane contemplating a rather new-looking mound, which was decorated, not with the conventional vases of flowers or growing plants, but with a large framed photograph of a rather good-looking man with a leonine head.

'What a curious idea,' said Jane, looking up at the woman who approached her through the tombs and dimly recognising her as the one in brown who had been holding the vase of dead flowers, 'to have a photograph of oneself on one's tomb. I wonder if it is usual. It seems to be rather a delicate thing – perhaps one would really prefer to be remembered for oneself alone, for one's simple goodness, though it might be a kindness to posterity if one were particularly handsome, as this man appears to have been.'

'Appears to have been!' Miss Morrow gave a short laugh. 'But he still is, or thinks he is. The photograph is of Fabian Driver, and that is his wife's grave.'

'Fabian Driver,' Jane repeated, something about lions and eagles going round in her head. 'Is his wife recently dead?'

'Nearly a year ago. We thought at first that the photograph

was put there temporarily until he could get a stone put up, but he seems to have come to the conclusion that he need not go to that expense after all. People are used to seeing it there now.'

'Perhaps his wife would have liked it better than a stone,' Jane suggested.

'Well, it is something for her, poor soul. I suppose even a photograph is better than nothing. You see, her husband was more interested in other women than he was in her. I believe that does sometimes happen. Her death came as a great shock to him – he had almost forgotten her existence.' Miss Morrow imparted this information in a cool, detached tone; there was nothing secretive or gossiping about her manner. 'He takes flowers to the grave sometimes,' she went on, 'flowers of a particular kind that are said to have been her favourites, but I often wonder if they really were.'

'You think he may be confusing her preferences with somebody else's?' Jane asked in an interested tone.

'Well, it seems quite likely. He is one for the grand gesture and has no time for niggling details.'

'And what now? Does he live alone?'

'Yes. In a pretty house on the village green. He is an inconsolable widower.'

'What does he do for a living?'

'Oh, there is some business in the City which belonged to his father-in-law. Whatever it is it doesn't seem to require his attendance every day of the week. He is often here, apparently doing nothing.'

'I feel it a good thing that I should have this information,' said Jane, walking with Miss Morrow towards the church. 'Canon and Mrs. Pritchard told us so little about the people here.'

'Yes, some things must be known,' said Miss Morrow. 'It is no use nodding and pursing lips and saying dark things, and as you were by the grave I felt I could tell you. It is not the sort of thing one can talk about in the church. I was to ask you if you

28

would care to supervise the decorating, though I imagine that you would have stayed in church if you had wanted to.'

'It isn't really much in my line,' said Jane. 'I'm not very good at arranging flowers at the best of times and I have had little experience of fruit and vegetables. Coming from a town parish, we didn't really have much at Harvest Thanksgiving. Sometimes we even had to have artificial fruit – I see you look shocked, but I think there was some excuse for us; London suburban gardens don't burgeon as they do here.'

'Perhaps I was thinking of Roman Catholic churches in Italy and Spain,' said Miss Morrow apologetically; 'those dusty bunches of artificial flowers. But I can see that fruit might be different; it would be easier to keep it clean.'

'Something made me slip away when I saw everybody there in the church,' said Jane. 'I'm afraid it's a fault in me and a great disadvantage for a clergyman's wife, not to be naturally gregarious. But I should really like to meet them all,' she added with more confidence than she felt.

'Well, I am Jessie Morrow,' said the little brown woman. 'I suppose you would describe me as that outmoded thing, a "companion". Miss Doggett, my employer, is a vigorous old lady who has no need of my services as a companion but rather as a sparring partner. The other two ladies are connected with the church.'

'You mean they are deaconesses?' Jane asked.

'No, they are widows who do a good deal of church work. Actually they run a tea-shop with home-made cakes and that sort of thing.'

They stepped back into the church and introductions were made. The ladies had now been joined by others and there was a confusion of fruit, vegetables and flowers everywhere. Dahlias and chrysanthemums blossomed in unlikely corners, marrows tumbled off window ledges, spiked arrangements of carrots and parsnips flaunted themselves against stained glass.

'I hope we shall have *Let us with a gladsome mind*,' said Jane.

'It is such a fine hymn. In many ways one dislikes Milton, of course; his treatment of women was not all that it should have been.'

'Well, they did not have quite the same standards in the old days,' said Miss Doggett, frowning. 'Of course we shall have the usual harvest hymns, I imagine. *We plough the fields and scatter,*' she declared in a firm tone, almost challenging anyone to deny her.

The corners of Miss Morrow's mouth lifted in a half-smile. 'Not without our galoshes,' she murmured, looked down at her thin glacé kid shoes, damp from walking among the tomb-stones.

Mrs. Crampton and Mrs. Mayhew looked up from the font in surprise.

'Miss Morrow was telling me that you run a tea-shop,' said Jane. 'I do hope you do lunches too. I have to send my husband out for lunch at least twice a week!'

'Yes, it is difficult to manage sometimes,' said Mrs. Crampton.

'And the clergy are always with us where meals are concerned,' sighed Jane.

'Of course, a man must have meat,' pronounced Mrs. Mayhew.

'Certainly he must,' said a pleasant voice in the porch.

Jane looked up to see a tall, good-looking man of about forty, with a marrow in his arms, coming towards them.

'Oh, Mrs. Cleveland, have you met Mr. Driver yet?' asked Miss Doggett, taking command of the situation, as if the other ladies might not be equal to making the introduction.

'No, I don't think I have,' said Jane, taking in at a glance the rather worn, perhaps ravaged – if one could use so violent a word – good looks, the curly hair worn rather too long and touched with grey at the temples, also the carefully casual tweed suit and brogued suède shoes, which gave the impression of a town-dweller dressed for the country.

'This is a great pleasure,' said Fabian as they shook hands.

Jane looked up at him frankly and then lowered her eyes, embarrassed at being confronted by such an excellent likeness of the photograph she had just been looking at on his wife's grave. She felt that she knew more about him than one usually does on a first meeting, remembering Miss Morrow's words about his having been more interested in other women than in his wife and the possibility of his taking the wrong flowers to the grave. That might be a stumbling block between them, she felt, the photograph and the infidelities, but perhaps there might come a time when they would speak frankly of these things and even laugh, though, when one came to think of it, neither graves nor infidelities were really any laughing matter.

'What a fine marrow, Mr. Driver,' said Miss Doggett in a bright tone. 'It is the biggest one we have had so far, isn't it, Miss Morrow?'

Miss Morrow, who was scrabbling on the floor among the vegetables, mumbled something inaudible.

'It is magnificent,' said Mrs. Mayhew reverently.

Mr. Driver moved forward and presented the marrow to Miss Doggett with something of a flourish.

Jane felt as if she were assisting at some primitive kind of ritual at whose significance she hardly dared to guess.

'We are so much looking forward to hearing our new vicar's first sermon,' said Fabian gallantly, looking at Jane rather intently.

'Nicholas isn't one of these dramatic preachers,' she said quickly, feeling a little confused.

The ladies looked interested, as if hoping that she might be guilty of further disloyalties, but Jane recollected herself in time and said: 'Of course, he's a very good preacher; what I meant was that he doesn't go in for a lot of quotations and that kind of thing.'

'Much wiser not to,' agreed Miss Doggett. 'Simple Christian teaching is what we want, isn't it, really?'

Jane had to agree, but she was conscious that Miss Doggett's tone was a little patronising and was not surprised when she went on to add that Canon Pritchard had been a very fine preacher, '. . . most eloquent. Such a fine mellow voice and never at a loss for a word. . . .'

'Nicholas is never at a loss for a word, and his voice is very mellow; I think one could call it that,' said Jane, feeling ridiculous now, and wishing she could think of some excuse to leave the gathering.

'I'm sure we shall find it to our liking,' said Fabian kindly.

'And now I really must be going,' said Jane. 'There is the meal to see to,' she added vaguely, remembering that both Flora and Mrs. Glaze were at the vicarage that morning, so that her presence there was really quite unnecessary.

'Yes, of course,' said Mrs. Crampton sympathetically.

'Why, here is your husband now,' said Miss Doggett. 'How nice of him to come and see us. We shall work all the better for this encouragement.'

'Oh, there you are, darling,' said Jane, stepping backwards on to a heap of vegetables. 'I was just going to see about lunch. Goodbye, everybody,' she said, leaving Nicholas to make his own impression. She had noticed that he seemed a good deal more at ease with the decorators than she had been, but perhaps that was to be expected.

She hurried away down the church path and found Fabian at her side.

'I don't feel I can do much good there,' he explained. 'I too must see about lunch.'

'Do you cook for yourself then?'

'I live alone, you know. Since my wife died . . .'

'Yes, of course, Miss Morrow told me.'

'Really? What did she say?'

'Oh, how sad it was and all that sort of thing,' said Jane rapidly with her eyes on the ground.

'Yes, I think she knows. She is a very understanding person in her way.'

'And do you like cooking and looking after yourself?' asked Jane in a brighter tone.

'One manages,' said Fabian; 'one has to, of course.'

The use of the third person seemed to add pathos, which was perhaps just what he intended, Jane thought.

'You and your husband must come and have a meal with me one evening,' Fabian went on.

'We should love to,' said Jane, pausing to open the vicarage gate.

'Goodbye, then.' Fabian walked slowly away.

He is going back to cook a solitary lunch, thought Jane, or perhaps it will just be beer and bread and cheese, a man's meal and the better for being eaten alone.

'I've just met Mr. Driver,' she said to Flora as she entered the house. 'He is a widower and lives alone. I felt quite sorry for him going back to eat a rather miserable lunch.'

There was a bark of laughter from Mrs. Glaze, who was dusting in the hall.

'I don't think Mrs. Arkright would thank you for calling it that, madam,' she said.

'Mrs. Arkright?'

'Yes, she goes in and cooks Mr. Driver's meals, and a very good cook she is. I dare say he'll be having a casserole of hearts to-day,' said Mrs. Glaze in a full tone.

'A casserole of hearts,' murmured Jane in confusion, thinking of the grave and the infidelities. Did he eat his victims, then?

'My nephew the butcher had hearts and liver this week, madam, but I didn't know if you liked hearts. Not everybody does.'

'No, I don't think my husband does,' said Jane.

'The vicar doesn't like hearts? Oh, I must remember that.' Mrs. Glaze nodded her head and stopped in her dusting as if to let the fact sink into her memory.

'But Mr. Driver gave me to understand that he did his own cooking,' she said.

'Well, madam, I dare say he might make a cup of coffee or boil an egg; you know how men are.'

'Yes, of course,' Jane agreed. 'The church is going to look very nice, I think.'

'Oh, Mother, you always say that,' said Flora, Mrs. Glaze having left them alone together. 'And you never really notice.'

'No, I notice the things one shouldn't,' said Jane.

She thought of this again the following evening when she and Flora were sitting in their pew at Evensong and she found herself regretting that they were not sitting further back, where they could have had a better view of the congregation. Fabian Driver was on a level with them at the other side. When they came into the church he had looked up and half smiled at Jane; it was the sort of smile one could give in church or to a very intimate friend. Miss Morrow and Miss Doggett and a few elderly ladies in yellowish brown fur coats were in the front pews. But apart from them Jane could see hardly anybody. It was not until the time for the collection came and a bag was handed to her that she realised that it must be Mr. Mortlake standing there, deferential yet expectant, appearing confident of the folded note or couple of half-crowns that would be slipped into it. But Jane had been taken unawares and a desperate fumbling in her purse produced only a threepenny bit and two pennies. She felt almost as if she should apologise to the tall, elderly man with the beaky nose waiting so patiently there, for surely he must have seen her miserable offering.

'Oh, dear,' she whispered to Flora, 'I hadn't got the right money. I'm sure he noticed.'

But Flora wasn't really listening to what her mother said. Her eyes were fixed on the back of the young man in one of the front pews who had read the second Lesson. Tall, with fairish wavy hair and a thin, spiritual-looking face; he looked a little tired, perhaps even hungry. She must persuade her mother to ask him to supper some time.

I suppose that's the one Mr. Mortlake doesn't like reading

the Lessons, Mr. Oliver or some such name, thought Jane, trying to get him clear in her mind. But she soon lost interest, and found herself turning her attention to Mr. Driver and wondering, though very faintly, if he might perhaps do for her friend Prudence?

## Chapter Four

✖

P RUDENCE, unlike Jane and her family, had attended no kind of Harvest Thanksgiving service, and got up on Monday morning thinking of nothing but the week's work ahead of her and the rapture and misery and boredom of her love for Arthur Grampian.

When she reached the vague cultural organisation where she worked for him, she found that Miss Trapnell and Miss Clothier, who worked in the same room, had already arrived. Miss Trapnell was putting on her mauve office cardigan, while Miss Clothier arranged some leaves of an indefinite species in a jar on top of the filing-cabinet. Miss Trapnell's garment was shrunken and not altogether clean, but she did not believe in wearing 'good' clothes for the office. Prudence often wondered when she blossomed out in these so-called 'good' clothes which she was reputed to possess and what company was considered special enough to deserve them. Both Miss Trapnell and Miss Clothier were of an indeterminate age, though it was rumoured that Miss Clothier had passed her fiftieth birthday. There existed between the three of them a kind of neutral relationship and they banded together against the inconsiderateness of their employer and the follies and carelessness of the two young typists. Besides the three women and the two girls there was also a young man, Mr. Manifold, a kind of 'research assistant' who had a little room to himself and kept to his own mysterious business.

Prudence sat down at her table and wished as she always did that she could have a room of her own. Her status, though somewhat indefinite, was higher than that of Miss Trapnell and Miss Clothier, but they had been there longer, which gave them a slight advantage. If one were asked point-blank it would really be difficult to say what any of them, even Dr. Grampian, actually did; perhaps the young typists' duties were the most clearly defined, for it was certain that they made tea, took shorthand and typed letters which did not always make sense. However, on this Monday morning Prudence put on her pale-blue-rimmed interestingly-shaped spectacles, took a bundle of proofs and a typescript from a wire tray, and began to apply herself to them. Miss Trapnell went to the filing-cabinet and put some pieces of paper into a file, and Miss Clothier drew a small card index towards her and began moving the cards here and there with her fingers, as if she were coaxing music from some delicate instrument.

'I wonder if we might have one bar of the fire on?' asked Miss Clothier at last.

'Oh, it isn't cold,' said Miss Trapnell. 'Do you find it cold, Miss Bates?'

Prudence disliked being called 'Miss Bates'; if she resembled any character in fiction, it was certainly not poor silly Miss Bates. And yet how could Miss Trapnell and Miss Clothier call her anything else? And how could she call them Ella and Gertrude?

'No. It doesn't seem cold,' she said.

'Well, of course I have been sitting here since a quarter to ten,' said Miss Clothier. 'So perhaps I have got cold sitting.'

'Ah, yes; you may have got cold sitting,' agreed Miss Trapnell. 'I have only been here since *five* to ten.'

Prudence, who had arrived at ten past ten, made no comment and indeed none was necessary. The hours of work were officially ten till six, but Prudence considered herself too highly educated to be bound by them. Her fine brain, which was now puzzling over a misplaced footnote, could not be expected to function under such stupidly rigid conditions. She always expressed herself as very willing to stay long after six o'clock should Dr. Grampian want her to, but he very seldom did, being only too anxious to hurry away to his club or even to his home.

And yet it had been on one of those rare late evenings, when they had been sitting together over a manuscript, that Prudence's love for him, if that was what it was, had suddenly flared up. Perhaps 'flared' was too violent a word, but Prudence thought of it afterwards as having been like that. She remembered herself standing by the window, looking out on to an early spring evening with the sky a rather clear blue just before the darkness came, not really seeing anything or thinking about very much; perhaps an odd detail here and there had impressed itself upon her mind – she liked to think that it had – the twitter of starlings, a lighted window in another building – and then suddenly it had come to her *Oh, my love* . . . rushing in like that. And as there had been at that time a temporary emptiness in her heart she had let it rush in, and now here it was with her always, a constant companion or a pain like a rheumatic twinge in the knee when one neared the end of a long flight of stairs. It was also on that occasion that Arthur Grampian had for a moment laid his hand on hers and said for no apparent reason, 'Ah, Prudence . . .' She had thought at the time that he might be going to kiss her, but it had not come to that; he had merely taken his hand away and said in his usual flat tone, 'Well, thank you, Miss Bates, I'm afraid I've kept you rather late. You'd better run along home now.' And so she had gone through these last months with nothing more than this 'Ah, Prudence . . .' to hug to her heart and take out and brood over numerous times a day. For nothing had happened since and he had never again even called her by her Christian name. He had gone to his club and home to his wife Lucy and his children Susan and Barnabas, and Prudence, for want of better material, had built up the negative relationship of which she had spoken to Jane at the Old Students' week-end, the negative relationship with the something positive that must surely be there underneath it all.

'Surely it must be tea-time, or is the milk late again?' said Miss Clothier. 'I had a very early breakfast this morning and I'm just dying for a cup of tea.'

'You can hardly call it the cup that cheers,' said Miss Trapnell. 'If only those girls wouldn't pour it all out at once and then leave it standing for about ten minutes. I've told them I don't know how many times.'

'It would be better if we made the tea ourselves,' suggested Prudence.

'But, Miss Bates, we couldn't do that,' said Miss Clothier in a shocked tone. 'It wouldn't do at all.'

'No; I suppose it wouldn't,' Prudence agreed.

But at that moment a sound was heard outside the door and a pretty girl of about seventeen dressed in the height of fashion pushed her way through the door carrying a tray from which poured a stream of weak-looking tea.

'Oh, Marilyn, why don't you put the cups and saucers separately on the tray?' said Miss Clothier fussily. 'Then you wouldn't slop it all into the saucers.'

'Sorry, Miss Clothier,' said the girl cheerfully. 'I was hurrying to get tea over before *He* came in.'

'But Dr. Grampian will want a cup when he comes,' said Miss Clothier.

'He's had it, then. We've run out of tea; that's why I had to make it so weak. I couldn't add any more water to what's left in the pot.'

'I'm sure that shouldn't have happened,' said Miss Trapnell sharply. 'It isn't the end of the ration period yet. We *can't* have used all the tea.'

Somebody was heard walking past the door.

Marilyn threw up her hands in a comical gesture. 'What did I tell you? There he is!'

'But surely there's some Oxo or Nescafé or something,' said Prudence in a faint voice. She had no wish to become involved in this trivial controversy, but the thought of Arthur having to go without his elevenses was quite unbearable. Not that the tea was even drinkable.

'Mr. Manifold has a tin of Nescafé, but he always makes it himself and keeps it locked up in his cupboard.'

'Then somebody must go and ask Mr. Manifold if he would mind Dr. Grampian having a little of it,' persisted Prudence.

Miss Trapnell and Miss Clothier turned away and busied themselves with their files and card-indexes with an air of it being none of their business.

'Oh, Miss Bates, *I* couldn't ask Mr. Manifold,' giggled Marilyn. 'I don't mind making it if you'll ask him, Miss Bates.'

'Very well, then.' Prudence rose from her table and followed Marilyn out of the room.

Miss Trapnell and Miss Clothier exchanged glances.

'Would you like a biscuit, Miss Clothier?' asked Miss Trapnell in a rather ceremonial voice. She opened a little tin and offered it to her companion. 'These are Lincoln cream. My grocer always saves them for me.'

'Thank you,' said Miss Clothier. 'I wonder if Dr. Grampian would like one?'

'I shan't offer them. He gets a good lunch at his club and I expect he had a good breakfast.'

'Miss Bates might not like it if you were to give him biscuits,' said Miss Clothier obscurely.

'There would be nothing in it if I did,' said Miss Trapnell. 'I believe I have offered him one before now when the occasion called for it. Naturally, I shouldn't go out of my way to do it.'

'Oh, no. I certainly wouldn't take the trouble that Miss Bates does. Dr. Grampian isn't really the kind of man I should fancy for myself.'

'You'd think Miss Bates could do better. After all, she's very good-looking and smart. Besides, Dr. Grampian is married.'

'Well, what is there for her here?' asked Miss Clothier. 'She obviously thinks herself too good for Mr. Manifold.'

Prudence knocked at Mr. Manifold's door, and then was annoyed at herself for doing so. After all, it wasn't his bedroom; she had a perfect right to walk straight in.

He was a thin, dark young man in the late twenties who kept himself very much to himself, either because he was naturally of a retiring disposition or because he felt his position as the only man in the office apart from Dr. Grampian. It was thought that he sometimes unbent with the typists, but Prudence did not like to imagine what form this unbending could take.

At Prudence's entry he looked up from his table, where he seemed to be sorting out sheets of paper covered with his spidery writing.

'I hear you have a tin of Nescafé,' she began rather aggressively.

'Yes, I have,' he said unhelpfully.

'Well, I was wondering if you would lend it for Dr. Grampian to have some.'

'But isn't he going to have tea? The girls have only just made it.'

'No, there isn't enough tea. The ration was used up and no more water could be added to the pot. You see, there wasn't enough tea to begin with and it would be impossibly weak if water was added,' said Prudence, despising herself for going into such a long, tedious explanation.

'Well, personally, I like weak tea,' said Mr. Manifold, 'when I drink it at all, which isn't often. Still I suppose Gramp should have some coffee to keep him awake,' he added on a sarcastic note, opening a drawer in his table and taking out a tin. 'Mind you return it, though.'

'Of course,' said Prudence scornfully. 'Thank you very much.' She didn't like the way Mr. Manifold called Arthur Grampian 'Gramp'. It was just the kind of silly, obvious name he would think of, and she suspected that the girls also used it among themselves.

She took the tin to Marilyn, who made the coffee and went to Dr. Grampian's door with it. Prudence heard her go in and presumably place the cup on his desk, but she was not to know that it lay there untouched until it was removed by the cleaner who came in that evening, and she returned to her proofs with the feeling of having done something more worthwhile than emending footnotes and putting in French accents.

The morning wore on and Dr. Grampian did not send for her. At twelve Miss Clothier got up to go to her lunch, again remarking that she had been here since a quarter to ten and really felt quite hungry. Some time after that Miss Trapnell produced a packet of sandwiches from her hold-all and took out the green openwork jumper she was knitting. At half-past twelve Dr. Grampian was heard to leave the office. At a quarter to one Prudence went out for her own lunch.

On her way to the restaurant she passed Arthur Grampian's club, with its noble portals, into which undistinguished-looking but probably famous men could be seen hurrying. She imagined Arthur himself in conversation with professors and bishops. But did they talk? she wondered. Wasn't it quite likely that they concentrated solely on the business of eating? Men alone, eating in a rather grand club with noble portals – and women alone, eating in a small, rather grimy restaurant which did a lunch for three and sixpence, including coffee. While Arthur Grampian was shaking the red pepper on to his smoked salmon, Prudence was having to choose between the shepherd's pie and the stuffed marrow.

While she ate she turned the pages of a book of Coventry Patmore's poems; the Blackbird was breaking the Young Day's heart as her fork toyed with her food. But the book remained open there, and after a while she stopped reading and became conscious of herself sitting alone at a table that could have held two. She was still young enough – and when does one become

41

too old? – to wonder if people were looking at her and asking themselves, 'Who is that interesting-looking young woman, sitting alone and reading Coventry Patmore?' But it was altogether unlikely in this kind of restaurant, she realised, where it was obvious that people were eating seriously and with too much concentration to notice anybody else.

'Is this seat taken?' asked a man's voice.

Prudence looked up suspiciously. 'No,' she said in rather a nervous tone.

The man took off his raincoat and sat down. He was middle-aged with a small moustache. Prudence handed him the menu without looking at him. She felt she couldn't bear it if he should begin to talk to her.

'You must have a good lunch,' said a woman's voice from the next table. They were evidently together, but had failed to find a table for two. 'It'll be pretty late before you get your supper.'

'Well, I don't feel much like eating. Seven-thirty to eight the visiting hours are. I suppose I could get a snack before that.'

'Madge will be looking forward to seeing you,' said the woman. 'But you mustn't expect to see her looking too grand, you know.'

'No, it'll be a shock to the system, won't it, the operation? She won't feel like much, but I thought I'd take her a few grapes. . . .'

The lump in Prudence's throat made it difficult for her to speak, but she managed to offer to change places so that the man and woman could be at the same table. They thanked her and the change was made. Prudence sat for the rest of the meal, listening to her neighbours' conversation, her eyes full of tears. Disliking humanity in general, she was one of those excessively tender-hearted people who are greatly moved by the troubles of complete strangers, in which she sometimes imagined herself playing a noble part. The man sitting at her table, who had at first appeared to be a bore or even a menace, was now proved to be an object of interest. There was both nobility and pathos about him.

She was just walking to the cash desk to pay her bill when she noticed a young man sitting at one of the tables. It was Mr. Manifold. He was eating – perhaps 'tucking into' would describe it better – the steamed pudding which Prudence had avoided as being too fattening. She had never seen him eating before and now she averted her eyes quickly, for there was something indecent about it, as if a mantle had fallen and revealed more of him than she ought to see. Of course the women in the office had known that he lunched somewhere – indeed, they had even speculated on where he went; perhaps the vastness of the Corner House swallowed him up or the manly security of a public-house lapped him round. Prudence hurried out of the restaurant feeling disturbed and irritated. Had he ever been there before, she wondered? She hoped he wasn't going to make a habit of frequenting the places she went to. It would be annoying if she had to change her own routine.

When she got back into her room, Miss Trapnell and Miss Clothier were sitting virtuously in their places, occupied with the same rather indefinite tasks as before lunch. Prudence settled down to her proofs again and began to feel sleepy; she even took a few minutes' nap, covering her eyes with her hand. Outside all was quiet; Dr. Grampian did not come in again. No visitors called. At a quarter to four Miss Trapnell and Miss Clothier began to speculate on the possibility of tea – whether it would be punctual or not. Eventually the clatter of the tray was heard and Gloria, the other typist, brought it into the room. Miss Trapnell opened her tin of biscuits, Miss Clothier took a slice of homemade cake from a paper bag; Prudence ate nothing, but lit a cigarette. And so the hours went on until it was a quarter to six.

'I think I am justified in leaving a little *before* six to-night,' declared Miss Clothier. 'I arrived here at *twenty* to ten this morning and was sitting down to work at a quarter to.' She looked at Prudence and Miss Trapnell as if challenging them to contradict her.

'Oh, certainly,' said Prudence in a bored way.

'Well, I think I shall stay till six,' said Miss Trapnell, 'although I was actually here between ten and five to ten this morning, so I could really leave a *little* before six. But I think I'll just finish what I am doing; it's rather unsatisfactory to leave a piece of work half-done.'

'I quite agree! But sometimes one has to make a break if a thing can't be finished within a reasonable time,' said Miss Clothier. 'I shouldn't at all mind staying until *half past* six if I thought I could finish what I've been doing, but to do that I should have to stay until about eleven o'clock' – she gave a little laugh – 'and I'm sure Dr. Grampian wouldn't expect me to do that.'

Prudence swallowed down her irritation. How could they presume to know what he expected?

'He seems to expect little and yet much,' said Miss Trapnell obscurely. 'One wouldn't like to fall short.'

'He has never complained about *my* work,' said Miss Clothier in rather a huffy tone.

'Oh, I didn't mean to suggest anything like that,' said Miss Trapnell with a look at Prudence; they both found Miss Clothier a little 'difficult' at times.

'Won't you miss your train if you don't hurry?' suggested Prudence.

'There are other trains,' said Miss Clothier. 'I shouldn't like anyone to think I was a clock-watcher.'

'But surely we are all that to some extent,' said Prudence. 'We should hardly be human if we didn't notice when it was tea-time or feel glad when the end of the day came.'

'Well, I am certainly going now,' said Miss Trapnell, gathering her things together. 'Don't stay too late, Miss Bates,' she added in a jocular tone. 'We shouldn't like to think of *you* being here till eleven.'

At last they had both gone. Prudence finished the page she was reading and then began to prepare to go home. But she did it rather slowly. Sometimes Dr. Grampian came in at six o'clock and worked quietly by himself until dinner-time. But to-night was evidently not to be one of those evenings. Prudence had given up hope as she went out of the door and heard a step behind her.

'Did you enjoy your lunch, Miss Bates?'

It was Mr. Manifold. There was a hint of roguishness in his tone. So he had noticed her after all.

'Neither more nor less than usual,' said Prudence. 'It isn't the kind of place where one gets an *enjoyable* meal.'

'Well, I thought I'd try it,' said Mr. Manifold, walking by her side. 'But I could have eaten it all twice over.'

'You men have such enormous appetites,' said Prudence, conscious of being rather kittenish.

'You seemed more interested in your book than in the food,' said Mr. Manifold. 'What were you so deep in?'

'Just Coventry Patmore,' said Prudence coldly.

'Ah, Coventry Patmore. Just your cup of tea, I should think.

*'My heart was dead,*
*Dead of devotion and tired memory . . .*

Look, that's my bus and I think I can get it if I run. Do excuse me, won't you. Goodbye!'

Prudence remained rooted to the spot; really, there was no other way to describe it. That he should even have *heard* of Coventry Patmore! And then to quote those lines, those telling lines. What was it he had said? Just your cup of tea, I should think. . . . What exactly did he mean by that? It sounded almost as if he had studied her and thought about her and what her tastes were likely to be, as if he had noticed things about her, perhaps even her feeling for Arthur Grampian. It was most annoying and disturbing. She pushed her way angrily on to a bus and stood huddled with the others inside.

She had calmed down by the time she arrived at her flat. As if it mattered what Geoffrey Manifold thought about her! He was a dull young man who kept his private tin of Nescafé locked in a drawer. It was impertinent of him to ask her what she had been reading. She wished now that she hadn't told him.

There was a letter on the mat when she got in. It was from Jane, a bubbling, incoherent sort of letter full of underlinings.

'Dearest Prue, such *richness* here! I suppose you would say that we are really getting *settled*, though I still don't seem to have unpacked all my clothes and have just been *burrowing* in a trunk to find Nicholas a *clean surplice*! If only they could have them made of paper and just throw them away when they're dirty – or even of *nylon* – I dare say American clergymen do. I always remember when I went to Dresden as a girl and attended the American church there, it was the best heated building in the town and there were little gold stars on the ceiling! Anyway, such *richness*! The secretary of the parochial church Council is called Mr. Mortlake; he is a tall dignified gentleman with the look of an eagle about him and he is also a *piano tuner*. There seems to be a kind of feud between him and a young man, a bank-clerk who sometimes reads the Lessons. Flora finds him rather attractive, I believe. Oh, to be young again! Then there is Mr. Fabian Driver, a disconsolate widower but very fascinating. I believe he eats the hearts of his victims *en casserole*. He looks more like a lion, or *lyon*, so we are surrounded by the noblest of God's creatures.'

Prudence read on, for there was much more in the same strain. At the end she managed to disentangle the news that Jane hoped to come up to Town soon 'ostensibly to visit Mowbrays and buy holy books', but she insisted that Prudence should meet her for lunch somewhere, when she would tell her 'all about everything'.

She put the letter back into its envelope and poured herself a gin and French. She always enjoyed getting home in the evening to her pretty little flat with what Jane called its 'rather uncomfortable Regency furniture'. When she had finished her drink she went to the kitchen and started to prepare her supper. Although she was alone, it was not a meal to be ashamed of. There was a little garlic in the oily salad and the cheese was nicely ripe. The table was laid with all the proper accompaniments and the coffee which followed the meal was not made out of a tin or bottle.

It had been a trying day, Prudence decided, though she could not have said exactly why. No sign of Arthur Grampian, the slightly upsetting lunch – that poor man would be sitting at Madge's bedside now, leaning slightly forward in his chair, waiting for her pale lips to move in speech – the impudence of Mr. Manifold, the perpetual irritation of Miss Trapnell and Miss Clothier – any one of these things would have been enough and she had had them all. So she decided to go to bed early and read a book. It was not a very nice book – so often Miss Trapnell or Miss Clothier asked her 'Is that a nice book you've got, Miss Bates?' – but it described a love affair in the fullest sense of the word and sparing no detail, but all in a very intellectual sort of way and there were a good many quotations from Donne. It was difficult to imagine that her love for Arthur Grampian could ever come to anything like this, and indeed she was hardly conscious of him as she read on into the small hours of the morning to the book's inevitable but satisfying unhappy ending.

## Chapter Five

✖

JANE KEPT the thought of a day in London as a treat to buoy her up as she went about doing those tasks in the parish that seemed within her powers. She kept thinking of all the things she would tell Prudence when she saw her and even began to speculate on where they should have lunch and what they should eat. The day after she had written to Prudence, Mrs. Glaze was, for some mysterious reason which Jane did not dare to ask, unable to come, so that the problem of meals had to be solved by Jane herself, as Flora had gone out for the day to visit a school-friend.

'I think, darling,' she said, going into Nicholas's study just before lunch-time, 'it would be better if we had lunch *out* to-day.'

Nicholas looked over the top of his spectacles with a mild, kindly look, obviously not having heard what she said.

Mild, kindly looks and spectacles, thought Jane; this was what it all came to in the end. The passion of those early days, the fragments of Donne and Marvell and Jane's obscurer seventeenth-century poets, the objects of her abortive research, all these faded away into mild, kindly looks and spectacles. There came a day when one didn't quote poetry to one's husband any more. When had that day been? Could she have noted it and mourned it if she had been more observant?

> *'What doth my she-advowson fly*
> *Incumbency?'*

she murmured. Unsuitable, of course, but she loved the lines.

'What, dear?' said Nicholas, not looking up this time.

'I don't know,' said Jane. 'I've forgotten what I wanted to say.'

'You did say something. Something about going out.'

'Yes, lunch. I really think it would be better if we went out to-day.'

'Why to-day especially?'

'Well, you see, Mrs. Glaze isn't here and neither is Flora, and I really don't know what we should have,' said Jane a little desperately.

'Couldn't we open a tin or something?'

'A tin of *what*? That's the point.'

'Oh, meat of some kind. Spam or whatever you call it.'

'But, darling, there isn't Spam any more. It came from America during the war and we don't get it now.'

'Then there isn't anything to eat in the house? Is that what you're trying to tell me?' asked Nicholas quite good-humouredly.

'Yes, that is the position. Mrs. Glaze did say something about there being sausages at the butcher if one went *early*, but I'm afraid I forgot, and now it's nearly half-past twelve,' said Jane guiltily.

'Well,' said Nicholas, standing up, 'we may as well go out. Should we go now?'

Jane put on an old tweed coat which hung in the hall – the kind of coat one might have used for feeding the chickens in – and they went out together. They stood uncertainly outside the front gate, wondering which direction to go in, and then wandered off past the church with no clear idea of where they were to have their meal.

'*I* know,' said Jane suddenly. 'Mrs. Crampton and Mrs. Mayhew! They run a café, don't they? The Spinning Wheel, I think it is.'

'The Spinning Wheel,' repeated Nicholas doubtfully. 'That doesn't sound as if it would provide us with lunch. Are you sure it isn't just one of those places that sells home-spun scarves and things like that?'

'No, I'm certain they do provide meals as well. In fact, I had a conversation with them about it in church when they were doing the Harvest Festival decorations.'

Eventually they came to the Spinning Wheel, and although there were a number of home-made-looking objects of an artistic nature in the window, there was also a menu written in a gentlewoman's flowing hand pinned up at the side of the door.

'It looks very quiet,' said Jane as they stood on the threshold; 'there's nobody here at all.'

'Perhaps people don't lunch till one,' Nicholas suggested.

'No, that may be it. Shall we sit in the window? Then we shall be able to see what happens.'

They chose a table in the window and sat down to look out at the deserted street.

'I expect they were all early at the butcher's and got sausages,' said Jane, 'and now they are all eating toad-in-the-hole.'

'I don't think I should like *that*,' said Nicholas in a more definite tone than his usual one.

There was a movement behind them, and Jane looked up to see Mrs. Crampton herself standing by the table.

'Good morning, vicar, and Mrs. Cleveland,' she said. 'What would you like?' She handed them a menu which offered them a choice between toad-in-the-hole or curried beef.

'Oh, dear,' Jane burst out, 'I'm afraid I don't like curry and my husband can't take toad, so could we just have the soup and a sweet, perhaps?'

'How would you like an egg and some bacon?' said Mrs. Crampton, lowering her voice.

'That would be fine,' said Nicholas.

'Could you really manage that?' asked Jane.

'Oh, yes, we can sometimes, you know, but not for everyone, of course. And you'd like the soup, would you?'

They said that they would, and Mrs. Crampton hurried away behind a velvet curtain at the far end of the café.

'Why did you say, "my husband can't take toad"?' asked Nicholas, shaking with suppressed laughter. 'It sounded so very odd.'

'I don't know. I think I wasn't conscious of having said it until I did. I must have thought she would expect me to say something like that.'

Mrs. Crampton brought the soup, which they finished, and there was a long silence. Neither Jane nor Nicholas spoke and nobody came into the café. After a time Jane heard sounds from behind the velvet curtain, the low mumbling of voices and the hiss of frying. At last Mrs. Crampton emerged from behind the velvet curtain carrying two plates on a tray. She put in front of Jane a plate containing an egg, a rasher of bacon and some fried potatoes cut in fancy shapes, and in front of Nicholas a plate with *two* eggs and rather more potatoes.

Nicholas exclaimed with pleasure.

'Oh, a man needs eggs!' said Mrs. Crampton, also looking pleased.

This insistence on a man's needs amused Jane. Men needed meat and eggs – well, yes, that might be allowed; but surely not more than women did? Perhaps Mrs. Crampton's widow-hood had something to do with it; possibly she made up for having no man to feed at home by ministering to the needs of those who frequented her café.

Nicholas accepted his two eggs and bacon and the implication that his needs were more important than his wife's with a certain amount of complacency, Jane thought. But then as a clergyman he had had to get used to accepting flattery and gifts gracefully; it had not come easily to him in the early stages. Being naturally of a modest and retiring nature, he had not been able to see why he should be singled out.

'This is delicious,' said Jane, hoping that Mrs. Crampton wasn't going to stay and watch them eat their meal.

'Do you find that many people come here for lunch?' asked Nicholas.

'Well, we have a few regulars, you know, and "casuals" as we call them. Mr. Oliver is one of our "regulars" – he always comes at a quarter past one. He works in the Bank, you know, and I don't think his landlady does lunch for him; just breakfast and an evening meal.'

'Poor Mr. Oliver,' said Jane, scenting pathos. He certainly looked very pale reading the Lessons on Sunday evenings, but perhaps that was just a trick of the lighting. She hurried to finish her egg and bacon in case he should come in and see them at it without being able to have it himself.

'Ah, here he is.' Mrs. Crampton opened the door with a

gesture of welcome and Mr. Oliver took his seat at a small table in the corner. He nodded and poured out a glass of water. She then disappeared behind the velvet curtain.

'Good morning, vicar,' said Mr. Oliver, 'or good afternoon, perhaps, though it always seems morning until one has had lunch.'

Nicholas introduced Jane to Mr. Oliver and they began a rather stilted conversation across the café. Jane was embarrassed because Nicholas had not yet finished his last egg, and hoped Mr. Oliver wasn't noticing.

'You must come and have tea with us one Sunday,' said Jane. Flora would certainly like to meet him, though she might be a little disappointed in him. He did not appear to have much to say for himself and his suit was of rather too bright a blue to be quite the thing, Jane felt. Still, tea would be quite easy to manage, and they arranged that he should come the very next Sunday.

Mrs. Crampton now returned and set down before Mr. Oliver a plate laden with roast chicken and all the proper accompaniments. He accepted it with quite as much complacency as Nicholas had accepted his eggs and bacon and began to eat.

Jane turned away, to save his embarrassment. Man needs bird, she thought. Just the very best, that is what man needs.

'Does Mr. Fabian Driver ever come here, I wonder?' she said to her husband.

'Fabian Driver? How on earth should I know?' said Nicholas indulgently.

They ate their sweet – stewed plums and rice pudding – and drank a cup of surprisingly good coffee. Then Nicholas called for the bill. 'I do hope you are coming to the whist drive,' said Mrs. Crampton. 'I can sell you some tickets.'

'Whist drive?' asked Nicholas. 'Is there going to be a whist drive? I haven't heard anything about it.'

'Oh, not a *Church* whist drive,' said Mrs. Crampton, smiling. 'This is just in aid of Party funds, you know. It is not until early in December, but there will be a big demand for tickets. Mr.

Lyall himself has promised to be there and even Mrs. Lyall, if she can. It will be quite an occasion.'

'We should like to come,' said Jane. 'I haven't met our Member yet. May we have four tickets, please?'

'Miss Doggett is organising it, and Mrs. Mayhew and I are to be in charge of refreshments.'

'That is certainly an inducement for anyone to come,' said Nicholas in his best manner. They said goodbye and went out, leaving Mr. Oliver to his bird.

'If only I could get Prudence to come for that week-end,' said Jane. 'It might be just the thing for her.'

'I hardly think a village whist drive could do much for Prudence,' said Nicholas. 'I've often wondered why she doesn't take up social work of some kind.'

'Now you are talking like a clergyman, or like Miss Birkinshaw, our old tutor,' said Jane crossly. 'You imagine Prue "fulfilling herself" by sitting on some committee to arrange amenities for the "poor".'

'She doesn't go to church at all, does she?' asked Nicholas tentatively. 'That seems a pity.'

'Well, I suppose it does,' said Jane; 'especially in London, when you think what a choice there is.'

Nicholas sighed and left the subject.

Fabian Driver, doing his pre-lunch drinking in the bar of the Golden Lion, looked out and saw Nicholas and Jane walking home. He had a confused feeling of irritation and envy as he watched them. It must have been Jane's smiling up at her husband and the awful old coat she was wearing, the kind of coat a woman could wear only in her husband's presence, he thought. For a moment he was tempted to call out to them, to invite them in for a drink, even. But the moment passed, and anyway it was half-past one, time for Fabian to go home to what he called his 'solitary meal'.

'That was the new vicar and his wife,' he remarked to the lady behind the bar. 'I might have asked them in for a drink.'

53

'Oh, Mr. Driver!' she giggled.

'Well, what would have been so funny about it?'

'I was just thinking of the Canon and Mrs. Pritchard. You wouldn't have had them coming in here.'

'No, certainly not. Perhaps the Clevelands wouldn't have come either. I dare say they've been having lunch at the Spinning Wheel.'

There was nobody left in the bar now except Fabian. He sat idly, contemplating his reflection in the looking-glass framed with mahogany and surrounded by bottles.

'Mrs. Arkright'll be giving you what for if you don't hurry home to lunch,' said the lady behind the bar good-humouredly. 'I expect she's got something tasty for you.'

Fabian put down his glass. 'Well, yes, I may as well go.'

'That's it,' she said comfortably. 'I don't like to think of your dinner spoiling.'

No, Fabian thought, it wouldn't do for it to get spoilt. It did not occur to him that perhaps she was wanting to get her own meal.

He walked slowly down the main street, past the collection of old and new buildings that lined it. The Parish Church and the vicarage were at the other end of the village. Here he came to the large Methodist Chapel, but of course one couldn't go there; none of the people one knew went to chapel, unless out of a kind of amused curiosity. Even if truth were to be found there. A little further on, though, as was fitting, on the opposite side of the road, was the little tin hut which served as a place of worship for the Roman Catholics. Fabian knew Father Kinsella, a good-looking Irishman, who often came into the bar of the Golden Lion for a drink. He had even thought of going to his church once or twice, but somehow it had never come to any-thing. The makeshift character of the building, the certain discomfort that he would find within, the plaster images in execrable taste, the simplicity of Father Kinsella's sermons intended only for a congregation of Irish labourers and servant-girls – all these kept him away. The glamour of Rome was obviously not *there*.

There remained only the Church of England, and here there was at least a choice between the Parish Church and Father Lomax's church – in the next village, but still within reasonable distance. It was natural to Fabian's temperament to prefer a High Church service, incense and good music, vestments and processions, but Father Lomax discouraged idle sightseers and expected his congregation to accept the less comfortable parts of the Faith – going to Confession, and getting up to sing Mass at half-past six on a winter morning. So there was really nothing for it but to go to the Parish Church, where, even if the service was less exotic, the yoke was easier. Also, the Parish Church was older and had some interesting wall tablets and monuments. Fabian often imagined a tablet to himself put up in the church, though he never stopped to consider who should put it up or why.

His own house was one of several standing round the little green with its chestnut trees and pond which formed the real centre of the village. As he pushed open the gate and walked up the path, bordered now with fine pompom dahlias, he saw that Mrs. Arkright in her hat and apron was standing in the open doorway.

'Oh, Mr. Driver,' she said reproachfully, 'I was wondering what had happened to you. I've a piece of steak for you and I didn't want to start grilling it until you came. We can't afford to spoil meat nowadays, can we?'

Fabian went into the little hall and then out of the drawing-room french windows into his garden, which was a long stretch of grass with a fine walnut tree in the middle of it, and at the end a vegetable patch and a group of apple trees.

Next door to him on one side was the doctor and on the other Miss Doggett and Miss Morrow. Miss Morrow was in the garden now, cutting early chrysanthemums which grew near to the fence separating the two gardens.

'Ah, cutting flowers,' said Fabian.

'Yes, cutting flowers,' said Miss Morrow, in a bright tone.

Yes, she was undeniably cutting flowers, thought Fabian irritably. He wished he hadn't come out into the garden, for he found it difficult to make conversation with her. When his wife had been alive he had hardly noticed Jessie Morrow; indeed, if possible, he had noticed her even less than he had noticed his wife. Miss Doggett he knew, of course, but Miss Morrow had appeared always in her shadow, a thing without personality of her own, as neutral as her clothes.

Lately, however, he had become more conscious of her, though he could not have said exactly why or in what particular way. She did not seem to speak to him more than she ever had, but when he was with her he felt uncomfortable, as if she were laughing at him, or even as if she knew things about him that he didn't want known.

'Would you like some apples?' he asked, to break the silence. He glanced vaguely up at a tree.

'Thank you, but we really have plenty,' said Miss Morrow, indicating their own apple trees with a gesture.

Fabian felt rather foolish, for indeed Miss Doggett's garden had far more apple trees than his.

'Perhaps you would like some quinces when they are ripe?' she suggested. 'Our tree always does very well. You haven't a quince tree, have you?'

'Alas, no. Constance was so fond of quinces,' said Fabian sadly.

Constance was so fond of quinces! thought Miss Morrow scornfully. As if Fabian had known or cared what Constance was fond of – why, Miss Doggett had several times offered her quinces and she had always refused them!

'Mr. Driver! Mr. Driver!' Mrs. Arkright came out on to the lawn calling. 'Your steak's ready!'

'Ah, my steak.' Fabian smiled. 'You will excuse me, Miss Morrow?'

'Of course. I shouldn't like to keep you from your steak. A

man needs meat, as Mrs. Crampton and Mrs. Mayhew are always saying.' She waved her hand in dismissal.

Fabian hurried away, conscious of his need for meat and of the faintly derisive tone of Miss Morrow's remark, as if there were something comic about a man needing meat.

The dining-room was in the front of the house and was furnished with rather self-conscious good taste, a little too carefully arranged to be really comfortable. The general effect, as might have been expected, was Regency.

The steak was tender and perfectly cooked, as were the potatoes and french beans. Constance had not appreciated good food. She had been a gentle, faded-looking woman, some years older than Fabian. She had been pretty when he had married her and had brought him a comfortable amount of money as well as a great deal of love. He had been unprepared for her death and outraged by it, for it had happened suddenly, without a long illness to prepare him, when he had been deeply involved in one of the little romantic affairs which he seemed to need, either to bolster up his self-respect or for some more obvious reason. The shock of it all had upset him considerably, and although there had been several women eager to console him, he had abandoned all his former loves, fancying himself more in the rôle of an inconsolable widower than as a lover. Indeed, it was now almost a year since he had thought of anybody but himself. But now he felt that he might start again. Constance would not have wished him to live alone, he felt. She had even invited his loves to the house for week-ends, and two women sitting together in deck-chairs under the walnut tree, having long talks about him, or so he had always imagined, had been a familiar sight when he happened to be looking out of an upper window. In reality they may have been talking of other things – life in general, cooking or knitting, for the loves always brought knitting or tapestry work with them as if to show Constance how nice they really were. But they would be talking a little awkwardly, as two women sharing the same man generally do; there would inevitably be some lack of spontaneity and frankness.

After lunch Fabian went upstairs and into the room which had been Constance's. It was almost like a room in a Victorian novel, where nothing belonging to the departed had been touched, but it was laziness and lack of enterprise rather than sentiment which had left clothes still hanging in the wardrobes and the silver-backed brushes and mirror still on the dressing-table. Perhaps he would ask somebody to help him to sort out these things and give them away. The new vicar's wife, Mrs. Cleveland, might do it. She seemed to be a sensible sort of person. He could not ask Miss Morrow or anybody who had known Constance and his behaviour towards her to help him. He made up his mind to ask Jane Cleveland about it the next time he saw her.

By now he had moved over to the window and was looking out. Miss Morrow was still at the bottom of the next door garden. Surely she couldn't have been cutting flowers all this time? Suddenly, to his astonishment, he saw her glance up at his house and wave her hand, but the next time he looked she was gone, so that afterwards he was not sure whether she had really waved to him or whether he had imagined the whole incident.

## Chapter Six

✖

'MOTHER,' said Flora the following Saturday, 'don't forget that Mr. Oliver is coming to tea to-morrow. You said you'd asked him when you saw him having lunch the other day.'

'Why yes, so I did,' said Jane. 'Well, I suppose Mrs. Glaze might make a cake or we might get some from the Spinning Wheel.'

Mrs. Glaze seemed a little uncertain about whether she would be able to make a cake and Jane thought she detected some unwillingness in her manner.

'I don't suppose he gets very good food at his lodgings,' she said, to encourage Mrs. Glaze. 'I always feel so sorry for young men living in lodgings, especially on a Sunday afternoon. I wonder if he has a sitting-room with an aspidistra on a bamboo table in the window and a plush table-cloth with bobbles on it,' Jane mused, forgetting her audience, 'and some rather dreadful pictures, perhaps, even photographs of deceased relatives on the wall.'

'Mrs. Walton has given him a very nice front room,' said Mrs. Glaze, 'and there is a plant on a table in the window – an ornamental fern it is, a beautiful thing, better than he deserves.'

Jane changed the subject hastily. Perhaps it was not quite the thing to ask Mr. Oliver to tea. Nicholas had seemed a little uncertain after she had done it. 'Are you going to ask all of them separately?' he asked rather fearfully. 'Shall we never have a Sunday afternoon in peace?'

'Of course, but Mr. Oliver seemed quite a nice young man and as he lives by himself in lodgings I thought it would be a kindness,' said Jane. 'I certainly don't intend to ask all the Parochial Church Council, if that's what you mean.'

'Well, dear, I suppose you could hardly do that,' said Nicholas, 'I don't want Mortlake and Whiting and the others to feel in any way slighted, though.'

'Oh, we'll have a cup of tea and some buns after the next P.C.C. meeting,' said Jane airily; 'that will make up for it.'

'Can you eat and drink in the Choir Vestry?' asked Flora.

'We could have the meeting here, I suppose,' said Nicholas; 'there'd be plenty of room. Though,' he added doubtfully, 'it might be unsuitable to be lolling about in armchairs.'

'Well, they needn't loll,' said Jane; 'and there would probably be fewer disagreements and less unpleasantness if they were more comfortable. People don't realise the importance of the body nowadays – oh, I know the seventeenth-century poets did,' she added hastily, 'but not quite in the way I mean.'

'No, not quite,' said Nicholas, darting a fearful glance at her, for indeed he was not sure what she might quote, and with Flora in the room one must draw the line somewhere. 'Anyway,' he concluded, 'we shall have to see how things go.' He ambled off into his study conscious of having taken an easy way out, if it was a way out at all.

The next day after lunch Flora got out the best tea service and began washing the cups and plates, for it was some time since they had been used. Lovingly she swished the pink-and-gold china in the hot soapy water and dried each piece carefully on a clean cloth. Tea could be laid on the low table by the fire, she decided, with the cloth with the wide lace border. Mrs. Glaze had eventually been persuaded to make a Victoria sandwich cake, there were little cakes from the Spinning Wheel and chocolate biscuits, and Flora intended to cut some cucumber sandwiches and what she thought of as 'wafer-thin' bread and butter. It would be a much better tea than was usually served at the vicarage; she only hoped her mother wouldn't spoil it all by making some facetious comment. She got everything ready, went up to change her dress and tidy herself, and then settled down by the fire with a nice Sunday afternoon kind of novel from the library. Jane was sitting on the other side of the fire with her feet up on a pouffe; there was a book open on her lap and the Sunday papers were spread out at her side, but she was not reading; she had 'dropped off', as she frequently did on a Sunday afternoon, and her head was drooping over against the back of the chair; her mouth was slightly open too. She had just been reading the review of a novel where a character was said to 'emerge triumphantly in the round', and somehow this had set her nodding. She was conscious of Flora coming into the room and she seemed to remember that she had said something about having cleaned the bath. 'But surely Mr. Oliver won't want to have a bath at four o'clock in the afternoon,' she had said. After that all was blessed oblivion until the cruel shrilling of the front-door bell startled her into uttering a cry and sitting bolt upright in her chair.

'That must be him,' said Flora, her tone betraying signs of agitation also, 'but it's only half-past three.'

'Quickly, let me get out of the room,' cried Jane. Diana and her nymphs bathing could not have felt more embarrassed when surprised by Actaeon as Jane did at this moment. She gathered up the Sunday papers and fled from the room.

Flora hurried to the front door and found Mr. Oliver standing there. He was wearing a dark suit, either in honour of tea at the vicarage or perhaps in anticipation of reading one of the Lessons at Evensong. Seen at close quarters, he was naturally rather less pale and spiritual-looking than he had appeared in the kinder light of the church.

'I'm afraid I'm rather early,' he said. 'Mrs. Cleveland just said tea and I wasn't quite sure what time to come.'

'Oh, you're not at all too early,' said Flora enthusiastically. 'Do come in. Perhaps you'd like to leave your raincoat in the hall.'

'Yes, thank you. I thought it safer to bring it. The sky looked rather overcast as I was leaving my lodgings, and I thought I felt a drop as I came up the drive.'

Flora looked up at the ceiling. 'I expect we need rain for the harvest,' she said.

'But the harvest is gathered.'

'Yes, of course, it must be. We've had Harvest Festival, haven't we?' And Mr. Oliver had looked so beautiful against the autumnal background – the sheaves of wheat, the great jars of Michaelmas daisies and chrysanthemums, the grapes on the lectern.

Flora led the way into the drawing-room. It was empty.

'I'm afraid it looks rather untidy,' she said, going over to Jane's chair, plumping up a cushion and gathering up an odd sheet of one of the Sunday papers. 'I'm afraid my father isn't in yet – he's taking the Boys' Bible Class.'

There was a pause. What could she say next? Flora wondered. Mr. Oliver did not seem to be very easy to talk to. She almost wished that her mother would come back; at least there would not be silence then.

Mr. Oliver was looking round the room hopefully. He had noticed the table laid with a lace-edged cloth and a rather pretty tea-set, so there would be tea, and perhaps quite soon. He had not imagined himself alone with the vicar's schoolgirl daughter; in fact, he had hardly realised her existence until she came to the door. He had hoped to have a profitable talk with the vicar and perhaps with Mrs. Cleveland too; otherwise he would have preferred to be in his lodgings, looking over the Lesson he was to read that evening and perhaps practising some of it aloud. Mrs. Walton, his landlady, always had her wireless on very loudly on Sunday afternoons, so that he could raise his voice without fear of being heard or of making himself ridiculous.

'I am going up to Oxford next week,' said Flora, to break the silence.

'Really, Miss Cleveland? Have you relatives there?'

'No. I mean I am going to the University.'

'Ah, to study. What subject, may I ask?'

'English Literature,' said Flora rather stiffly.

'Oh, I see.' Mr. Oliver did not appear to have anything to say about English Literature and Flora was glad when there was a sound at the door and Jane came into the room.

'Mr. Oliver, how nice! I'm so glad you were able to come.'

Flora looked at her mother in astonishment. She had spent the time that had elapsed between her rushing from the room and her meeting with Mr. Oliver in improving her appearance, or rather in altering it, for it was difficult to say whether the garments she now appeared in were any more suitable for the occasion than those she had been wearing before. Her dress, a patterned navy foulard with long sleeves, was really too light for October and was a little crushed, for, as Flora rightly guessed, it had been put away in a drawer since the last warm weather. She had also taken the trouble to change into silk stockings and a pair of very uncomfortable-looking navy shoes with pointed toes and high heels. Her face had been hastily dabbed with powder of rather too light a shade.

Mr. Oliver rose to shake hands.

'I do hope my daughter has been entertaining you,' said Jane easily. 'I was suddenly called away,' she added, thinking as she said it that this was the kind of thing some clergy wrote in parish magazines when people had died. Called away or called home, they said.

'I expect you're very busy, and the vicar too,' said Mr. Oliver.

'Ah, here is Nicholas coming in now,' said Jane, stepping carefully to the window in her tight shoes. 'Now we can have tea. Darling, go and put the kettle on, will you? I think everything else is ready.'

Flora went quietly from the room and Nicholas came in, rubbing his hands together and looking vaguely benevolent.

'Ah, good afternoon, Oliver, very glad to see you,' he murmured. 'Tea not ready yet?' he said, in the way men do, not pausing to consider that some woman may at that very moment be pouring the water into the pot. 'Teaching those lads is thirsty work.'

'Flora is just making it, dear,' said Jane, soothingly. 'Here she is.'

Mr. Oliver sprang up to help her with the tray and soon they were comfortably settled round the fire.

Conversation did not flow very easily at first. There was too much passing of sandwiches and enquiries about who took sugar. Jane hardly ever remembered what even her own family's preferences were in this respect. When she had discharged her duties, she began to ask Mr. Oliver about his work. It must be so interesting working in a bank, she thought.

'Interesting?' he echoed. 'Well, yes, it is in a way, I suppose.'

'I always think of the medieval banking houses in Florence; great times those must have been,' went on Jane rather wildly.

'I should think there have been a good many changes since then,' observed Nicholas dryly. 'What department do you work in?'

'I'm in the Executor and Trustee Department at the moment,' said Mr. Oliver.

'How that must put you in mind of your own mortality!' said Jane, clasping her hands under her chin in rather an affected way. 'You must see the worst and the best sides of people too – I believe it always comes out over money. Are you shut up in a room at the back of the bank, then? We shouldn't be able to go in and peer at you over the counter.'

'No, I am not visible to passers-by,' said Mr. Oliver with a faint smile.

'What a disappointment,' said Jane, echoing her daughter's thoughts, for Flora had been very much cast down when she realised that it would not be possible to see him by going into the Bank on some pretext or other. It was not, unfortunately, the one where the Clevelands had their account. But it didn't really matter very much, she decided; she was beginning to fall out of love with him already. He was not so very interesting after all, and had hardly given her a glance. It had been nice of him to help her with the tray, but any man with reasonable manners would have done the same. Now he was talking to her father about the Parochial Church Council, a most boring subject. Something about Mr. Mortlake and Mr. Whiting. That was a kind of fish that always had its tail in its mouth, Flora thought, wanting to giggle. Apparently there was some complication about something, nothing 'overt', whatever that might be, nothing had been said but the feeling was there. Nicholas was just nodding and saying 'really' or 'oh dear' as if he didn't much want to be talking about it at all, but Mr. Oliver's voice was going on and on. It was rather that kind of voice.

Jane wished he would go, so that she could have a fourth cup of tea, take off her tight shoes and finish reading the book reviews, but the party did not break up until Nicholas suddenly looked at his watch and it was discovered that they must all be getting ready for Evensong.

In church Mr. Oliver again appeared glamorous, seen in the distance and the dim light; Flora's love came flooding back, so that she could hardly bear to look at him. His voice when he read the Lessons sounded different from when he was talking about the Parochial Church Council in the afternoon. She was reminded of a poem she had once read somewhere, something about my devotion more secure, woos thy *spirit* high and pure. . . . If she could find it, she would copy it out into her diary.

At supper afterwards Jane and Nicholas discussed what their visitor had been saying about Mr. Mortlake and Mr. Whiting.

'I couldn't quite follow,' said Jane; 'it all seemed rather obscure. For a moment I almost thought it was something to do with the men's lavatory in the church hall, the cistern or something, but how could that be?'

'Well, there is more to it than that,' said Nicholas guardedly. 'Though that does come into it. I'm wondering,' he went on quickly, fearing his wife's ready laughter, 'whether it was perhaps a mistake to ask Oliver to tea. If Mortlake and Whiting got to hear of it, there might be feeling.'

'Then we'll have them all to tea in turn,' said Jane comfortably, 'though goodness knows what we shall talk about. I should think they would be even more difficult than Mr. Oliver.'

'Well, the Bank and the Church aren't always the easiest combination – I mean, the two together.'

'We should have asked him about his home,' said Jane regretfully, 'his mother and sisters. I'm sure he has sisters.'

'We didn't touch on his war career, either,' said Nicholas. 'That would have been a topic of conversation.'

'His triumphs in the Army,' said Jane.

'I don't think he served with any particular distinction.'

'I meant his triumphs with women,' Jane explained. 'He might

65

have had those, but I suppose they were hardly suitable topics of conversation for a vicarage tea party. Even the water-tank in the church hall was more in keeping.'

Nicholas sighed. 'Yes, one does rather long for the talk of intelligent people sometimes – people of one's own kind, I mean.'

Jane laughed. 'Oh, that would be too much! Besides, we might not be equal to it now.'

## *Chapter Seven*

JANE STOOD on the platform waiting for the train which was to take her to the junction where she would change to the London train. It was a cold November day and she had dressed herself up in layers of cardigans and covered the whole lot with her old tweed coat, the one she might have used for feeding the chickens in. Her hat, however, was quite smart, out of keeping with her other garments, since it had been bought for a wedding and seldom worn since. It was black and of quite a becoming shape, though the dampness of the day had made its veil droop rather sadly round her face.

She paced up and down the platform, humming to herself, looking at the gardens which bordered the station, wondering whether Nicholas really minded her missing the Mothers' Union tea. He had seemed quite amenable to her going up to London to have luncheon with Prudence, though he had smiled a little at her serious excuses, the visit to Mowbray's to buy suitable books for Confirmation presents and perhaps even to get some Christmas cards in *really good time*, and had told her to enjoy herself.

'After all,' Jane had said, 'I don't really feel so very much of a mother, having only *one* child, and you know how bad I am at presiding at meetings. It would be far more suitable if somebody like Miss Doggett were to do it, though I suppose spinsters aren't eligible, really.'

'Good morning, Mrs. Cleveland . . .' A firm voice called out the greeting from some distance away. It was Miss Doggett herself approaching at a steady pace. But just as she came near to Jane, she seemed to hesitate. Her mouth opened and she glanced round as if to make sure that they were not overheard, then said in a low confidential tone, 'I hope you'll excuse me for mentioning it, Mrs. Cleveland, but I thought you might like to know.' She lowered her voice still more and almost whispered, 'Your underskirt is showing a little on the left side.'

'It's this wretched locknit,' said Jane rather too loudly and gaily, so that Miss Doggett recoiled a little; 'it does *sag* so. Still, there's nothing I can do about it now. The train's coming.'

They got into an empty carriage together and sat rather stiffly on opposite sides by the window. Miss Doggett produced a safety pin from her bag.

'You could take it up at the shoulder, perhaps,' she suggested, offering the pin.

'Thank you,' said Jane, who had had no intention of doing anything about her sagging slip, 'I suppose I ought to do something, especially as I am going to London. People might notice,' she added unconvincingly, for who among the many millions – six, was it, or eight? – would notice that a country vicar's wife had half an inch of underskirt showing on the left side?

'Well, it is feeling right oneself that's the important thing,' said Miss Doggett, stroking her musquash coat. 'I am going up to my dressmaker for a fitting.'

'How grand that sounds, having clothes specially fitted so that they are exactly your shape and nobody else's,' said Jane impetuously.

Miss Doggett, whose figure was rather an odd shape, known to dressmakers as 'difficult', seemed as if she did not quite know how to take Jane's remark, but she must have decided that she was obviously much too unworldly to mean any offence, so decided not to take umbrage.

'I suppose you have to go to London on business,' she said quite pleasantly. 'You will be sorry to miss the Mothers' Union tea. I believe it is quite an event.'

'Yes, I am sorry,' said Jane quickly; 'but you know, I feel so unlike a mother when I am at these functions. I am so very undomesticated. They are all so splendid and efficient and have really quite wonderful ideas. Do you know, a mother in our last parish had one of her hints published in *Christian Home*.'

'Really?'

'Yes. It was a use for a thermometer case, if you had the misfortune to break your thermometer, of course. A splendid case for keeping *bodkins* in!' Jane chortled with laughter.

An uncertain smile appeared on Miss Doggett's face. 'Well, well, I must remember that,' she said.

'Yes, do!'

There was a short pause. The last topic of conversation did not seem to lead very easily to anything else.

At last Miss Doggett said, 'I suppose you and the vicar are coming to the whist drive?'

'Oh, certainly,' said Jane. 'I do so very much want to meet our Member. I have heard he is very charming.'

'Yes, and his principles are very sound.'

'I often wonder whether people born into his station of life can really know how others live,' said Jane thoughtfully. 'I'm always reminded of that verse in *We are Seven* – something about a little child that lightly draws its breath, what can it know of death? Do you see what I mean?'

Miss Doggett obviously did not, but she went on to repeat that Edward Lyall's principles were very sound and that of course his father and his grandfather had been Members of Parliament before him.

'He is not married?' asked Jane, trying to keep her voice neutral.

'No, he does not appear to be.' Miss Doggett sounded puzzled for a moment. 'He is thirty-two, but of course a man in his position couldn't afford to make a hasty or unsuitable choice. His wife would have to be quite exceptional – one could hardly expect him to marry a very *young* girl, either,' she added with a glance at Jane.

'Certainly not,' Jane agreed. 'I have no hopes in that direction.'

'Well, it would *hardly* be suitable,' said Miss Doggett. 'Your daughter . . .'

'Has just gone up to Oxford, where she is surrounded by young men. A man of *twenty*-two would seem old to her,' said Jane gaily. But was she failing in her duty as a mother, she wondered, by not entertaining hopes of Edward Lyall as a possible husband for Flora? He would be more suitable for Prudence, if anybody, but the truth was that one hardly considered members of his Party as being within one's own sphere; it would have seemed presumptuous to regard them as possible husbands for one's relations and friends.

'What is Mrs. Lyall like?' asked Jane bluntly.

'Well, of course she is not one of us,' said Miss Doggett. 'You may have heard that she goes to Father Lomax's church, which seems a pity.'

'Oh, well, Nicholas is the last person to mind a thing like that. He and Father Lomax were at Oxford together. I often think I would prefer a High Church service myself, but of course clergy wives have to be very careful, you know. They have to be sitting there in their dowdy old clothes in a pew rather too near the front – it's a kind of duty.'

Again Miss Doggett had no ready answer. 'Of course,' she went on after a while, 'Mrs. Lyall is not very sound politically either. I have heard that there are tendencies the other way. . . .' She moved her hands about in a vague gesture.

'The other way?' Jane echoed. 'Yes; I see what you mean. Rome and Russia.'

'Oh, not *Russia*,' said Miss Doggett in a shocked tone. 'After all, her son was educated at Eton and Balliol, and Mrs. Lyall herself is of quite good family.'

'Well, thank you for telling me,' said Jane in a reassuring tone. 'I shan't indicate in any way that I have heard when I meet Mrs. Lyall.' Then, seeing that Miss Doggett was looking very puzzled, she added, 'About the tendencies the other way, I mean.'

They sat in silence in their corners for a moment or two, then Jane said, 'I do like your companion, Miss Morrow, so much.'

'You like Miss Morrow?' Miss Doggett sounded surprised. 'Well, she is really a distant relation more than a companion. Her mother was my cousin. I felt I had to do what I could for her when she was looking for a post.'

'That is a difficult position to be in, especially when there's a relationship,' said Jane. 'She seems such a bright, intelligent sort of person – she told me quite a lot about the village.'

'You mean about the people in the village?' said Miss Doggett sharply. 'Yes, Jessie certainly has her eyes open.'

'She told me a good deal about Mr. Driver,' said Jane. 'About his wife and other things.'

'Ah, the other things,' said Miss Doggett obscurely. 'Of course, we never *saw* anything of those. We *knew* that it went on, of course – in London, I believe.'

'Yes, it seems suitable that things like that should go on in London,' Jane agreed. 'It is in better taste somehow that a man should be unfaithful to his wife away from home. Not all of them have the opportunity, of course.'

'Poor Constance was left alone a great deal,' said Miss Doggett. 'In many ways, of course, Mr. Driver is a very charming man. They say, though, that men only want *one thing* – that's the truth of the matter.' Miss Doggett again looked puzzled; it was as if she had heard that men only wanted one thing, but had forgotten for the moment what it was. 'Ah, here we are at the junction,' she said, gathering her things together with an air of relief. 'You will need to hurry to catch the London train – they don't allow much time.'

The remainder of Jane's journey was shorter and less interesting. She thought idly about Fabian, turning him over in her mind as a possibility for Prudence, but in no time the train was slowing down under the great glass roof of the London terminus and she was gathering together her bag and umbrella and unread book and newspaper.

She was to meet Prudence at a quarter to one and found that when she got to Piccadilly she still had some time to spare. So, in anticipation of lunch or perhaps to tantalise herself by looking at dainties she would most certainly not be eating, she wandered into a large provision store and moved slowly from counter to counter, her feet sinking into the thick carpet, her senses bemused by the semi-darkness and the almost holy atmosphere. She finally stopped in the middle of the floor before a stand which was given over to a display of *foie gras*, packed in terrines of creamy pottery, some of them ornamented with pictures.

A tall man, rather too grandly dressed for his function, Jane thought, came up to her.

'Can I help you, madam?' he asked quietly.

'Well, now, I wonder if you could,' said Jane.

'I shall certainly endeavour to, madam,' said the man gravely.

'The point is this. How can a clergyman's wife afford to buy *foie gras*?'

'It would seem to be difficult,' said the man respectfully. 'Let us see now.' He took down a card from the stand. 'The smallest size is fourteen and ninepence.'

'Yes,' said Jane. 'I saw that. But I shouldn't really want the smallest size. Those large decorated jars have taken my fancy.'

'Ah, madam, those are one hundred and seventeen shillings,' said the salesman, rolling the words round his tongue.

'Well, I'm sorry to have wasted your time like this,' said Jane, moving away. 'I should like to have bought some.'

'To tell you the truth, madam, I don't care for it myself,' said the salesman, bowing Jane out of the door, 'and my wife doesn't either.'

And, comforted by these words, Jane moved out into the street feeling that she had been vouchsafed a glimpse of somebody else's life. She wondered about the man as she walked to meet Prudence – perhaps he was a churchwarden or sidesman somewhere, there had been something about his bearing that suggested it; in a way he had reminded her of Mr. Mortlake.

Jane realised that she had killed too much time and was now a little late, for Prudence was already waiting at the vegetarian restaurant where they were to have lunch. The place was crowded and they found themselves sitting at a table with two women, under the photograph of the founder of some system of diet in which the restaurant specialised. He was bearded and wore pince-nez, which seemed suitable.

Prudence ordered a raw salad while Jane chose a hot dish of strange vegetables. Conversation was a little difficult at first, since the women already at the table were engaged in an interesting family tale which Jane and Prudence could not help listening to. Indeed, it would have seemed impolite to start a conversation of their own, and they contented themselves with murmurs and glances. Jane noticed a woman wearing heavy silver jewellery and an orange jumper – she looked the kind of person who might have been somebody's mistress in the nineteen-twenties. She was also interested in two foreign gentlemen at the next table, arguing vigorously.

'Prue,' said Jane when they were at last alone at their table, 'I do so want you to come down and stay with us the week-end after this one,' said Jane. 'Flora will just be back, and there's going to be a kind of political whist drive where you'll meet simply everybody.'

Prudence hoped that her horror did not show in her face. She disliked going away from home in the autumn and winter. Other people's houses were so cold, and she knew from experience that Jane and her family lived in an uncomfortable, make-shift way. The food wasn't even particularly good; it seemed that Jane would stop to admire a smoked salmon in a window or a terrine of *foie gras*, but in the abstract, as it were; her own catering never achieved such a standard even on a lower scale.

'I don't know if I shall be able to manage *that* week-end,' she said warily. One's married friends were too apt to assume that one had absolutely nothing to do when not at the office. A flat with no husband didn't seem to count as a home.

'Oh, Prue, do come! I'm sure it will be fun, and it will do you good to get away from London.'

'Well, I dare say I could – though the idea of a whist drive fills me with dismay.'

'But we needn't play – or at least not seriously,' said Jane. 'You know I'm no good at anything but patience, and not always very good at that. But I feel it will be a drawing-together of the threads – we shall see the place all of a piece as it were.'

'Have you met any interesting people – people of one's own type, I mean?' asked Prudence cautiously.

'Yes, in a way. There's Miss Morrow and Fabian Driver – I think I told you about him in my letter.' Jane was too wise to appear anything but casual in her tone as she mentioned this eligible widower. She knew that the pride of even young spinsters is a delicate thing and that Prudence was especially sensitive. There must be no hint that she was trying to 'bring them together'.

'Yes – you said something about him eating the hearts of his victims,' said Prudence, equally casual. She realised that Jane might have some absurd idea in her mind about 'bringing them together', but determined not to let her see that she suspected or that she entertained any hopes herself. So they were both satisfied and neither was really deceived for a moment. The conversation went on smoothly – Jane revealed that Fabian was good-looking and quite tall, about five foot eleven which was really tall enough for a man, and that he had a nice house.

At last Prudence looked at her watch and said she must be getting back to her office.

'Are you supposed to take only an hour for your lunch?' Jane asked.

'Good Heavens, no,' said Prudence impatiently. 'I can take as long as I like – Arthur never minds and I'm not answerable to anyone else.' It gave her a peculiar pleasure to speak of Dr. Grampian casually by his Christian name – Jane was the only person with whom she could do it.

'Funny how I thought his name was Adrian,' said Jane, as they walked out into the street. 'Won't the other women who work with you be jealous, though, if you take a longer lunch-time than they do?'

'I don't know. I'm not really interested in what they think.'

'I'm sure I should be horribly conscious of it,' said Jane rather complacently. 'I should feel their eyes on me. I should pretend I'd been in the lavatory or something.'

'One has to have the courage of one's convictions,' said Prudence.

'I suppose they are like the weaker brethren,' said Jane. 'One ought perhaps to think of them like that, being led astray by one's own actions or example.'

'Really, Jane, you talk as if I were doing something wrong,' said Prudence crossly. 'And anything less like the weaker brethren than Miss Trapnell and Miss Clothier couldn't possibly be imagined. They certainly wouldn't like to hear themselves described like that.'

They stopped outside the building where Prudence worked and made some final arrangements about the week-end. They were just about to part when a man came up to them and said 'Good afternoon' to Prudence.

'Jane, I don't think you've met Dr. Grampian,' she said rather nervously. 'This is a friend of mine, Mrs. Cleveland,' she explained.

Jane said 'How do you do' and shook hands, her glance resting

74

with interest on the man before her. So this was Arthur Grampian. Certainly, now that she saw him, she realised that the name Adrian, with its suggestion of tall, languid elegance, would have been entirely unsuitable. He was of middle size, almost short, and gave an impression of greyness, in his clothes and face and in the pebble-like eyes behind his spectacles. Whatever did Prue see in him? she wondered, conscious as she asked herself of the futility of her question. Arthur Grampian and his wife Lucy – one mustn't forget his wife Lucy, though it was obvious that Prue did. But this insignificant-looking little man . . . Oh, but it was splendid the things women were doing for men all the time, thought Jane. Making them feel, perhaps sometimes by no more than a casual glance, that they were loved and admired and desired when they were worthy of none of these things – enabling them to preen themselves and puff out their plumage like birds and bask in the sunshine of love, real or imagined, it didn't matter which. And yet Prudence's love didn't seem to have had any very noticeable effect on Arthur Grampian; he made nervous conversation about the weather, and smiled and nodded in a rather vague way, as if he didn't really know who either of the women really were.

At last Jane broke away and went off in search of suitable books for Confirmation presents. Prudence stood in the lift with Arthur Grampian, holding herself rather stiffly apart from him as if afraid that their sleeves might touch.

'Getting on all right, Miss Bates?' he asked as the lift stopped and they got out at their floor.

No, no, nothing is all right, everything is wrong, Prudence wanted to call out, but instead she merely answered, 'Yes, I think so. Do you want to see me about anything?'

Perhaps a note of hope had sounded in her tone, for he looked startled and seemed to clasp his brief-case to his breast and step backwards and away from her as he said, 'Want to see you about anything? No, I don't think so. I'm sure everything is going all right.'

And so he hurried into his room and Prudence into hers.

Miss Trapnell and Miss Clothier were in their places, their appointed places it seemed, like something in a hymn, or the wise virgins in the Bible. Not much hope of *them* sparing any oil from their lamps.

> O, *happy servant he,*
> *In such a posture found,*

thought Prudence with irritation, noticing Miss Clothier's casual glance at her watch.

'I was meeting a friend I haven't seen for some time,' she heard herself say weakly, 'so I'm afraid I'm rather late. I shall have to stay on a bit to make up for it.'

'Oh, meeting a friend is rather different,' said Miss Trapnell with excessive geniality. 'I'm sure Dr. Grampian would have no objection to any of us taking a longer lunch-hour for a reason like that.'

'As a matter of fact, I met him coming in,' said Prudence, 'so I was able to introduce my friend.' She disliked the way she kept referring to Jane as 'my friend', almost as if she hoped to give the impression that she had been lunching with a man.

Jane, in the meantime, was wandering round a religious book-shop, glancing at their selection of new novels; so absorbed was she that half an hour passed by like a minute and then it was time for her to go to the station for the train back. It would have been nice to have tea in the Corner House or gone, rather wick-edly, to a Solemn Evensong with lots of incense, she thought. But as it was, she hadn't even time to buy the Confirmation presents. Really, except for looking at the jars of *foie gras*, having lunch with Prudence and seeing Dr. Grampian for the first time, her day had been wasted.

## *Chapter Eight*

PRUDENCE was in the train on her way to spend the week-end with the Clevelands. It was Friday evening and she sat rather crushed up in her corner, for the half-empty carriage which she had chosen so carefully for herself had filled up at the last moment with men in bowler hats and over-coats, carrying despatch-cases and evening papers. Prudence looked at them with resentment, almost with loathing; she wished she had a spray of freesia or lily-of-the-valley to hold under her nose so that she wouldn't smell their horrible pipe smoke – she hated men who smoked pipes. As it was, she had drenched her handkerchief in expensive French scent, for going to stay with Jane always drove her to extremes, and she would take her best clothes rather than her most suitable. Besides, there was this whist drive at which they were supposed to appear, with its promise of a young Member of Parliament and an eligible widower; presumably one would have to dress up for that.

Although she disliked going away in the winter, it was a relief to be leaving London and her flat. The blankness of the last few weeks, with Arthur Grampian taking even less notice of her than usual, combined with the approach of winter, had brought her down to a rather low state. I have given him the best years of my life, she thought, and he doesn't even know it. He was immersed in his work and his club and going home every evening – or so one imagined – to his wife Lucy, and she was saying, 'Well, dear, had a good day?' or whatever it was that wives said to their husbands when they returned home in the evening.

The train slowed down and Prudence gathered her things

together rather fussily, for this was the junction where she had to change. She stood up and prepared to lift her suitcase down from the rack, but before she could do so the man sitting next to her had jumped up and taken it down for her. Prudence thanked him, experiencing that feeling of contrition which comes to all of us when we have made up our minds to dislike people for no apparent reason and they then perform some kind action. Now she gave him her most charming smile and thought of him enjoying a pipe in the train on his way home, a good husband and father. She noticed that he had some cakes in a white cardboard box – taking them home for the children, she supposed; she could hardly bear it . . . she left the carriage, her eyes full of tears.

Jane was to meet her at the junction, ostensibly to 'show her the way', but really because she loved an excuse to go on a little journey. She peered at the people stepping down from the train and then ran forward to greet Prudence and to hurry her over the bridge.

'The train won't be a minute,' she said. 'How lovely it is to see you and how lovely you smell. What is it?'

Prudence murmured the name a little self-consciously, for she knew that her French accent was not good and the name was of an amorous kind that sounded a little ridiculous when said out loud. Anyway, it would convey nothing to Jane. She gritted her teeth for Jane's peal of laughter, which came almost before she had finished speaking.

'What names they think of! And really they're all made from coal-tar. Does Dr. Grampian like it?'

'I don't know – I don't use it in the office, really.'

'No, of course not, just a little eau-de-Cologne or a light toilet water – you see, I read the women's magazines when I go to the dentist. How *is* Dr. Grampian?'

'Oh, just as usual,' said Prudence evasively.

'Which seems to be rather sad and shy, unless he was frightened of me,' said Jane.

'Wasn't he as you'd imagined him?' asked Prudence in a stifled voice.

'No, but of course people never are. It reminds me of that poem about two men looking out through prison bars, one seeing mud and the other stars – do you know it?'

'Yes.' Prudence couldn't help smiling at Jane's absurdity. 'But it doesn't seem very appropriate.'

'Well, perhaps not, but it conveys the general idea. Obviously you see him quite differently from me – I'd imagined a big, tall, dark man, a sort of Mr. Rochester.'

'He is rather good-looking, though, don't you think?'

'Yes, in a way, but if you think him so that's the main point after all. Some hollow in the temple or a square inch of flesh on the wrist that's all it need be, really. . . .'

A little train came puffing along the platform, and Jane and Prudence got in.

'The vicarage is some way from the station,' said Jane, 'but I've asked one of Nicholas's lads to meet the train and carry your case for you.'

The boy took hold of the case, swung it up on to his shoulder and ran off with it at a great pace. Jane and Prudence followed more slowly, picking out landmarks, or rather Jane enthusiastically pointed them out while Prudence dutifully peered through the moonless darkness at the shapes of buildings – the gasworks, the Golden Lion where Fabian Driver did his pre-lunch drinking, the chapel with the Temperance Hotel next to it and the Spinning Wheel Café opposite; then on to the older part of the village with the church, the village green, the pond and the more picturesque houses, and at last to the vicarage with its green-painted gate and the laurels in front of Nicholas's study window.

'Here we are,' said Jane. 'It's quite a nice house, though not as old as the church. Of course, it's enormous, with too many rooms, impossible to heat adequately.'

Prudence shivered. She was wondering if there would be a

79

glass of sherry or a drop of gin waiting; she was so used to that little comfort at the end of a day's work and one seemed to need it even more in strange surroundings.

They were in the hall now with the old coats hanging up and the piles of parish magazines waiting to be delivered. The place felt damp and chill. Nicholas came out of his study with his spectacles pushed halfway down his nose and greeted Prudence.

He used to be so attractive, she thought, but being a clergyman and a husband had done their worst for him, rubbed off the bloom, if that was the right word. He murmured something conventional about the journey and the shortening days so that Prudence was reminded of the silly old joke about winter drawers on.

'You'll want to see your room,' said Jane. 'We haven't put you in the *proper* spare room – it seemed so very vast and cold – but in one of the smaller ones. Here we are.' She flung open the door of what seemed to Prudence, who was used to a boxlike, centrally-heated flat, a very large, bare-looking room with a bed in one corner, a chest of drawers, a chair and an old-fashioned marble-topped washstand. There were a few books on a little table by the bed, but no reading lamp, Prudence noticed quickly, just a light hanging rather too high up in the middle of the room. The floor was covered with shabby linoleum on which two small rugs had been placed in strategic positions, one by the bed and the other before a little looking-glass which hung on one wall.

Darling Jane, thought Prudence, noticing a rather rough arrangement of winter flowers in a little jar on the bedside table, a solitary rose, a few Michaelmas daisies and a dahlia.

She lit a cigarette and began to unpack her case. She felt happier with her own possessions around her, her hot-water bottle in its pink cover, her turquoise blue wool housecoat, her bottles and jars on the chest of drawers and Arthur Grampian's photograph, cut from some learned periodical, on the bedside table.

'Prue,' Jane's voice called, 'supper will be ready in a minute! I've just been trying to open a bottle of sherry, but the corkscrew's gone in all crooked – do be an angel and help me with it.'

Prudence ran downstairs with a lighter heart. It was a good sherry, too, the kind one would hardly have expected Jane to buy.

'I remembered you liked it like this,' said Jane, 'so I asked the man for a very *pale* sherry and he said, "You mean very *dry*, madam" – of course, I always forget these things.'

'Aren't you going to have any?' asked Prudence, seeing Jane fill glasses only for herself and Nicholas.

'No, I don't really like it, you know. I've got out of the way of drinking. It seems rather terrible, really.'

'Not at all, my dear,' said Nicholas conventionally.

'I've been such a failure as a clergyman's wife,' Jane lamented, 'but at least I don't drink; that's the only suitable thing about me.'

'Well, clergymen's wives don't really drink, do they?' said Prudence, contemplating the topaz colour of her drink under the light. 'That doesn't seem to be one of their vices.'

'So even my not drinking isn't an advantage,' said Jane. 'I might just as well take to it, then.' She poured herself a full glass of sherry.

'I shouldn't have it if you don't like it,' said Nicholas in an anxious tone. 'It seems a pity to waste it.'

Jane flashed him a look which Prudence caught. She supposed that marriage must be full of moments like this. She looked round the large, cold drawing-room, inadequately furnished, and imagined what she would do to such a room.

'These curtains aren't quite long enough,' said Jane, following her glances, 'and they don't really meet across the windows. Canon Pritchard was rather a wealthy clergyman – they had long crimson velvet curtains and a curtain over the door too; of course, they *would* keep the draughts out, but luckily we don't feel the cold.'

Prudence remembered other houses where Jane and Nicholas had lived and the peculiar kind of desolation they seemed to create around them. They certainly did not appear to feel the cold, but she was glad that her black dress had a tartan stole to wrap round the shoulders.

'Ah, there is supper,' said Jane. 'I can hear Flora taking it in. Mrs. Glaze doesn't oblige us in the evenings.'

'Flora is shaping very well as a cook,' said Nicholas. 'I don't know where she gets her talent – certainly not from either of us. She will make a good wife for somebody one of these days.'

'But men don't want only that,' said Jane, 'though perhaps the better ones think they do. I was talking to Miss Doggett in the train the other day . . .' Her sentence trailed off vaguely, for perhaps she too had difficulty in remembering what it was that men wanted.

'How has Flora enjoyed her first term at Oxford?' Prudence asked.

'One hardly knows,' said Jane in rather a flat tone. 'I had expected her to be so enthusiastic. The new work, the wonderful atmosphere of Oxford in the autumn, the walks up to Boar's Hill and Shotover and all those lovely berries we used to gather, and then going to St. Mary's on Sunday evenings . . . Oh, it was all so thrilling!'

'But, darling, it's probably different now,' said Nicholas.

'Yes, I suppose it's a mistake to think one can live one's youth over again in one's children,' said Jane sadly.

'Has she fallen in love?' Prudence asked.

'She doesn't say. Of course, she's met a lot of young men, but there doesn't seem to be anyone special yet.'

Prudence smiled a little complacently, remembering her own first term. Why, the very first week somebody had fallen in love with her, poor Cyril, saying rather pompously, 'Male and female created He them,' when she had refused to kiss him good-night. And after that, barely a month later, Philip, sending flowers every day . . .

'Well, shall we go in to supper?' Nicholas suggested. 'Prudence, you had better sit with your back to the fire. Only one of the bars seems to be working, I'm afraid. Something must have gone wrong with the other, but I have no idea what it can be.'

Flora had prepared a very good meal, a chicken casserole with rice and french beans followed by a lemon meringue pie. Prudence had hardly seen her apart from a brief greeting on the doorstep, and was surprised to find her attractive-looking and nicely dressed, almost a grown-up person. She did not join very much in the conversation, but was busy with the food. Prudence could see that she was growing away from Jane, leading her own secret life. Afterwards the women went into the kitchen to wash up, leaving Nicholas in his study, preparing Sunday's sermon. At least Prudence supposed he must be doing this, for her imagination was unequal to the task of penetrating behind the closed door of a clergyman's study.

Later, when she was in her hard bed, reading by the light of a candle which Jane had given her, she heard the murmur of him and Jane talking together in their room, which was next to hers. Husbands took friends away, she thought, though Jane had retained her independence more than most of her married friends. And yet even she seemed to have missed something in life; her research, her studies of obscure seventeenth-century poets, had all come to nothing, and here she was, trying, though not very hard, to be an efficient clergyman's wife, and with only very moderate success. Compared with Jane's life, Prudence's seemed rich and full of promise. She had her work, her independence, her life in London and her love for Arthur Grampian. But tomorrow, if she wanted to, she could give it all up and fall in love with somebody else. Lines of eligible and delightful men seemed to stretch before her, and with this pleasant prospect in mind she fell into a light sleep.

Later, however, she awoke with the realisation that married people did not understand the importance of the full hot-water bottle. Hers was now thin and cold and she had not had her usual hot bath before going to bed. For a moment she wondered whether she could creep downstairs and refill her bottle, but it seemed to be too much trouble and she did not want to wake anybody up. So she draped her fur cape over the bed and then, a sudden inspiration, one of the little rugs from the floor over her feet and lay curled up under the weight of all these clothes, waiting for sleep.

## Chapter Nine

✠

'SHOULD we have something to eat before we go, do you think?' Jane asked. 'I believe refreshments are provided, but they may not be till rather late.'

'Perhaps a glass of sherry and a biscuit?' suggested Prudence hopefully. 'One doesn't really want much to *eat* . . .' but *how* we need a drink, she continued to herself; the idea of facing this whist drive without one was quite terrifying.

'Oh, yes, that would be the thing,' said Jane quickly, with her head bent. She found herself quite unable to look at Prudence, whose eyelids were startlingly and embarrassingly green, glistening with some greasy preparation which had little flecks of silver in it. Was this what one had to do nowadays when one was unmarried? she wondered. What hard work it must be, always remembering to add these little touches; there was something primitive about it, like the young African smearing himself with red cam-wood before he went courting. The odd and rather irritating thing about it was, though, that Nicholas was gazing at Prudence with admiration; it was quite noticeable. So it really did work. Jane studied her own face in the looking-glass above the sideboard and it looked to her just the same as when Nicholas used to gaze at it with admiration. Would he look at her with renewed interest if she had green eyelids? she wondered, but her thoughts were interrupted by his voice asking about the glass of sherry. Were they going to have one or not?

'I've got it here,' said Flora; 'and a few sandwiches. I think we'd better start soon.'

'Why, how nice you look, darling,' said Jane in a surprised mother's voice. 'That's the dress you made, isn't it?'

'Yes. I did make it,' said Flora quickly, embarrassed by her mother's comment and fearing worse to come. 'Does anybody want a sandwich – they're only cheese, I'm afraid.'

'It's a charming dress,' said Prudence, wishing she could feel more natural with Flora. It was awkward when one's friends' children suddenly became grown-up people. 'You look like, oh, something Victorian, that striped silk and the locket and the way you've done your hair. There was a picture very like that in last month's *Vogue*,' she went on, anxious to please.

'Oh, but your dress is much nicer,' Flora burst out, 'and the colour of your nail varnish is so lovely. What is it?'

So we're two women talking together, thought Prudence with surprise and a little dismay. She was glad when Jane made some joking remark about not liking Flora to use nail varnish, thus turning her into a child again.

'We really ought to be going,' said Nicholas. 'It starts at eight, you know.'

'We can be a *little* late,' said Jane, 'though not as late as the party from the Towers. It would be a serious social error if we were to be later than the Lyalls.'

'I suppose the villagers will be there already,' said Prudence, glancing at her watch.

'Yes, the old order hasn't changed that much. Edward Lyall isn't one of these new-fangled Members of Parliament. His ancestors have represented this place for generations.'

They set out, Jane in her old tweed coat, Prudence in a fur cape. The hall was practically next door to the vicarage, so there was little time in which to compose oneself. Suddenly a door was pushed open and there was a noise of talk and laughter and chairs scraping on the wooden floor. Looking around her,

Prudence realised at once that she was overdressed. Her green-and-gold shot taffeta cocktail party dress was out of place here, where most of the women were in long-sleeved wool or even coats and skirts. Her fur cape was the only one in the little cloakroom where they hung their coats.

'I think I'll wear it round my shoulders,' she said. 'It doesn't seem very warm.'

'You'll be boiled,' said Jane cheerfully. 'And it will get in the way of the cards.'

They went out into the hall and stood vaguely around, but only for a moment. Mrs. Crampton and Mrs. Mayhew were upon them, Prudence was being introduced, and within a matter of seconds she found herself sitting down at a table with three others.

'You must be Mrs. Cleveland's friend that's come to stay,' said a woman in a dark felt hat trimmed with a bird's body. 'I'm Mrs. Glaze and this is my nephew' – she indicated a fresh-faced young man – 'and this is Mr. Mortlake. We're all great churchgoers and we like the vicar so much.'

'Oh, good,' said Prudence nervously.

'Canon Pritchard was a good man in his way, but we didn't care for his lady,' said Mrs. Glaze. 'Much too interfering. There's none of that from Mrs. Cleveland.'

'No, I don't suppose there is,' said Prudence. 'She usually gets on well with people.' She wished they wouldn't talk quite so much, for it was many years since she had played whist and she found she had to concentrate. Her partner, Mrs. Glaze's nephew, the butcher, was taking no part in the conversation, but the others kept up a continual flow, most of it about people she didn't know or had just heard Jane mention.

It was a relief to find herself at a table with Jane, and Mr. Oliver and Mr. Whiting, who were also apparently church-people.

'They will be arriving soon,' said Mr. Whiting, 'the party from the Towers, I should say. I hope Mr. Edward will give us a few words. We need that bit of encouragement these days.'

'Does he usually give a few words?' Jane asked.

'Yes, Mrs. Cleveland; he usually has a message. And then we adjourn for refreshments. After that he takes a hand himself and Mrs. Lyall too, but the poor lady has very little notion of how to play.' He shook his head, and gathered in a trick.

'She's a good sort, though,' said Mr. Oliver. 'She's got the right ideas, though of course she can't go against the party openly.'

'If you can call them the right ideas,' said Mr. Whiting, glaring at Mr. Oliver. 'Personally, I shouldn't.'

'Well, you know my views,' said Mr. Oliver truculently.

'We've certainly heard them often enough,' said Mr. Whiting. Jane and Prudence exchanged a look.

'Well, we all have different views,' began Jane, but fortunately it was not necessary for her to continue with her platitudes, for at that moment a hush seemed to strike through the hall, cards were laid down and faces turned towards the door.

A slight, dark young man, with a pale, interesting face and hair worn rather too long, stood on the threshold. He was accompanied by a middle-aged woman in a black lace dress, who looked about her anxiously.

'There they are!' said Mr. Whiting, raising his hands and bringing them together in a clap which was taken up by the rest of the hall.

'Is it usual to clap one's Member?' whispered Jane to Prudence. 'I should have thought the time would be *after* he had said a few words or given his message.'

Edward Lyall acknowledged the applause by a wave of his hand and a charming smile which seemed to include everybody.

'Thank you, my friends,' he said in a ringing voice; 'thank you. It gives me great pleasure to be among you to-night and to see so many of you here in this good cause. As I drove down from the House this evening to be with you I found myself wondering what I could say to you, what encouragement I could give you.'

'He might well find himself wondering,' said Mr. Oliver in a low tone, but he was silenced by an angry look from Mr. Whiting.

Edward Lyall's smooth voice flowed on. Political speeches at such gatherings tend to have a certain sameness about them, and Edward Lyall's message to his constituents had nothing particularly original about it. Jane found herself noticing his continual references to the 'burden' and began to wonder whether this word was more used by clergymen or politicians. Indeed, after Edward had been speaking for about ten minutes, she came to the conclusion that his words might almost have been coming from a pulpit. Would he perhaps end with a prayer?

'And now, my friends, I have talked long enough. You didn't come here to listen to me, I know. And I'm not ashamed to admit that as I drove down from the House to-night I found myself looking forward to Mrs. Crampton and Mrs. Mayhew's excellent refreshments' – he turned to those ladies and smiled – 'so I won't keep you from them any longer.' He ended with a reference to 'these austere days' and flung in an extra burden for luck, as it were, and then he really had finished. Jane and Prudence found themselves being borne forward on a tide of people surging towards the refreshments and their beloved Member.

'I suppose we should wait to be introduced,' said Jane, looking over to where Edward Lyall and his mother were waiting, as if to receive presentations. 'It's a pity they're standing right in front of the refreshments, though. We could at least have made a start on those.'

'Surely not before *they* start,' said Prudence. 'They aren't eating anything yet.'

'Ah, Mrs. Cleveland . . .' Miss Doggett, in her purple woollen dress, seemed to take command of the situation. 'Let me introduce you to our Member.'

Jane followed meekly and shook hands first with Mrs. Lyall

and then with her son. He had an appropriate word for her, if not exactly a message, and she found herself liking him very much, falling a victim, as she put it, to his easy charm of manner. Refreshments now began to be offered and many ladies came up to him with plates of sandwiches and other delicacies. Jane saw Mrs. Mayhew offer a plate rather furtively and heard her say in a low voice, 'Oyster patties – specially for you. I know how much you like them.' The situation interested and amused her; there was something so familiar about it and yet for a moment or two she could not think what it was. The hall, the trestle tables, the good-looking young man, the ladies surrounding him . . . where had she seen all this before? Then it came to her. It was usually curates who were accorded such treatment, but this parish had no curate. Edward Lyall, therefore, was a kind of curate-substitute. The idea pleased her so much that she wanted immediately to tell somebody about it, but she found herself standing next to his mother and felt she could hardly reveal her thought. What should she say to Mrs. Lyall, a gentle-looking person with a rather long, melancholy face?

Fortunately, Mrs. Lyall started first.

'Edward is so tired,' she said; 'it's really a nice rest for him to come down here. That speech yesterday took a lot out of him.'

That speech? Jane never followed the proceedings of Parliament, but she could imagine quite well what a young man of his party might have said, so she said cheerfully, 'Yes; it must have done. Very fine, I should think it must have been. That bit about Youth and the Empire,' she hazarded.

'Yes, everyone was very pleased. I'm glad to see him doing so well, though of course, as you may have heard, I don't always agree with everything he says.' There was a little worried frown on Mrs. Lyall's face, which made Jane say in a hearty reassuring voice, 'Oh, no, of course one doesn't. There's good and bad on each side, isn't there?'

'I'm so glad to hear you say that, because it's just what I feel.'

'After all,' said Jane, warming to the subject, 'Members of

89

Parliament are only human beings, aren't they? We all make mistakes, even the best of us, whichever the best may be.'

She realised that she had spoilt her little message of cheer by throwing in this last obscurity, for the worried frown appeared again on Mrs. Lyall's face.

'If only one could take the good from *both* sides,' said Mrs. Lyall sadly. 'Still, I do feel that things are not quite as they used to be.'

'No,' Jane agreed. 'There have been many changes in the last few years.'

'Especially since the war,' went on Mrs. Lyall. 'I think of it often, especially at breakfast-time.'

'At breakfast-time?' Jane echoed.

'Yes, all those dishes on the sideboard. When my husband was alive, we'd have three or four different hot dishes and cold ham when there were only the three of us at breakfast.'

'Ah, yes,' said Jane eagerly; 'kidneys and bacon and scrambled egg and boiled eggs, perhaps haddock too, not to mention porridge. I used to read about it in novels about Edwardian country house parties.'

'Now we've done away with all that,' said Mrs. Lyall, 'and it's such a relief. I just have tea and toast. Edward likes coffee and a cereal of some kind. He might have a boiled egg or a rasher of bacon occasionally. . . .'

Jane turned away, feeling that she was not worthy to receive these sacred revelations of his tastes. Others ought to have been listening and they apparently were, for Miss Doggett's voice chimed in, saying, 'I think a man needs a cooked breakfast, especially after an all-night sitting in the House. I can imagine Mr. Lyall needing a cooked breakfast then. Can't you, Jessie?' She turned to her companion and spoke rather sharply for, as Jane had noticed, Miss Morrow was smirking a little as if there were something funny being said.

'Men seem to need a lot of food at all times,' said Miss Morrow in a rough, casual tone.

'Sometimes,' said Mrs. Lyall, on what seemed a reproachful note, 'Edward is too tired to eat breakfast when he's been in the House all night.'

'Oh, dear . . .' Mrs. Mayhew and Mrs. Crampton had now joined the little group round Mrs. Lyall.

'Perhaps a nourishing milk drink would be best at a time like that?' suggested Mrs. Crampton. 'Benger's or Ovaltine . . .'

'Or a more drastic remedy,' said Miss Doggett boldly. 'Brandy, perhaps?'

'Yes, one does feel that in cases of fatigue, something really strong is needed,' said Mrs. Mayhew.

'I always think one should have brandy in the house,' said Mrs. Crampton.

'Does she mean in the house or in the House?' said Miss Morrow to Jane. 'I think we can safely leave them to their worship now, don't you?'

'Yes,' Jane agreed. 'Why, what have you got there?' she asked, seeing that Miss Morrow appeared to be secreting a paper bag behind her back.

'Oyster patties,' whispered Miss Morrow. 'I like them too. I thought I would eat them when I got home in the privacy of my bedroom. I took these when nobody was looking, or, rather, nobody who mattered. I think Mr. Oliver saw me, but with his views he could hardly disapprove. Would you like one?'

'No, thank you,' said Jane. She looked rather anxiously round the hall to see that Prudence and Flora were all right. The latter was talking to Mr. Oliver, but Prudence was standing in an incongruous little group, which consisted of Mrs. Glaze, Nicholas and the two churchwardens. She did not look as if she were enjoying herself very much, and she had been promised at least a glimpse of Fabian Driver, Jane realised, and there was no sign of him as yet.

'I wonder what can have happened to Mr. Driver?' she said to Miss Morrow. 'Doesn't he usually put in an appearance at these affairs?'

'Oh, yes,' said Miss Morrow. 'He will be coming along when he judges the time is ripe.'

'Ripe?' echoed Jane in a puzzled voice. 'How can it be ripe, and for what?'

'A good entrance. He has to time his appearance carefully – it mustn't be too soon after the arrival of Edward Lyall, otherwise he wouldn't be noticed.'

'Surely he wouldn't consciously think of it like that,' said Jane, laughing. 'I expect he likes to have a leisurely dinner and then come along.'

'Yes; Mrs. Arkright has left him a cold bird – pheasant, I believe – with a salad, and he will take his time over the meal, but he will take more time than is really necessary.'

'What a lot you know about him,' said Jane, looking at Miss Morrow with new eyes. What she saw was unremarkable enough; the birdlike little face with long nose and large bright eyes, the ordinary dark blue crepe dress with a cheap paste clip at the neck.

'Well, living next door, you get to know these things. I knew Constance, his wife, of course. One can know a lot about men through their wives.'

'Oh, dear . . .' Jane considered herself ruefully. 'Yes, I suppose one can. What was she like?'

'Older than he was, not a very interesting person really; she was a good needlewoman.'

Miss Morrow's tone was dry and Jane did not feel she had gleaned very much about Constance Driver from this bare description. Surely he will come soon, she told herself, anxious for Prudence's evening, and very soon after this he did come, walking in slowly, his leonine head held rather high, looking around him with an air almost of surprise.

Miss Morrow smiled sardonically. Jane advanced towards him and he greeted her.

'I want you to meet Miss Prudence Bates,' she said. 'She is staying with us for the week-end.'

So this is Fabian Driver, thought Prudence, putting on a rather cool social manner. She had a natural distrust of good-looking men, though they seemed to offer a challenge which she was never unwilling to accept. Fabian's glance when they shook hands was so penetrating that something of her poise deserted her. She had often enough had men look at her like that, and perhaps it is a thing that women cannot have too much of. She returned his glance and held it.

'How do you do?' he murmured.

Jane, watching from the side, thought 'Oh, goody,' in a childish sort of way. It was going to be all right. The way he had looked at her was most promising. *By our first strange and fatal interview* . . . she said to herself.

Prudence and Fabian drew a little apart from the whist players, who had now started again, Edward Lyall and his mother among them.

'Have you been playing?' Fabian asked.

'Only a little,' said Prudence, with a laugh. 'I'm afraid I've forgotten all I ever knew about it, though.'

'I like to look in at these affairs,' said Fabian. 'One has a certain responsibility, living in a small community.'

'Yes, I suppose so.'

There was a pause. It's like being at a cocktail party without anything to drink, thought Prudence.

'Would you like a sandwich?' she asked, offering a dejected-looking plate.

'No, thank you. I had dinner before I came. I was wondering, though,' he looked deeply into her eyes, 'whether we might slip out and have a drink? Would you like one?'

'Yes, I certainly would. The strain of making conversation with so many people has quite worn me out.'

'Had you a coat or something? It's rather cold outside.'

'I had a little fur.' Prudence made a helpless gesture round her shoulders. 'We left it somewhere when we came in.'

Fabian retrieved her cape from a pile of tweed coats and they went out together. The pub was just the other side of the pond. They seemed almost to run towards it and were soon sitting by a blazing fire. Most of the villagers were at the whist drive and the bar was deserted. Fabian asked Prudence what she would like to drink and she told him with no false modesty or beating about the bush. Mild-and-bitter or light ale, which she did not like, anyway, would have seemed unworthy of the occasion. But their conversation did not improve very much even with strong drink, though they gradually became more relaxed and their eyes met so often in penetrating looks that it did not seem to matter that they had little to say to each other, or that Prudence found herself doing most of the talking. She had spent many such evenings in her life and always enjoyed them; the time passed pleasantly until it was time to go home.

'I'm afraid it's rather dark in the country,' said Fabian, taking Prudence's arm. 'I shall have to guide you.'

'I can see quite well, thank you,' said Prudence in her cool voice. 'I like walking in the dark.'

'I will see you to your door,' said Fabian.

'Well, that is kind of you. I'm not quite sure where the vicarage is from here.'

'Just the other side of the pond. But it's quite easy to get lost in a strange place. My house is just here.' He indicated a gate.

'How nice. Jane tells me it is a lovely house.'

Fabian sighed. 'Yes, I suppose it is, but I'm a lonely person.'

Prudence, her perception a little blunted by whisky, did not smile. She looked up at his face and found his profile pleasing. Poor, lonely Fabian. . . . She began to wonder if he would kiss her outside the vicarage gate.

'Good night, Mr. Driver,' a loud countrywoman's voice broke in on her thoughts, and she realised that they were passing the village hall, from which a crowd was now emerging. So it was unlikely that he would have the opportunity to kiss her good night. She wondered if she would have enjoyed it if he had.

'We must meet in London,' Fabian was saying as he let go of her arm. 'Perhaps you could have lunch with me or something? Or we might go to a theatre and have dinner.'

'That would be very nice.'

'May I write or telephone you, then? Is your name in the book?'

'Oh, yes.'

'Miss Bates – Miss Prudence Bates.' He took her hand as if he would kiss it, but his gallant gesture was interrupted by the appearance of Miss Doggett and Miss Morrow, who called out 'Good night' and went on their way muttering.

Fabian sighed. 'Ah, well . . . good night, my dear,' and Prudence walked up the vicarage drive alone.

Inside the vicarage the family had assembled in Nicholas's study.

'We felt like a cup of cocoa,' said Jane brightly. 'Would you like one?'

'No, thank you,' said Prudence, blinking her eyes in the light.

'No, perhaps not – you had a drink with Fabian, I imagine.' Jane tried to keep her voice flat and uninterested.

'Yes, I did.'

'What did you have?'

'Whisky.'

Jane made a face. 'How horrid! Was Fabian in good form?' she asked, yielding to temptation.

'Good form? Well, I don't know. We talked about Italy and Coventry Patmore and Donne and various other things.'

'Coventry Patmore and Donne! He has never talked like that to me – you *must* have got on well.'

'I thought him rather pleasant,' said Prudence in an offhand way. Really, now she came to think of it, though, it was she who had brought Coventry Patmore and Donne into the conversation.

I wonder if he kissed her, Jane thought. She was surprised to hear that they had had what seemed to be quite an intelligent conversation, for she had never found Fabian very much good in that line. She had a theory that this was why he tended to make love to women – because he couldn't really think of much to say to them – but she could hardly reveal her thought to Prudence.

'Edward Lyall is charming, don't you think?' she went on. 'I thought he looked rather tired to-night. It must be exhausting to be admired like that, and one feels that politicians aren't quite so used to it as the clergy are.'

Nicholas smiled down into his cocoa.

Prudence agreed that Edward Lyall was good-looking. Flora busied herself removing the cups, but said nothing. To-night she had known the exquisitely painful sensation of a moment's unfaithfulness to Mr. Oliver, whose place in her affections had not yet been taken by any undergraduate. Edward Lyall's pale, even slightly hollow, cheek had touched her imagination. But everyone had been rather horrid to Mr. Oliver, and that had touched her heart. She scarcely knew which she would think about before she went to sleep that night.

Jane stood up and stretched her arms. She hoped it had been a good evening. Perhaps Fabian and Prudence could meet in London. She began to plan lunches and dinners for them. Really, she was almost like Pandarus, she told herself, only it was to be a courtship and marriage according to the most decorous conventions. Fabian was a widower and Prudence was a spinster; there wasn't even the embarrassment of divorce. No, when she thought it over, Jane decided that she was really much more like Emma Woodhouse.

# Chapter Ten

✠

'Do you suppose Miss Bates has any love life?' asked Marilyn idly one morning after Prudence had been staying with Jane. 'She's quite attractive still, really.'

'I wonder how old she *is*,' said Gloria. 'About thirty, do you think?'

'Oh, yes, must be. I hope I die before I'm thirty – it sounds so old.'

'Forty must be worse,' said Gloria sensibly. 'I shouldn't like to be forty. Miss Trapnell's over forty, I should think, and Miss Clothier too.'

They brooded silently for a moment over this horror.

'Manifold's thirty,' said Marilyn in a brighter tone. 'It doesn't seem so bad for a man.'

'And Gramp's forty-eight this year,' said Gloria. 'I looked him up in *Who's Who*.'

'Fancy him being anybody,' giggled Marilyn. 'You wouldn't think it to look at him. Forty-eight! That makes him nearly twenty years older than Miss Bates. When she was a baby, he was grown-up. Fancy that! How do you think the passion's going these days?'

They discussed Miss Bates's passion for Dr. Grampian for some moments, after which they came to the conclusion that any feeling one might have for such an elderly man – and in the office too – could hardly be counted as love life. They regarded themselves as much more fortunate in having friends of their own age who had nothing to do with their work.

'I suppose I'd better make the tea,' said Gloria, getting up and taking the kettle to fill it. 'It's my turn to-day.'

'Are you going to make Manifold's Nescafé?'

'No, he can make it himself if he wants it. I don't mind

boiling water for him – he can have what's left over from the tea.'

In another room Prudence sat with Miss Trapnell and Miss Clothier, discussing the possibility of tea being ready within the foreseeable future.

'Five-past eleven,' said Miss Trapnell. 'I hope they've put the kettle on.'

'I thought I heard a sound,' said Miss Clothier, opening her tin of biscuits.

'What kind of a sound?' asked Prudence idly.

'The sound of running water.'

'Did you say rushing water?' asked Miss Trapnell seriously.

'No, no; *running* water,' said Miss Clothier impatiently. 'As if somebody was filling a kettle.'

Footsteps were heard outside the door. They paused for a moment.

'Ah,' said Miss Trapnell.

'Look here, Miss Bates!' Mr. Manifold burst into the room and confronted the three women.

I suppose he hides his feeling of inferiority under this blunt and rather ill-bred manner, thought Prudence, hardly looking up from what she was doing. After a moment she did glance up in what seemed to him her cool, maddening way.

She saw him standing by her side, holding a bundle of galley proofs. Corduroy trousers, plaid shirt and tweed jacket – why must he dress like an undergraduate? she thought with irritation. And the dear boy was so cross about something. His eyes were blazing.

'Have I done something?' she asked.

'Yes, or at least I think so,' he faltered, disarmed by her coldness. 'Didn't you write up these notes of mine for Gramp?'

'I may have done. Let me see.' Prudence held out a hand for the proofs. 'What's it all about? Ah, yes,' she smiled. 'It was most obscure – Dr. Grampian and I had a very difficult time with it. We couldn't make out what you meant.'

'Well, it wasn't what you've put,' said Mr. Manifold rather more meekly now. 'Perhaps I didn't make it quite clear.'

'No, I don't think you can have done. Oh, good, here's tea. Stay and have yours here and then we can talk it over.'

'I don't want any tea.'

'Oh, no. You don't like it, do you? Gloria will make you some Nescafé, won't you, Gloria?'

'All right, Miss Bates,' said Gloria rather sulkily.

'I don't want anything, thank you,' said Mr. Manifold. 'I'll make it myself later, if I do.'

'You really ought to have something,' said Miss Clothier. 'Won't you have a biscuit?'

'Thank you. I am rather hungry as a matter of fact.'

'I'll just slip out and tell Gloria to make you some Nescafé,' said Miss Trapnell.

Mr. Manifold sat down by Prudence and together they discussed the corrections that would have to be made.

'You see, it isn't really quite what's written here,' he explained. 'You've over-simplified it.'

'Really?' Prudence assumed an interested tone and looked up into his clear hazel eyes as if she understood every word he was saying. 'I'm afraid we've got it wrong, then.'

'One doesn't want to be misrepresented.'

'No, of course not. I'm sorry.'

'Oh, that's all right. I only thought for a moment . . .'

'What did you think?' Prudence looked up at him again. Really, his eyes were beautiful, she thought. Her voice had taken on an absent-mindedly intimate note as if she were not in the office at all.

Mr. Manifold looked surprised. Then he smiled and something like a blush flooded into his pale cheeks. Prudence turned away to hide a smile and he hurried out of the room.

'Why, he didn't finish his Nescafé,' she exclaimed after he had gone.

'I suppose he forgot it,' said Miss Trapnell.

'Being with you must have put it out of his mind,' said Miss Clothier.

'Being with *me*?'

'Yes, I always think he rather likes you, Miss Bates.'

Prudence laughed. 'Well, really, what an extraordinary idea!' But, why not? What could be more natural? She was attractive and intelligent, even 'desirable'; it was not at all surprising that Geoffrey Manifold should find her so.

When the telephone rang and she was summoned into the presence of Dr. Grampian she went to his room feeling light-hearted and confident, ready to be admired by him too.

He was sitting at his desk with a glass of water and some tablets before him. Prudence felt a pang that she was not as moved at the sight as she would have been a few weeks ago.

'Ah, Miss Bates,' he said, opening the bottle and shaking a few tablets out on to the desk.

'Aren't you feeling well?' asked Prudence, her tone softening. We must love them all, she thought, and perhaps we should make a special effort with those for whom our love is growing cold.

'I suppose I am as well as I ever am,' said Dr. Grampian in a colourless tone. 'But things have been rather trying lately.'

Prudence wondered what things. Men did not have quite the same trials as women – it would be the larger things that worried him, his health, his work, perhaps even his wife Lucy. Was she being unsatisfactory in some way? Prudence felt that she could hardly ask.

'I think you and Manifold between you could manage to do something with this . . .' he went on, taking up a thick folder of type-written foolscap, turning over the pages and marking certain paragraphs with a pencil. Prudence appeared to be attending to him, but her thoughts were wandering to the evening she was to spend with Fabian. Their acquaintance had prospered since the evening they had met at the whist drive. Luncheons and dinners, with the appropriate foods and wines, had turned it into quite a romantic love affair.

When the time came to leave the office, Prudence was ready to go before six o'clock had struck.

'Being with Dr. Grampian always takes it out of me,' she explained. 'I'm really quite exhausted.'

Miss Trapnell nodded sympathetically. 'Contact with a brilliant mind like that must be very tiring,' she agreed. 'You have to be so very much on your mettle.'

Prudence remembered the bottle of tablets and the fingers turning the pages of the typescript and her own silence, filled with thoughts of Fabian, and had the grace not to pursue the subject further.

She was to meet Fabian at a Soho restaurant which they usually frequented, but luckily there was time for her to go back to her flat first to change her dress and give herself a suitable evening face.

He was waiting for her with a spray of red roses, her favourite flowers. He found it pleasant to be taking an attractive woman out to dinner again – ten months was a long time to be away from it all, he had hardly realised how much he had missed it, and was gratified to find that he had not lost his old touch. And this time there was the added pleasure of a clear conscience; it was a very long time since he had been able to take out another woman without the nagging guilty feeling at the back of his mind, the picture of Constance, sitting in a deck-chair under the walnut tree, doing her needlework.

'My darling,' he said as they sipped cocktails, 'how very lovely you look to-night. I've been so longing to see you again.'

Prudence took a larger gulp of her drink. She had thought his words rather banal, disappointing, even. Her imaginary evenings with Arthur Grampian had not been quite like this, but probably he would have been just as dull when it came to the point. Perhaps nothing could be quite so sweet as the imagined evenings with their flow of sparkling conversation, but it was not the kind of thing she could very well say to Fabian. All the same, she told herself sensibly, he would probably make quite a good husband for her. He was the right age, they had tastes in common and she enjoyed his company. Also, and this was not unimportant, he was good-looking. They would make a handsome couple.

'Now we must have something nice to eat,' said Fabian, studying the menu. 'What would you like, my dear?'

Prudence chose what she would have, perhaps more carefully than a woman truly in love would have done, and Fabian made his choice, which was equally deliberate and not quite the same as hers.

The chicken will have that wonderful sauce with it, thought Prudence, looking into Fabian's eyes. She had ordered smoked salmon to begin with, and afterwards perhaps she would have some Brie, all creamy and delicious.

'Have you seen Jane lately?' she asked.

'Oh, yes. I quite often see her,' said Fabian. 'We are great friends. I find her a most delightful person.'

'Yes; dear Jane. She is rather wonderful, and yet in a way she's missed something. Life hasn't turned out quite as she meant it to.'

Fabian looked blank.

'She seems quite happy,' he ventured.

'*Seems*, well, yes . . .'

Fabian found Prudence's tone disconcerting; it was as if no woman could be really happy even when she was being taken out to dinner. He felt he ought to say something profound, but, naturally enough, nothing profound came out.

'I mean, she leads a useful kind of life – work in the parish and that kind of thing,' he went on vaguely.

'But she's really no good at parish work – she's wasted in that kind of life. She has great gifts, you know. She could have written books.'

'Written books? Oh, good heavens!'

'Well, what's wrong with that?' asked Prudence rather sharply.

'I always think women who write books sound rather formidable.'

'You'd prefer them to be stupid and feminine? To think men are wonderful?'

'Well, every man likes to be thought wonderful. A woman need not necessarily be stupid to admire a man.'

Prudence thought a little sadly of her admiration for Arthur Grampian, now perhaps in the past. She could not pretend that she really admired Fabian in quite the same way. But when the wine came, golden and delicious, her heart warmed towards him and by the time they were drinking black coffee and brandy she felt that perhaps she really did admire Fabian. After all, what was a brilliant mind and some rather dull books that nobody could be expected to read? Not so very much really when compared with curly hair, fine eyes and good features.

'I shall have a dark, lonely journey home,' said Fabian softly. 'It seems very sad that we have to part.'

'Yes, it does,' said Prudence thoughtfully; 'but evenings have to come to an end.'

'They need not,' Fabian began, but then he remembered that Prudence could not be quite like all the others. There was the complication of her being a friend of Jane Cleveland's. Somehow one did not play fast and loose with the friend of one's vicar's wife, he thought solemnly.

'Perhaps some other time . . .' said Prudence uncertainly.

'I'll see about getting you a taxi, then.'

While Prudence was waiting in the foyer, a tall young woman in a tweed suit came up to her.

'Hullo, Prue! I saw you in the distance, but you wouldn't look at me.'

'Why, Eleanor, what are you doing here?'

'My dear, I've been having dinner with J.B. He's off to the

Middle East to-morrow. We didn't leave the Ministry till after nine – there were *things to see to*, you know.'

Eleanor's tone, mysteriously important as always, made Prudence a little envious. How wonderful it must be to work for somebody who really needed you, who couldn't get off to the Middle East unless you were there to see to things. J.B. couldn't do anything without Eleanor. She stood now, beaming, tweedy and efficient, while J.B., a tall worried-looking man with an excessively bulging briefcase, got his coat from the cloakroom.

'We must lunch one day,' said Prudence rather feebly.

'Oh, yes, let's. Give me a ring some time.'

Going home by herself in the taxi, Prudence thought of Eleanor and her other contemporaries at Oxford, all neatly labelled in Miss Birkinshaw's comfortable classification. 'Eleanor, with her work at the Ministry, Mollie with the Settlement and her dogs, and Prudence . . .' Well, what about Prudence? Prudence with her love affairs, that was what Jane used to say, and perhaps, after all, it was true. She would put the red roses in a glass on her bedside table and take them into the office in the morning.

## *Chapter Eleven*

✖

NOW THAT there was a feeling of spring in the air, Fabian decided that he really ought to do something about 'poor Constance's things'. Also, the entry of Prudence into his life made it seem unsuitable that nothing should have been done about them before.

It was Mrs. Arkright who managed to spur him to some definite action. She was always saying to her friends what a shame it was that all those good things of poor Mrs. Driver's should be still lying in the drawers and wardrobes, and now that another spring with its attendant cleaning and tidying was approaching it really did seem as if she ought to say something to Mr. Driver. Last spring it had been different, of course; the bereavement was too fresh in his mind, poor man, but now it really was time that he pulled himself together.

Jane Cleveland heard all about this from Mrs. Glaze.

'It's just over the year now,' she said. 'I was looking in the paper last week to see if there'd be anything, but there wasn't.'

'In the paper?' Jane asked. 'But why should there be?'

'In Memoriam,' said Mrs. Glaze rather stiffly. 'It's nice to put something.'

'Oh, in the local paper, of course,' said Jane, remembering the long column of pathetic, limping verses commemorating Gran and Dad and the rest of the dear departed.

'You'd have thought there might be something,' went on Mrs. Glaze. 'Mrs. Arkright passed the same remark to me only yesterday. You'd think he'd remember her.'

'I don't suppose he forgot,' said Jane, 'but people don't always show their feelings in the same way, do they.' And sometimes, she added to herself, they don't have the feelings one would expect.

*A long sad year has passed today*
*Since my dear Connie was taken away . . .*

Was that the kind of thing Mrs. Glaze and Mrs. Arkright would have found suitable, nodding their heads and saying it was 'nice'?

'That sort of thing shouldn't really be necessary for Christians,' she began firmly; 'if we believe, as we should . . .' But then, she thought, weren't we all, even the most intelligent of us, like children fearing to go into the dark, no better than primitive peoples with their ancestor cults, the way we went to the cemetery on a Sunday afternoon, bearing bunches of flowers? But she couldn't say all this to Mrs. Glaze, standing at the kitchen table in her hat and apron, making pastry.

'At least he's going to get her things sorted out; that's

something,' said Mrs. Glaze. 'Mrs. Arkright said why not let Miss Doggett and Miss Morrow do it – they're nice ladies and they were friends of poor Mrs. Driver.'

'Or Mrs. Crampton and Mrs. Mayhew,' suggested Jane, 'though they might be too busy at the Spinning Wheel.'

'Well, four ladies might be a bit too much even for Mr. Driver,' said Mrs. Glaze with a laugh. 'Perhaps there should be a married lady, though. He might have asked you, but I told Mrs. Arkright, I didn't think you would be much of a one for tidying.'

Jane hung her head. 'No, not for tidying, perhaps,' she agreed. But was her status as wife of the vicar of the parish to count for nothing? She could hardly add that her insatiable curiosity might also render her eligible for the position. 'When are they going to do it?'

'On Saturday afternoon – that seemed the best time.'

'I should have thought a morning might be better,' said Jane.

Mrs. Glaze looked a little shocked. 'We have our work in the morning, madam,' she said importantly. 'Mrs. Arkright will be there to do the tea, of course.'

'So tea is to be provided?'

'Well, they'll need tea. There's a lot of things to be sorted.'

'Yes, of course,' said Jane slowly, her mind on plans for being there herself. A casual call? A request to borrow a lawn-mower in the depths of winter? How was she to manage it? No doubt something would occur to her when the time came.

On the chosen Saturday afternoon Miss Doggett and Miss Morrow left their house at about a quarter past two. Miss Doggett had considered the occasion important enough to give up her afternoon rest and was rather more grandly dressed than a call next door seemed to warrant, in a skunk cape and large hat of the type known as 'matron's', trimmed with brown velvet and little tufts of feathers. Miss Morrow wore her grey tweed coat and had a plaid scarf over her head.

They went up to Fabian's front door and rang the bell. Mrs.

Arkright in her apron and a purple turban opened the door and showed them into the dining-room, where Fabian was still at the table drinking his coffee. He sat with his head bowed, gazing into his cup, one cheek resting on his hand. It seemed a suitable position for him to be in, making it appear that a mere week or two and not a whole year had elapsed since poor Constance's death.

'You will forgive me if I don't join you,' he said in a low voice. 'I should find it . . .'

'Oh, very painful, of course. We quite understand,' said Miss Doggett briskly. 'We'll get to work straight away.'

'Most of the things are upstairs,' said Fabian in the same low voice. 'In the large room overlooking the garden and some in the room next to it. I shall stay here . . .' He drew towards him a bowl of white hyacinths which stood on the table and began to sniff at the flowers absent-mindedly.

Miss Doggett and Miss Morrow went quietly out of the room. Once out of his presence, however, their steps became noticeably brisker and there was an eagerness about their bearing which they did not attempt to conceal.

'Now for it,' said Miss Morrow, almost running up the stairs.

'Really, Jessie,' said Miss Doggett, whose step was slower than her companion's only because she was a much older and heavier woman. 'I wonder if Mr. Driver would object to our lighting the gas-fire,' she said as they opened the door and sensed the chill of the big room overlooking the garden. 'It's rather cold in here. Poor Constance always used to say this room was damp.'

'He'd jolly well better not object,' said Miss Morrow, lighting the fire and then removing her coat and scarf. 'On what principle are we to sort out these things? Distressed gentlewomen and jumble? Or should there be more and subtler distinctions?'

'No. I should think that is what Mr. Driver would wish, and what poor Constance herself would have wished,' said Miss

Doggett, opening the wardrobe. 'Oh, dear, here is her mus-quash coat! She never had it remodelled, though I often sug-gested to her that she should. Mr. Rose could have done it for her as he did my cape.' She stroked the strands of skunk which still hung from her shoulders, for the room had not yet warmed up in spite of the flaring and popping gas-fire.

'I can just see her in that coat,' said Jessie, looking at the long brown coat with its narrow shoulders and old-fashioned roll collar. She remembered Constance's long, pale face with the worried grey eyes and the fair, wispy hair drawn back into a rather meagre little knot on the nape of the neck. 'And, oh dear, here are all her shoes, long and narrow and of such good leather. Just the thing for the gentlewomen.'

'She was much too good for him,' said Miss Doggett, taking a pair of the shoes into her hand. 'I often wondered how they ever came to be married. These lizard courts – they cost eight guineas, I remember Constance telling me. She had to have them specially made, such a very narrow foot she had.'

Miss Doggett was still holding the shoes when Jane came into the room carrying a khaki canvas hold-all.

'I came round on the offchance of getting a bit of jumble,' she said, bringing out the words she had been rehearsing on her way from the vicarage. She had decided to appear in the simple rôle of a vicar's wife seeking jumble, and hoped it sounded convincing. Mrs. Arkright, who had opened the door, had looked a little suspicious, but Miss Doggett and Miss Morrow appeared to accept her without question.

'Jumble's on the bed,' said Miss Doggett. 'We have put the things we think might do for the distressed gentlewomen on the chaise-longue.'

'How very suitable to put them there!' Jane burst out. 'I suppose this was Mrs. Driver's room?'

'Yes, and she had the little room next door as a kind of workroom – she kept her sewing machine there and her em-broidery things.'

'These were her books?' Jane asked, going over to a small bookcase which was fixed on to the wall near the bed.

'I suppose so,' said Jessie, 'though Constance didn't seem to be much of a reader. She had a novel from the library sometimes.'

'Or a good biography,' added Miss Doggett.

'You mean a life of Florence Nightingale or the memoirs of some Edwardian diplomat's widow,' Jane murmured. 'But these are mostly books of poetry. Was this what she read secretly, I wonder?'

'Oh, I don't think Constance was the kind of person to go in for that sort of thing,' said Miss Doggett in a shocked voice.

'People do seem to be ashamed of admitting that they read poetry,' said Jane, 'unless they have a degree in English – it is permissible then. It has become a kind of bad habit, but one that is excused. I wonder what she made of Mr. Auden and Mr. MacNeice? Perhaps the seventeenth century was more to her taste, as it is to mine. Odd to think that we may have had that in common.' She took a book from the shelf and began to examine it in the hope of finding an interesting inscription on the fly-leaf. Nor was she disappointed, for on it was written in a fine, intelligent-looking hand

F. from C., 18th April, 1935

*My Love is of a birth as rare*
*As 'tis for object strange and high . . .*

She closed the book quickly and slipped it into the canvas hold-all. This must not go to the jumble sale. Marvell – *A Definition of Love* – had poor Constance's love been begotten by Despair upon Impossibility? Jane wondered. But then of course when writing an inscription one did not always consider the appropriateness or otherwise of the rest of the poem. 1935 – Fabian would have been in his early twenties and Constance some years older – it must have been at some moment during their courtship. Jane wondered when she had taken her gift back, if it had been a conscious action performed on some special occasion, perhaps after some particularly painful infidelity on Fabian's part, or whether the book had just got into the shelf of its own accord, as it were, as books do when they are no longer particularly treasured.

'Do you suppose he really wants any of these books?' she asked in a rather rough tone.

'Well, perhaps we had better ask him,' said Miss Doggett, 'though he did say he'd rather we used our own judgment.'

'I'll go and ask him if you like,' said Jessie, hurrying from the room.

She found Fabian downstairs huddled over the fire in the drawing-room. He did not seem to be doing anything in particular, though *The Times* was folded back at the crossword and there were a few words filled in. It was difficult, Jessie thought, for him to know what he ought to be doing while she and the others were upstairs. There was rugby football or dance music on the wireless, but neither of these would be suitable listening, and the Third Programme had not yet started. Perhaps some Bach on the radiogram or a little work in the garden, but the earth was still bare and hard and it did not look as if anything would ever grow again.

'Mrs. Cleveland wants to know about the books,' she began.

'What books?'

'On the shelf by the bed.'

'Oh, let her do what she likes with them – take them herself or have them for a jumble sale – I don't care.'

'Poor Fabian. What are you doing?' Jessie laid a hand on his head and looked down into his face. 'Just brooding?'

'I don't know what to do,' he said. 'The whole thing is most painful to me.'

'Yes, you are having the pain now,' Jessie said. 'Women are very powerful – perhaps they are always triumphant in the end.'

'What do you mean?'

'Oh, you wouldn't understand!' She dropped a light kiss on his brow and hurried away.

If Fabian was surprised by her action he gave no indication of it. After all, it was by no means the first time that a woman had paid him a little spontaneous tribute; it might be considered as no more than his due. He stood up and looked at his face in the mirror framed in a design of gilded cupids which hung over the mantelpiece. Its dim surface gave back an interesting, shadowy reflection. He began to think about Jessie Morrow – more in her than met the eye – a deep one – his thoughts shaped themselves into conventional phrases. She had an unexpectedly sharp tongue; there was something a little uncomfortable about that. She was so badly dressed, usually in tweeds that had never been good. It would be interesting to see her transformed in the way that the women's magazines sometimes glamorised a dowdy woman. No doubt Prudence would be able to make some suggestions. . . . Fabian's thoughts now turned to her, but his evenings in her company, though delightful, seemed to have little reality at the moment. Wine, good food, flowers, soft lights, holding hands, sparkling eyes, kisses . . . and upstairs those three women were sorting out poor Constance's things. Altogether he was glad when Mrs. Arkright announced that she had laid tea in the dining-room.

'I thought the ladies would prefer to sit round the table,' she explained.

They were summoned from upstairs and came down eagerly enough. Jane began to wonder if they were to have a meat tea or fish and chips as a reward for their hard work, but she was quite satisfied when she saw the hot buttered toast and sandwiches and several different kinds of cake.

'We're nearly through,' said Miss Doggett briskly. 'There are one or two small personal trinkets, we thought perhaps . . .'

'Oh, no . . .' Fabian bowed his head into his hands, 'not that . . .'

'Somebody had better pour out tea,' said Jane sensibly, wondering when Fabian would raise his head.

'You, of course, Mrs. Cleveland,' said Miss Doggett.

'I always do it rather badly,' said Jane. 'The ability to pour tea gracefully didn't come to me automatically when I married. I wish you would do it, Miss Doggett.'

'Very well, if you wish,' said Miss Doggett.

Fabian had by now raised his head and was taking a piece of hot buttered toast.

Mrs. Arkright came into the room bearing an iced walnut cake on a plate. 'Mrs. Crampton and Mrs. Mayhew have just called,' she explained. 'They thought Mr. Driver might like this cake. It's his favourite, I know.'

'How kind,' said Fabian, rousing himself. 'Are they at the door? Do ask them to come in so that I can thank them.'

'No, sir. They hurried away,' said Mrs. Arkright.

Jane reflected how much more delicate their behaviour had been than hers and bowed her head. Still, she had perhaps done some good by saving poor Constance's gift from prying eyes, and she had certainly collected a lot of useful jumble.

Miss Doggett and Jessie too could feel that they had done something both for Fabian and for the distressed gentlewomen, and Jessie had privately earmarked one or two garments for herself and planned to alter them suitably and add them to her wardrobe.

Conversation at tea was not very brilliant. Jane was thinking too much about Constance and the book, Jessie about Fabian, and Fabian himself about the oppressive presence of three not particularly attractive women at his table, and also about Jessie's strange behaviour earlier in the afternoon. He hoped she wasn't going to become a nuisance in any way. They still had a little more sorting out to do, but he decided against offering them sherry when they had finished. It might go to their heads, he decided, and then they might all behave foolishly. He could easily make it understood that he was really too much upset to prolong the painful business any longer. He would have a half bottle of St. Emilion with his dinner, and after that he might write a letter to Prudence.

'Well, it's a very satisfactory thing to have done,' declared Miss Doggett as they stood outside Fabian's gate in the cold night air. 'I expect Mr. Driver is very relieved to have it settled. We shall be going in to-morrow to parcel up the things for the gentlewomen.'

'Well, I suppose I must be getting home,' said Jane. 'Poor Mr. Driver – it seems unkind to leave him all alone this evening.'

'Yes,' Miss Doggett agreed. 'One does feel that men need company more than women do. A woman has a thousand and one little tasks in the house, and then her knitting or sewing.'

Jane, who did not seem to have these things, made no answer.

'A man can have his thoughts,' suggested Miss Morrow.

'Perhaps they do not care to be left alone with those,' said Jane. 'I often wonder when I leave Nicholas in his study.'

'But surely, Mrs. Cleveland, a clergyman must be different. He would be thinking out a sermon or a letter to the Bishop.'

'Yes, he ought to be doing things like that,' said Jane vaguely. 'Well, I mustn't keep you talking in the cold. Good night.' She wandered away in the direction of the vicarage, but when she reached the church she lingered a while by the churchyard wall, thinking of eighteenth-century poets and charnel-houses and exhumations by the light of flickering candles. Then she saw that there was a light in the choir vestry. No doubt Nicholas was doing something there; there was a meeting of some kind or perhaps a choir practice. Then she remembered that he was away from home that evening, at some ruridecanal conference, something that went beyond the narrow confines of the parish. Mrs. Glaze was to have left her something simple and womanish for her evening meal, the kind of thing that a person with no knowledge of cooking might heat up.

She crept up to the window where the light was and stood

outside it for a moment. People seemed to be talking inside – men's voices were raised in what sounded like an argument. Jane felt like some character in a novel by Mrs. Henry Wood. But she was the vicar's wife and as such surely had a right of entry to the choir vestry. So she went boldly up to the door and opened it.

'Good evening,' she said. 'I saw a light and heard voices so I thought I'd look in.'

'Good evening, Mrs. Cleveland.' Mr. Mortlake stood before her, obviously angry at being disturbed and looking rather terrible.

'Good evening.' Mr. Oliver stood up and looked a little taken aback. The third member of the party, Mrs. Glaze's nephew, the butcher, said nothing. To-morrow, thought Jane, we may have to face each other over a tray full of offal or a few chops scattered between us, so perhaps silence is the best thing.

'I could hear your voices from outside,' she observed pleasantly. 'Were you having an argument about something?'

'We were discussing a little matter,' said Mr. Oliver in a soothing tone; 'nothing of any importance, really.'

'There was some disagreement,' said Mr. Mortlake.

'A difference of opinion, you might say,' ventured Mrs. Glaze's nephew.

'Well, I'm sure you ought not to disagree about things,' said Jane. 'After all, you are all members of the Parochial Church Council, and in a way I suppose you are on hallowed ground here.'

'I wouldn't go so far as to say that, Mrs. Cleveland,' said Mr. Mortlake indignantly, so that she feared he must have misunderstood her.

'Well, perhaps not,' Jane faltered, for she was not really certain whether the choir vestry was in fact regarded as part of the church, 'but one doesn't like to think of any unpleasantness here. I know my husband would be sorry to hear about it.'

'I am not aware that there has been any unpleasantness,' said

Mr. Oliver in a hostile tone. 'We all have our own opinions and are entitled to them, I suppose.'

'Of course,' said Jane. 'Perhaps an outsider could help you to make up your minds, though.'

'Well, Mrs. Cleveland, we can hardly regard you as that,' said Mr. Mortlake unctuously. 'But we cannot burden you with our little petty differences. It is a matter altogether out of your sphere.'

Really, thought Jane, it was like one of those rather tedious comic scenes in Shakespeare – Dogberry and Verges, perhaps – and therefore beyond her comprehension. She suddenly saw them all in Elizabethan costume and began to smile. 'Oh, well, I suppose I shouldn't interfere,' she said. 'We women can't always do as much as we think we can.' She had imagined herself mediating and bringing them together so that they all went off and settled their differences over a glass of beer. She turned to go, half hoping that they would call her back, but they watched her in silence, until Mr. Oliver bade her good night and the others followed his example.

When she got home she found that Mrs. Glaze had left her a shepherd's pie, a dish she particularly disliked, to put in the oven. She waited hopefully for Nicholas's return, but when he eventually came she found herself talking only about the afternoon they had spent at Fabian's and not mentioning the episode in the choir vestry.

## Chapter Twelve

❖

IN HER early days Jane had once had a book of essays published and had somehow managed to become a member of a certain literary society of which she still sometimes attended meetings. These usually took place in the evenings, and were another excuse for Jane to absent herself from parish duties and to stay a night with Prudence at her flat. This particular meeting was to be a rather special one; it was the centenary of the birth of an author whose works Jane had never read, but who had died recently enough to be remembered by many persons still alive. This seemed a good reason for a literary society to be gathering together, as Jane explained to Nicholas, who had protested, though mildly enough, at her missing a meeting of the Parochial Church Council.

'I shouldn't do any good there,' said Jane guiltily, remembering her intrusion into the choir vestry a few weeks ago of which she had told him nothing.

'I should have thought the time could be more profitably spent in encouraging young authors rather than in celebrating dead ones,' Nicholas declared.

'But it does encourage them,' Jane said. 'They imagine that one day such a meeting might be held about them, and I suppose they wonder what will be remembered and hope it won't be something they'd prefer to be forgotten.'

Nicholas sighed and did not argue further, for he knew it was likely to be as profitable as most arguments with his wife. His poor Jane, he must let her go where she wanted to.

The society met at a house with vaguely literary associations, for it was next door to what had once been the residence of one of the lesser Victorian poets, who is, nevertheless, quite well represented in the *Oxford Book of Victorian Verse*.

Jane entered the house with rather less awe than on her first visit many years ago, and made her way to a room on the first floor where the meetings were held. It was a pleasant room with the air of a drawing-room about it, though the rows of chairs were set a little too close together for comfort. Jane stood in the doorway, looking to see if anyone she knew had arrived, and soon noticed her old college friend, Barbara Bird ('Miss Bird has her novels and her dogs,' as Miss Birkinshaw put it), sitting in the back row. She was wearing a shaggy orange fox fur cape and smoking a cigarette which she waved to Jane, indicating a vacant chair at her side.

'Freezing cold in here,' she said. 'Nice to see you, Jane.'

Jane sat down and looked around her. Here again, as when she went back to her old College, she found that she did not really look any more peculiar than the majority of the women present, most of whom were dressed without regard to any particular fashion. But it was a cold evening, so perhaps they had more excuse than the graduates who met in the summer. Jane herself was wearing her old fur lined boots and a tweed coat, underneath which an assortment of cardigans and scarves concealed a red woollen dress that Prudence had once given her.

'Better gathering than usual,' said Miss Bird; 'quite a few critics.'

'Such mild-looking men,' said Jane, seeing one of them taking his seat rather near the front. 'Perhaps they compensate themselves for their gentle appearance by dipping their pens in vitriol.'

Miss Bird then went on to tell Jane about what the critics had said about her latest novel, during which Jane's thoughts wandered, 'much incident and little wit' she heard dimly, and then Miss Bird's wheezy smoker's laugh ending in a paroxysm of coughing.

Why was it, Jane wondered, that there were usually more women than men at these gatherings? Were men less gregarious, less willing to listen to a lecture or talk from one of their kind, or was it something really quite simple, such as the lack of alcoholic refreshment, that kept them away? Certainly there were some men who attended regularly, and each had his little circle of what were presumably admiring women. Jane had not so far attached herself to any group; she preferred to wander freely and observe others with what she hoped was detachment.

To-night there were three speakers, an elderly female novelist, a distinguished critic and a beautiful young poet. Or perhaps he was not really so very young, Jane decided, though he was certainly beautiful, with brown eyes and a well-shaped nose. It is a refreshing thing for an ordinary-looking woman to look at a beautiful man occasionally and Jane gave herself up to contemplation, while the talk of the critic and the novelist flowed over her. The poet spoke last and had a soft, attractive voice which was totally inaudible at the back of the room. Miss Bird shamed Jane at one point by demanding in her gruff voice that he should speak up, which he did for the rest of his sentence, afterwards lapsing into soft inaudibility.

As the time drew on towards the usual hour for closing the meeting, Jane saw through a glass door at the back of the room the faces of two women anxiously peering. One of them was holding a coffee-pot. Perhaps they made their presence felt to the speakers in some way, for shortly after this the talk finished. There was a short, appreciative silence, a hasty vote of thanks and then the crowd proceeded to squeeze itself with as much dignity as possible through the narrow door to the room where the refreshments were to be served. Miss Bird again embarrassed Jane by pushing herself forward, knocking against a novelist of greater distinction than herself and seizing a plate of sandwiches and making off with it to a comparatively uncrowded corner.

'Didn't have any dinner,' she explained.

'Aren't you Miss Barbara Bird?' said a tall, youngish woman with large eyes and prominent teeth, addressing Jane.

'No. *I'm* not Barbara Bird,' said Jane. 'You won't ever have heard of me. This is Barbara Bird.' She indicated her friend.

The woman then gave her name, which was unknown to both Jane and Miss Bird, and the titles of the two novels she had published, neither of which seemed familiar.

'I think I've heard of them,' said Jane kindly. 'And now I shall look forward to reading them.'

'Oh, they're nothing, really,' said the young woman.

'One's first two books are really rather more than that,' said Miss Bird. 'After the first two or three one must be unselfish and consider one's public and one's publisher. I have just finished my seventeenth – "Miss Bird's readers know what to expect now and they will not be disappointed." '

Jane thought the young woman looked a little cast down, so she said, 'Oh, but I think one develops as one goes on. I feel sure I shouldn't have had Barbara's attitude if I had written more than one book. It was nothing you could possibly have read,' she went on hastily, seeing the puzzled look on the woman's face. 'A book of essays on seventeenth-century poets about fifteen years ago. The kind of book you might put in the bathroom if you have books there – with Aubrey's *Brief Lives*, and *Wild Wales* – really, I wonder why, now! It would be an interesting study, that.'

'It's been lovely meeting you and Miss Bird,' said the young woman. 'I was wondering, do you think I *dare* speak to *him*?' She indicated the young or not-so-young poet, who was surrounded by a little group. 'I found his talk so wonderfully stimulating.'

'Was it? We couldn't hear a word at the back,' barked Miss Bird.

'But do you think I should *dare* to tell him how much I enjoyed it?' the woman persisted.

'Of course,' said Jane sympathetically, realising how much she longed for a glance from those brown eyes. 'I expect he is used to being admired.'

'It was what he *said* really,' protested the young woman, though rather faintly.

'Yes, go on,' said Barbara Bird, almost giving her a push. She and Jane turned and watched their former companion approach the poet, linger on the edge of the circle and then plunge boldly in with an apparently paralysing effect, for the others immediately broke away, leaving her alone with him.

'The evening will have been made for her now,' said Barbara Bird not unkindly.

'Oh, yes,' agreed Jane enthusiastically, stepping backwards into a critic and causing him to upset his coffee over himself.

'I think it will be better to pretend I didn't notice,' she whispered to her friend.

'Yes, by all means. Look, he is being attended to. A woman is mopping at his trousers with her handkerchief.'

'This seems a good time to leave,' said Jane. 'The last impression will have been good – one woman rendering homage to a poet and another mopping spilt coffee from the trousers of a critic. Things like that aren't as trivial as you might think.'

Rather to Jane's surprise, their decision to leave seemed to break up the other little groups, and once outside in the dark square they were groups no more, but isolated individuals, each one going his or her own way. Barbara Bird took a taxi, the critic made his way to the Underground, the poet walked quickly away, while the young woman who had admired him, after a regretful glance after him, stood rather hopelessly at a request bus stop. Perhaps she had hoped that they might stroll to a pub together or continue their conversation – if such it had been – walking round the square. But once outside the magic circle the writers became their lonely selves, pondering on poems, observing their fellow men ruthlessly, putting people they knew into novels; no wonder they were without friends. Jane was reminded of Darley's *Siren Chorus* and found herself thinking of the last verse:

> *In bowers of love men take their rest,*
> *In loveless bowers we sigh alone;*
> *With bosom-friends are others blest,*
> *But we have none – but we have none.*

The swans in snowy couples and the murmuring seal lying close to his sleek companion. . . . Jane almost forgot where she was supposed to be going and came to herself just as she reached the stop for the bus that would take her to Prudence's flat. She enjoyed riding on the top of the bus, smoking a cigarette and looking into the lighted windows of the houses they passed, hoping that she might see something interesting. Mostly, however, the curtains were discreetly drawn, except occasionally in a kitchen where a man was seen filling a hot-water bottle (for his invalid wife or for himself? Jane wondered) or a woman laying the breakfast ready for the morning. Once they stopped outside a high, dark house and Jane found herself looking through the uncurtained window into an upper room, dimly lit, where a group of men and women were sitting round a large table covered by a dark green cloth. The glimpse was too fleeting to reveal whether it was a séance or a committee meeting. Would she ever pass that house again? Jane wondered. She doubted in any case whether she would have recognised it again.

Prudence's flat was in the kind of block where Jane imagined people might be found dead, though she had never said this to Prudence herself; it seemed rather a macabre fancy and not one to be confided to an unmarried woman living alone. Prudence came to the door quickly in response to Jane's ring; she was wearing a long garment of dark red velvet, a sort of rather grand dressing-gown, it seemed to Jane, who supposed it was a housecoat, the kind of thing to wear for an evening of gracious living. Not the sort of garment a vicar's wife could be expected to possess.

'Jane, how lovely to see you! Was it a good meeting? Let me take your bag – then perhaps you'd like a drink or some tea or Ovaltine?'

Prudence prided herself on being a good hostess and tried to think of everything that a guest could possibly need. Jane, while appreciating this and benefiting from it, thought the flat a little too good to be true. Those light striped satin covers would 'show the dirt' – the pretty Regency couch was really rather uncomfortable and the whole place was so tidy that Jane felt out of place in it. Her old schoolboy's camel-hair dressing-gown looked as unsuitable in Prudence's spare-room as Prudence's turquoise blue wool housecoat did at the vicarage.

'You've got a new dressing-gown,' she said, trying to keep

out of her tone the accusing note that women are apt to use to each other, as if one had no business to spend one's own money on nice clothes.

'Yes, I have. Red seemed a good colour for winter and people seem to think it suits me. You're quite sure you wouldn't like whisky? I actually have some – but then I know you don't really like it.' Prudence was fussing a little, almost as if she were nervous.

'No. Ovaltine for me, thanks,' said Jane. 'I hate the taste of whisky.' Had she entertained Fabian in her red velvet dressing-gown? she wondered. 'People' seemed to think it suited her, and 'people' said in that way often meant a man.

'Does Fabian like you in red?' she asked bluntly.

'Yes. I think so,' said Prudence rather vaguely.

'Has he seen you in that?'

'I can't remember really – he probably has.'

'I suppose it's all right in London,' said Jane, thoughtfully stirring her Ovaltine.

'How do you mean?'

'Well, to entertain a man in one's dressing-gown.'

'It isn't a dressing-gown,' said Prudence rather impatiently; 'it's a housecoat. And in any case I don't know what you mean by "all right".'

'No, it's a very decent garment really, with long sleeves and a high neck.' Jane picked up a fold of the full skirt and stroked the velvet. 'I suppose what I meant was would people think anything of it if they knew.'

Prudence laughed. 'Oh, really, Jane! It certainly isn't like you to worry about what other people would think.'

'No. I suppose it isn't. I was just thinking of you, really. A married woman does feel in some way responsible for her unmarried friends, you know.'

'Really? That hadn't occurred to me. In any case, I'm perfectly well able to look after myself,' said Prudence rather touchily.

'Darling, of course! I only wondered . . .' Jane paused, for really it was difficult to know how to ask what she wanted to know, assuming that she had any right to ask such a question. 'I suppose everything is all right between you and Fabian?' she began tentatively.

'All right? Why, yes.'

'I mean, there's nothing *wrong* between you,' Jane laboured, using an expression she had sometimes seen in the cheaper women's papers where girls asked how they should behave when their boy-friends wanted them to 'do wrong'.

'But I don't understand you, Jane. Did you think we'd quarrelled or something? Because we certainly haven't, I can assure you.'

'No, it wasn't that. I don't seem to be putting it very clearly, what I was trying to ask was, are you Fabian's *mistress*?' As soon as she had said it, Jane found herself wanting to laugh. It was such a ridiculous word; it reminded her of full-blown Restoration comedy women or Nell Gwynn or Edwardian ladies kept in pretty little houses with wrought-iron balconies in St. John's Wood.

Prudence burst into laughter, in which Jane was able to join her with some relief.

'Really, Jane, what an extraordinary question – you *are* a funny old thing! Am I Fabian's *mistress*? Is there anything *wrong* between us? I couldn't imagine what you meant!'

Jane looked up from her Ovaltine hopefully. 'I don't really know how people behave these days,' she said.

'Well, I mean to say – one just doesn't ask,' Prudence went on. 'Surely either one is or one isn't and there's no need to ask coy questions about it. Now, Jane, what about a hot-water bottle? Did you bring one with you?' Prudence stood up, slim and elegant in her red velvet housecoat.

Jane said, 'No, but I don't mind about a bottle, really I don't, though if you have a spare one it might be a comfort.' She felt a little peevish, as if she had been cheated, as indeed she had.

She also felt a little foolish – naturally, she should have known that Prudence was (or wasn't) Fabian's mistress.

'What about Arthur Grampian?' she asked. 'Is there still that negative relationship between you?'

'Oh, poor Arthur,' said Prudence lightly. 'He's a dreary old thing, in a way, but rather sweet.'

Jane clasped her hot-water bottle to her bosom and went to her room. She felt out of touch with Prudence's generation this evening.

## Chapter Thirteen

✗

JANE returned home feeling quite pleased with the result of her visit to London. The meeting of the literary society had been interesting, it had 'made a change', as people said, and she had enjoyed staying with Prudence. Though she was really no wiser than before about the exact relationship between Prudence and Fabian, it seemed that things were going well; the position was satisfactory, and no doubt their engagement would be announced quite soon, perhaps when the real spring weather came. Jane began to imagine Prudence settled in the village as Fabian's wife. It would be such a comfort to have her near and she would certainly make an admirable mistress – in the right sense, Jane told herself smilingly – of his house. She could give cultured little dinner parties with candles on the table and the right wines and food. She might even wear that becoming red velvet housecoat, which Jane had mistakenly called a dressing-gown. It would be perfectly suitable to receive guests in.

On the afternoon following her return, Jane received a message from Miss Doggett asking her if she would very kindly help her and Miss Morrow to pack up poor Mrs. Driver's things, which were to go to the distressed gentlewomen. Naturally, Jane accepted the invitation eagerly; they were to start at half-past three, after Miss Doggett had had her rest, so it could be assumed, Jane decided, that there would be tea at some time during the proceedings.

She found Miss Doggett and Miss Morrow already sorting out the clothes in the drawing-room when she arrived.

'I am going to send most of these things to the Society for the Care of Aged Gentlewomen,' said Miss Doggett. 'Not that poor Constance was aged herself, but one does feel that they need *good* clothes, the elderly ones.'

'Oh, yes,' Jane agreed; 'when *we* become distressed we shall be glad of an old dress from Marks and Spencer's as we've never been used to anything better.'

Miss Doggett did not answer, and Jane remembered that of course she went to her dressmaker for fittings and ordered hats from Marshall's and Debenham's.

'Miss Morrow and I, that is,' she added, hardly improving on the first sentence.

'*I* don't intend to be a distressed gentlewoman,' said Miss Morrow airily, 'though I have been one for the first part of my life, certainly.'

'Well, Jessie, I don't know that there is much that you can do about it,' said Miss Doggett comfortably. 'Of course, there may be something for you when I have passed on.'

'She may make a good marriage,' said Jane quickly, folding up a black wool dress rather badly. 'People can do that at any age, it seems.'

Miss Morrow looked almost smug, but said nothing.

'Oh, that reminds me,' said Miss Doggett. 'I had a letter from Mrs. Bonner who works at the Aged Gentlewomen headquarters and she told me a piece of interesting news. That nice Miss Lathbury has got married – what do you think of that?'

'Well, I never knew her,' said Jane. 'Did she work for the gentlewomen? And ought one to feel surprised at her marrying?'

'Yes,' said Miss Doggett. 'I was surprised. She seemed to

have so much else in her life. Her work there and in the parish – it seems that she was the vicar's right hand.'

'Who has she married?' asked Miss Morrow.

'An anthropophagist,' declared Miss Doggett in an authoritative tone. 'He does some kind of scientific work, I believe.'

'I thought it meant a cannibal – one who ate human flesh,' said Jane in wonder.

'Well, science has made such strides,' said Miss Doggett doubtfully. 'His name is Mr. Bone.'

'That certainly does seem to be a connection,' said Jane, laughing, 'but perhaps he is an anthro*pologist*; that would be more likely. They don't eat human flesh, as far as I know, though they may study those who do, in Africa and other places.'

'Perhaps that is it,' said Miss Doggett in a relieved tone. 'I read Mrs. Bonner's letter rather quickly. But the main thing is that he seems to be *most* suitable, good-looking and tall, Mrs. Bonner said. Over six feet tall, I think.'

'I never quite see why tallness in itself is so much sought after,' said Jane, 'though I dare say he has other qualities. I hope so for her sake.'

'He is a brilliant man,' said Miss Doggett. 'She helped him a good deal in his work, I think. Mrs. Bonner says that she even learned to type so that she could type his manuscripts for him.'

'Oh, then he had to marry her,' said Miss Morrow sharply. 'That kind of devotion is worse than blackmail – a man has no escape from that.'

'No, one does feel that,' Jane agreed. 'Besides, he would be quite sure that she would be a useful wife,' she added a little sadly, thinking of her own failures.

'I will go and get tea,' said Miss Morrow, slipping quietly from the room.

'Talking of marriages,' Miss Doggett began, 'I often wonder whether Mr. Driver will ever marry again.' She seemed to toss her sentence into the air hopefully for Jane to catch and throw back.

'Well, I suppose it is to be expected,' said Jane warily.

'That friend of yours, Mrs. Cleveland.' Miss Doggett hesitated. 'I was wondering . . .'

'Now, what were you wondering, Miss Doggett?' Jane asked.

'Whether they might marry,' said Miss Doggett firmly, winding up a ball of string.

'I really don't know,' said Jane. 'Of course, they have met and I think they like each other – it is difficult to see further than that.'

'I believe it would be an excellent thing,' said Miss Doggett. 'Mr. Driver is a lonely man.'

'He always seems to be telling people that he is,' said Jane.

'And your friend, Miss Bates – isn't that her name? – seems to be a very charming young woman.'

'Yes, she is certainly,' Jane agreed.

'You see, poor Constance was older than he is,' said Miss Doggett thoughtfully. 'One feels that if he were married to a young, attractive woman there wouldn't be any of those little – er – *lapses*. You see what I mean, of course.'

'Yes, I do see.'

'We know that men are not like women,' went on Miss Doggett firmly. 'Men are very passionate,' she said in a low tone. 'I shouldn't like Jessie to hear this conversation,' she added, looking over her shoulder. 'But you and I, Mrs. Cleveland – well, I am an old woman and you are married, so we can admit honestly what men are.'

'You mean that they only want one thing?' said Jane.

'Well, yes, that is it. We know what it is.'

'Typing a man's thesis, correcting proofs, putting sheets sides-to-middle, bringing up children, balancing the housekeeping budget – all these things are nothing, really,' said Jane in a sad, thoughtful tone. 'Or they would be nothing to a man like Fabian Driver. Therefore it is just as well that Prudence is an attractive young woman.'

There was a rattle of tea-things outside and Miss Morrow pushed open the door with a tray.

Conversation became more general during tea and ranged over parochial subjects, including the forthcoming meeting of the Parochial Church Council, of which Miss Doggett was a member. After tea the parcels were finished off and addressed and it was felt that a useful task had been accomplished.

As she walked out into the dusk of the March evening, Jane suddenly realised that spring was coming. Its arrival was less thrilling in the country than in London, and she wondered if Prudence was sensing it as she walked out of her office, noticing that the sky was a strange electric blue, that the starlings were twittering more loudly on the buildings; perhaps she was meeting Fabian that evening and he would have a bunch of mimosa for her.

But the next moment she knew that her fancy could not be reality, for she saw Fabian coming towards her through the blue dusk. Perhaps a sight of his beautiful, worn-looking face was what she needed on the first evening of spring. Her heart lifted for a moment in quite an absurd way as she prepared to greet him.

'A lovely evening,' she said; 'the first evening of spring. Have you been for a walk?' She raised her eyes to his.

'Yes, a short stroll. The rain seems to have kept off.' He tapped his umbrella on the ground.

'You take an umbrella for a country walk?' said Jane in astonishment.

'Yes, of course, if it looks like rain.'

'And you're wearing a hat and an overcoat and gloves,' Jane went on, and probably woollen underwear too, she added to herself.

'Yes, one is apt to catch cold at this time of year, I find,' said Fabian, slightly on the defensive, for he sensed her hostility.

'Oh, I never think of things like that,' said Jane, tossing her head. 'You'd better hurry in or the night air will harm you.' And with that she left him.

He looked after her as she went through the vicarage gate. No hat and that wild hair and that awful old coat and skirt. And lisle stockings too, he noted maliciously. He regarded it as an insult to himself that she should appear so carelessly dressed; he might perhaps have forgiven her if she had appeared at all confused or conscious of her shortcomings. Even Jessie Morrow, sharp though she was, did not take it amiss if he suggested some improvement in her appearance. He went in to his own house, smiling to himself, glad that he had not invited Jane Cleveland in for a glass of sherry.

When Jane got into the house she found Nicholas standing in the hall with a parcel in his hand. The absurd first-evening-of-spring feeling came back to her suddenly and she wondered if he had perhaps felt it too and brought her a present.

'Look,' he said undoing the wrapping. 'I thought I'd put them in my little cloakroom downstairs.'

On the table stood four soap animals in various colours, a bear, a rabbit, an elephant and a tortoise.

'Kiddisoaps, for children, really,' he explained. 'I shall arrange them on the glass shelf.' He went happily away, humming to himself.

If it is true that men only want one thing, Jane asked herself, is it perhaps just to be left to themselves with their soap animals or some other harmless little trifle?

'Darling,' she called out, 'what do you think. . . ?'

'I shall use the tortoise *first*,' her husband was saying in his little cloakroom.

'Fabian Driver takes an *umbrella* with him on a country walk and wears a hat and gloves.'

'Does he?' Nicholas emerged, beaming over his spectacles.

Beamy and beaky, mild, kindly looks and spectacles, Jane thought, whether in the Church or in the Senior Common Room of some Oxford College – it's all one really.

'There was a letter from Flora,' he went on. 'I haven't opened it yet.' He handed it to Jane.

Ah, Oxford in the spring, she thought, tearing open the letter to read Flora's news. Her letters were more interesting now than they had been. Work seemed to be going well, Miss Birkinshaw was 'rather remote', but next term she and her friend Penelope were to go to Lord Edgar Ravenswood for tutorials, which would be 'most stimulating' – 'imagine doing *Paradise Lost* with Lord Edgar!' Jane felt herself unequal to the effort of imagining it and passed on to the end of the letter, which was concerned with Flora's social life. She had been meeting a great many young men, as one still apparently did at Oxford; her favourite appeared to be somebody called Paul, of whom the letter was rather full. 'He is reading Geography and is rather amusing. . . .'

'Just imagine,' Jane called out to her husband. 'Flora has a young man called Paul who is reading Geography. And yet he is rather amusing!'

Nicholas appeared to find nothing strange in this, and Jane was left to ponder alone on the strangeness of anyone choosing to read Geography, which seemed to her, in her ignorance, a barren, dry subject, lacking the excitement of English or Classical Literature or Philosophy. Things are not what they were, she thought sadly, and at supper she felt very low, her spirits well damped down after the lift which the spring evening had given to them.

'Oh, I can understand people renouncing the world!' said Jane rather wildly as they sat down to a particularly wretched meal.

'Well, I should not mind renouncing cold mutton and beet-root,' said Nicholas evenly. 'That would be no great hardship.'

'We should not mind what we eat,' said Jane, 'and yet we do. That shows how very far we are from that state where we *might* renounce the world.'

Nicholas helped himself to more beetroot and they finished the meal in silence.

After supper Jane began rummaging in the drawer of her desk where her Oxford notebooks were kept, in which she had recorded many of her thoughts about the poet Cleveland. Creative work, that was the thing, if you could do that nothing else mattered. She sharpened pencils and filled her fountain-pen, then opened the books, looking forward with pleasurable anticipation to reading her notes. But when she began to read she saw that the ink had faded to a dull brownish colour. How long was it since she had added anything to them? she wondered despondently. It would be better if she started quite fresh and began reading the poems all over again. Then she remembered that her copy of the *Poems on Several Occasions* was upstairs and it seemed too much of an effort to go up and get it. How much could she remember without the book? A line came into her head. *Not one of all those ravenous hours, but thee devours* . . . If only she were one of these busy, useful women, who were always knitting or sewing. Then perhaps it wouldn't matter about the ravenous hours. She sat for a long time among the faded ink of her notebooks, brooding, until Nicholas came in with their Ovaltine on a tray and it was time to go to bed.

## *Chapter Fourteen*

THE NEXT meeting of the Parochial Church Council was to be held in the vicarage drawing-room as an experiment, for Nicholas, encouraged by his wife, imagined that an informal setting with comfortable chairs, the opportunity to smoke and possibly a cup of tea at some suitable point in the evening might create a more friendly atmosphere in which there was less likelihood of any unpleasantness.

It was arranged that Jane should slip out at a propitious moment and give the signal to Mrs. Glaze, who had consented to be in the kitchen that evening to make the tea and assist with the sandwiches and cakes. She had also agreed to answer the door-bell and admit the members as they arrived, while Jane and Nicholas waited, or perhaps cowered, in the dining-room until the time should come for them to emerge.

Mr. Mortlake, the Secretary, was the first to arrive, followed closely by the Treasurer, Mr. Whiting. They took their seats at the table facing the row of chairs and looked round the room critically, appraising the furnishings, which were less costly than those of their own homes, though in better taste, which they were unable to appreciate, since they noticed only the worm-eaten leg of a table or the broken back of a Chippendale chair.

'Chairs from the bedrooms,' said Mr. Mortlake laconically, pointing to a couple of white-painted, cane-seated chairs in the back row. 'Dining-room chairs would be more in keeping.'

'I expect they're sitting on them now, having their dinner,' said Mr. Whiting.

'Dinner isn't what they have,' said Mr. Mortlake. 'They have the big meal midday. Mrs. Glaze leaves something for them, whatever can be heated up, or a salad.'

'Ah, it was very different in Canon Pritchard's time,' said Mr. Whiting on a note of lamentation which seemed excessive for the triviality of the subject. 'Even during the war years they had the big meal in the evening. It seems more in keeping.'

'The dignity of the office,' said Mr. Mortlake. 'But then Mrs. Pritchard filled her position well. And she was a wonderful cook. I know that. They say Mrs. Cleveland hardly knows how to open a tin. It isn't fair on the vicar.'

'You never know, it might hold him back from promotion,' said Mr. Whiting. 'A man is often judged by his wife.'

'That evening she came to the choir vestry. It was most importunate . . .'

'She may have thought she was doing good,' said Mr. Whiting rapidly, lowering his voice at the sound of approaching footsteps. Although it was not the vicar or his wife but Miss Doggett who came into the room, the conversation could not be continued along its former lines, and changed to more uninteresting topics – the approach of spring, the drawing out of the days. By the time Mrs. Crampton and Mrs. Mayhew and Mr. Glaze had arrived, they were on to the subject of summer holidays.

It was at this moment that Jane and Nicholas chose to make their entry, Nicholas, as Chairman, taking his place at the table and Jane sitting down on one of the bedroom chairs at the back near the door.

'Well, is everyone here?' Nicholas asked in a brisk tone which he seemed to have assumed specially for the meeting.

'Mr. Oliver hasn't arrived yet,' said Mr. Mortlake.

'Oh.' Nicholas looked at his watch. 'Well, it is after half-past eight. Perhaps something has kept him. I think we should begin.' He stood up. 'Shall we say a prayer?'

They rose to their feet and bowed their heads. Jane tried very hard to realise the Presence of God in the vicarage drawing-room, but failed as usual, hearing through the silence only Mrs. Glaze running water in the back kitchen to wash up the supper things.

The meeting began with Mr. Mortlake's reading of the minutes. During this Mr. Oliver came in and sat by Jane at the back on the other bedroom chair. Mr. Glaze then stood up and gave a report on the water tank at the church hall. Something was blocked, dead leaves and dust had formed some kind of an obstruction; it was all highly technical. Jane could see that there was a puzzled frown on Nicholas's face as he tried to follow. She herself had given up any attempt to take an intelligent interest in the proceedings. It seemed that there was a particular kind of hat worn by ladies attending Parochial Church Council meetings – a large beret of neutral-coloured felt pulled well down to one side. Both Mrs. Crampton and Mrs. Mayhew wore hats of this type, as did Miss Doggett, though hers was of a superior material, a kind of plush decorated with a large jewelled pin. Indeed, there seemed to be little for the ladies to do but observe each other's hats, for their voices were seldom heard. Occasionally Nicholas would interpose with some remark, such as 'Now what do you feel, Miss Doggett? I am sure we should all like to hear your views on this point,' but as it was usually a matter such as the taxation of the Easter Offering, on which ladies could not be expected to have any sensible views, their comments amounted to very little and were soon disposed of and even made to seem slightly ridiculous by the men.

'And now we come to the parish magazine cover,' said Nicholas, gently but firmly curtailing Mr. Mortlake's dissertation on Income Tax. 'I believe everybody is not quite happy about it.'

'No, certainly not.' Jane, who was sitting by him, was quite startled by the violence of Mr. Oliver's protest. 'I must say I was most surprised to see the photograph of the lych-gate on the new cover. I was under the impression, and I may say that I believe others were too, that we had definitely decided to use the photograph of the high altar.'

'Yes, that was so,' said Nicholas hastily, 'but we did feel – the standing committee, that is – that as both photographs were equally suitable – you will remember I'm sure, Mr. Oliver, that we had great difficulty in deciding which we liked best – the Council would have no objection to our using the photograph of the lych-gate.'

'But why couldn't we have the high altar?' asked Miss Doggett bluntly. 'It seems to me to give a better idea of our beautiful old church.'

'Well, there were certain difficulties,' said Nicholas rather too weakly for a Chairman.

'Not to put too fine a point on it,' said Mr. Mortlake, 'the vicar and the churchwardens did feel, after considering the matter, that there was a danger of the cover of our magazine looking too much like that of St. Stephen's.'

'Well, really,' Jane burst out, 'I never heard anything so ridiculous. Even if the covers looked alike, there could certainly be no confusion over the contents. High Mass, Confessions and all that . . .'

Nicholas, who had thought it wiser to keep this matter of the magazine cover from his wife, smiled unhappily. She would never learn when not to speak, he thought, with rather less affectionate tolerance than usual. Not for the first time he began to consider that there was, after all, something to be said for the celibacy of the clergy.

Jane realised from Nicholas's laugh and the uncomfortable silence that followed that she ought not to have spoken. 'I wonder whether a cup of tea would help us to see things in better perspective,' she said quickly. 'I will just go and see Mrs. Glaze about it,' she added, hurrying from the room.

'A cup of tea always helps,' said Mrs. Mayhew in a rather high, fluty voice. 'It can never come amiss.'

'I shouldn't like to contradict a lady,' said Mr. Oliver, 'but I do feel that this is perhaps not quite the moment.'

'If you wouldn't like to contradict a lady, then why do it,' said Mr. Whiting, in something of a quandary, for he would have liked to agree with Mr. Oliver that this was perhaps hardly the time and place for a cup of tea.

'I think the best thing we can do is to take a vote on the matter of the cover,' said Nicholas hastily; 'then we can have the matter settled before the tea arrives.'

Everybody seemed willing to accept this suggestion, with the possible exception of Mr. Oliver, who sat looking sulky. There was a show of hands and the result was that everybody except Mr. Oliver voted in favour of having the photograph of the lych-gate on the magazine cover. Miss Doggett, who had raised a mild objection, confided to Mrs. Crampton and Mrs. Mayhew that of course she quite saw that it wouldn't do to have the picture of the high altar if there was any danger of their magazine being confused with that of Father Lomax's church.

'What a nice idea to have refreshments,' said Mrs. Crampton as the rattle of china was heard outside the door. 'We never had them in Canon Pritchard's time.'

'Well, it seemed a good idea,' said Jane from the open doorway. 'I always think when I'm listening to some of these tense, gloomy plays on the wireless, Ibsen and things like that, oh, if only somebody would think of making a cup of tea!'

'I hope our meeting doesn't strike you in that way,' said Mr. Whiting. 'They have usually been friendly affairs. There was never any necessity for a cup of tea in Canon Pritchard's time. We never had any unpleasantness then.'

'The Canon did have the knack as you might say of keeping certain people in their places,' observed Mr. Glaze.

'Do you mean blundering vicar's wives?' asked Jane pleasantly. 'Why, Mr. Oliver seems to have gone,' she exclaimed, standing with a cup of tea in her hand.

'I think he slipped out when you were bringing in the tea, Mrs. Cleveland,' said Mrs. Mayhew.

'He might have excused himself,' said Mr. Mortlake; 'but then one has ceased to expect these small courtesies from young men now.'

'I am sure I heard a nightingale the other night,' said Nicholas rather loudly. 'Would that be possible, Mr. Mortlake? Is the bird known to occur in these parts?'

Jane, who was sitting rather gloomily on a bedroom chair at the back, brightened up at the expression her husband had used – did birds *occur*? – but then lapsed into brooding silence again.

*O for a beaker full of the warm South,*

she thought sadly, clasping her hands round her teacup and looking into its depths. She sat thus for several moments, trying to see how much of the Ode she could remember, but the few lines that came to her did not bring her comfort –

*Fade far away, dissolve, and quite forget*
*What thou among the leaves hast never known,*
*The weariness, the fever, and the fret*
*Here, where men sit and hear each other groan . . .*

but in the next moment, they were all standing up and Nicholas was giving the Blessing and the meeting was over.

'Was it a success, having it here and with refreshments?' she asked him as the last footsteps scrunched away down the drive. 'Do you think it came off?'

'My dear, I wish you had not said what you did,' said Nicholas gravely.

'I, say anything?' Jane looked bewildered for a moment. 'But I always say what I think, and it *was* ridiculous all that fuss about the magazine cover and Father Lomax.'

'Yes, it was a small thing, but Mortlake and Whiting seemed to think it important. You cannot expect them to see things as we do.'

'Why should we always do what they want,' Jane burst out. 'Oh, if I had known it would be like this . . .' She ran from the room and into the downstairs cloakroom, where the sight of Nicholas's soap animals reminded her of her love for him and she might have wept had she not been past the age when one considers that weeping can do good or bring relief.

Instead she came back into the drawing-room and began moving chairs about rather aimlessly, not remembering where they had come from.

'If only you could have been a chaplain at an Oxford college,' she lamented. 'You're wasted here.'

'But, darling, you always said you wanted to be in a country parish. You were so pleased.'

'I know, but I didn't think it would be like this. I thought people in the country were somehow noble, through contact with the earth and Nature, I suppose,' she smiled; 'and all the time they're just worrying about petty details like water-tanks and magazine covers! – like people in the suburbs do.'

'We must accept people as we find them and do the best we can,' said Nicholas in too casual a tone to sound priggish. He stood up and began pacing about the room. 'Now I have thought of a wonderful idea. I am going to grow my own tobacco. Don't you think it would be interesting as well as a great saving?'

'Certainly, darling; what interests you do have in your life,' said Jane humbly. 'Shall we try to finish these sandwiches?'

And so they sat down on either side of the fire, two essentially good people, eating thick slices of bread spread with a paste made of 'prawns (and other fish)', Nicholas reading a book about tobacco-growing, and Jane wondering how she could make up for her tactlessness this evening. Perhaps by going to see Mr. Oliver and trying to reason with him, perhaps by visiting Mr. Mortlake, though even she shrank from that. She began imagining herself being shown into the front parlour, waiting, examining the photographs and ornaments . . . No, she had better leave well alone and concentrate on the things she *could* do, whatever they might be.

## Chapter Fifteen

✖

WHEN Miss Doggett reached home, she found, rather to her annoyance, that Miss Morrow was not there. Then she remembered that it was her evening out, for Jessie had insisted on having a definite free evening of her own, and that she had said she would probably go to the cinema. She had evidently gone out in a hurry, Miss Doggett decided, looking through the open bedroom door at the clothes flung down on the bed and the litter of cosmetics on the dressing-table. It seemed as if Jessie had been in doubt as to what to wear and also as if she had taken considerable trouble over her appearance, a thing she did not usually do. In this Miss Doggett was perfectly right, for no sooner had she left the house at a quarter to eight to go to the Parochial Church Council meeting than Jessie had hurried upstairs to her room.

To-night she was going to see Fabian. Not by invitation, for it would not have occurred to him to invite her in formally, but as a surprise. He often sat listening to the wireless in the evenings after he had had his dinner – she knew that. Sometimes he went out to the pub or the Golden Lion, but she would have to chance that.

She had a special dress she was going to wear, a blue velvet one which had belonged to Constance and which she had altered to fit herself. She knew that men did not notice things like that, but even if he did she was confident that she would be able to carry off any embarrassment successfully.

As she sat at the dressing-table, she felt like a character in a novel, examining each feature, the sharp nose, the large grey eyes and rather too small mouth. She worked carefully, smoothing on a peach-coloured foundation lotion, blending in rouge, powdering, outlining and filling in her mouth, shading her eyelids with blue and darkening her lashes. When she had finished she was quite pleased with the result. She was thirty-seven, older than Mrs. Cleveland's friend, Prudence Bates, but younger than poor Constance and than Fabian himself. She had always loved him, but it had not occurred to her until that autumn day in the garden when she had seen him looking out of the window that anything could be done about it. She was not the person to cherish a hopeless romantic love for a man, especially if he were free and lived next door, and now that Prudence Bates had come into his life Jessie felt that she must act quickly. It seemed to her entirely appropriate that she should lay her plans while Miss Doggett was at a meeting of the Parochial Church Council, discussing the parish magazine cover.

At a quarter to nine she left the house, looking carefully as she

139

stepped out of the gate to see whether anyone had observed her; but it was dark and there was nobody about. She opened Fabian's garden gate and then slipped quietly down the side of the house to the back, where the drawing-room french windows opened on to the garden. This evening they were lighted and the curtains not yet drawn; she saw Fabian in a velvet smoking jacket, sitting by the fire with a glass of some amber-coloured liquid – whisky, perhaps – on a small table at his side. There was a blotter on his knees and he appeared to be writing a letter.

Appeared to be writing was a correct impression, for he sat with his pen in his hand adding nothing to the few words he had already written. He did not find it easy to write to Prudence. To begin with, he had never been much of a letter-writer, and then her letters were of such a high literary standard, so much embellished with suitable quotations that he found it quite impossible to equal them. He felt that this was wrong; the man should be the better letter-writer, not the woman, though he remembered that he had never been able to equal Constance's either. It was ironical to think how much better she would have been able to answer Prudence's letter than he could himself. He thought that perhaps he should give up trying for this evening; he might stroll round to the Golden Lion for a nightcap later on; it was possible that the walk might give him some inspiration. It seemed to be quite a pleasant evening, he thought, going to the windows to draw the long dark green brocade curtains.

As he stood there he saw a figure move out of the shelter of a rhododendron bush – a woman whom he did not recognise stood there looking at him. For a moment he felt alarmed, and she smiled and he saw that it was Jessie Morrow.

'Why, what are you doing there in the gloaming?' he called out in a rather forced way. 'Won't you come in? Is Miss Doggett with you?' He was conscious as he said it of the incongruity of Miss Doggett lurking in bushes.

Jessie stepped in through the open french window and he

shut it and drew the curtains behind her. 'No. I am alone this evening,' she said, 'and I wondered if you were too, and if I would have the courage to call on you. Well, I did have, so here I am.'

'Sit down,' said Fabian, drawing up another chair to the fire. Now he could not possibly go on struggling with his letter to Prudence. 'What would you like now, a cup of tea or a hot drink of some kind?'

Jessie said nothing, but her eyes were fixed on the amber-coloured liquid on the little table.

'Would you like whisky?' Fabian's eyes lighted up and he fetched another glass. 'Somehow I didn't imagine you as liking it.'

'What did you imagine that I liked?'

'I don't know. I suppose I never thought.'

'You mean you never thought of me as a human being at all? As a person who could like anything?'

'Well, I don't know . . . but you seem different to-night.' Fabian looked at her, a little puzzled, appraising her. 'Your dress is becoming.'

'Yes, I think it is, and I'm glad you think so.'

'Constance had a dress rather like that once. Velvet, isn't it?'

'Yes – I think I remember it.' But fancy *him* remembering, she thought. It was a little unnerving the way men sometimes did – not that she feared he would recognise the dress as being the same one altered to fit her; it was just that an unsuspected depth had been revealed in him, and she realised that she might not know him quite so well as she had imagined she did.

'I think Constance would like to think of us sitting here together,' said Fabian. 'She was always very fond of you. You were very good to her.'

'Was I?' said Jessie in a rather brisk tone. 'I suppose I was better to her than you were. That wouldn't have been difficult.'

'What hurtful things you say! As if I didn't realise it. I am not quite so insensitive as you seem to imagine.'

141

'I'm sorry. My sharp tongue runs away with me sometimes.'
Jessie noticed without surprise but with a kind of comfortable
satisfaction that Fabian's arm had somehow placed itself round
her shoulders. She leaned her head back against his sleeve.

'It seems sometimes that we must hurt people we love,' said
Fabian, stroking her hair. 'Oscar Wilde said, didn't he. . . ?'

'Let's not bother about him,' said Jessie. 'I always think he
must have been such a bore, saying those witty things all the
time. Just imagine seeing him open his mouth to speak and then
waiting for it to come out. I couldn't have endured it.'

Fabian smiled. He hadn't been quite sure what it was that
Oscar Wilde had said, anyway.

Was he thinking of Constance or of Prudence? Jessie wondered. He had hurt one and he might be going to hurt the other.
How strange their names were, when one came to think of it,
Constance and Prudence. . . . Jessie was somehow a more comfortable name, without any reproach in it. Did he love Prudence,
anyway, and did she love him? Oh, well, thought Jessie as
Fabian bent his head to kiss her, even if she did she would soon
get over it.

## *Chapter Sixteen*

ⵝ

JANE was making the beds, a humble task that she felt was
within her powers. The window-cleaners had arrived shortly
after breakfast and it was a kind of game trying to evade
them. If I go down to the uttermost ends of the earth, Jane
thought, seizing a flattened pillow and beating it into roundness,
there they will find me. And sure enough here was the ladder
propped up against the sill, the sound of footsteps mounting
and then the face at the window, surprised, perhaps, to see the
vicar's wife making a bed. Mrs. Glaze should do the beds really,
but then she couldn't come very early, and by the time she

arrived there was the breakfast washing-up, the vegetables to do for lunch and the drawing-room to be sketchily mopped and dusted in case anyone should call. . . .

The face at the window was impassive now, but that seemed more unnerving than the surprised look, and suddenly Jane fled, leaving the bed half made and her husband's striped pyjamas lying on the floor. I suppose it may interest him to see the vicar's pyjamas, she thought, but was the window-cleaner a churchman? Now that she came to think of it, she couldn't remember ever having seen him in church. Perhaps he was a Roman or Chapel or went to the little tin-roofed Gospel Hall by the gasworks; or perhaps he was *nothing* – a frightening thought, like seeing into the dark chasm of his mind. Of course, it was just possible that he was merely High and carried a candle or swung a censer at Father Lomax's church. Yes; that was it. Jane saw him now through a cloud of incense, his rugged features softened . . .

'Nicholas!' she called out, but there was no answer from the study, and then she remembered that he had gone out immediately after breakfast, she couldn't remember where. Somebody was ill or dying; he had gone to play golf or perhaps to the church to see how the decorating was going; he had taken to looking in on a Saturday morning to encourage the ladies, and Jane felt that they really welcomed that more than her own uncertain help. Anyway, he was not here, so she could not confide her thoughts about the window-cleaner to him. . . .

'Madam!' Mrs. Glaze appeared at the foot of the stairs in her hat and flowered pinafore. 'Mr. Mortlake is here.'

'Mr. Mortlake? Good heavens!' Jane called out in agitation, her thoughts going back to the meeting of the Parochial Church Council and her outspokenness about the magazine cover. Had he come to see her privately about it? To reproach her for her interference?

'I have shown him into the drawing-room,' went on Mrs. Glaze.

'The drawing-room? Yes, certainly.' Jane smoothed back her tousled curly hair with her hands. 'I will come down.'

'Well, madam, I don't think you need disturb yourself.'

'Why, is the vicar with him?'

'Mr. Mortlake has come to tune the piano,' said Mrs. Glaze in a surprised tone.

'To tune the piano – of course!' Jane almost shouted.

She ran downstairs into the hall. There was his hat, a bowler of rather an old-fashioned shape, lying on a chair. Oh, the relief of it! He had come not to scold her, but to tune the piano! She wanted to rush in to him, to greet him with some exaggerated mocking gesture, '*Buon giorno, Rigoletto*,' posturing and bowing low. But he would not appreciate it or understand. So she seized his hat and placing it on her head, pirouetted round the hall singing,

> *O Donna Clara,*
> *I saw you dancing last night . . .*

From inside the drawing-room came the sound of Mr. Mortlake striking out single notes, cautiously, then rather impatiently. It would be some time before he ventured on to the rich chords and harmonies peculiar to his profession. Jane replaced the hat on the chair and opened the front door.

A young man, who had evidently been about to ring the bell, stood on the doorstep. He was rather flashily dressed and carried a large suitcase.

'Good morning, madam,' he said. 'Are there any old clothes for sale here?'

'This is the vicarage,' said Jane in a rather vague tone.

'Oh, I see . . .' His confidence seemed to leave him for a moment.

'So you wouldn't really expect any, would you?' Jane asked. 'Unless the ones I'm wearing would do?'

'The ladies like to keep old things to wear in the mornings,' he said, recovering his poise. 'I know that.'

'I expect I shall go on wearing these all day,' said Jane. 'My days don't really have mornings as such, not in that way, I mean.'

The young man edged away from her.

He thinks he has come to a private mental home, thought Jane, the patients are not dangerous, but are allowed to take walks in the grounds. 'I'm sorry I can't oblige you,' she said pleasantly. 'What a lovely morning it is,' she added as he wished her a hasty good morning and hurried out through the gate. And it certainly did seem to have improved, after that shock about Mr. Mortlake.

She would wander in the garden, thinking about what she should write. It was good to be alive, in the spring. Daffodils were out in the grass under the chestnut tree, which was showing sticky buds, and in the lane at the back of the church a plant with bright leaves and greenish flowers was flourishing. Dog's mercury – Jane remembered the name from childhood, a strange, rather sinister name . . . what was its derivation? she wondered. Was it perhaps a corruption of some other name? She went up to the chestnut tree and leaned her head against its trunk. Perhaps she could hear the sap rising and the flowers preparing to burst out of the buds. *Not one of all those ravenous hours, but thee devours?* Well, yes, that was true still, but it mattered less on a spring morning. She would cut some buds and bring them back into the house. They should stand in a great jar on the hall table, to show callers that there was hope at the vicarage. But she would need something to cut them with, some implement from the potting-shed, where the tools were kept. She ran over the lawn and round to the back of the house, but then she stopped.

A woman in a tailored costume and a fur was looking over the back gate, as if about to enter it. Behind her stood a stout, rosy-faced clergyman with white hair.

'Ah, Mrs. Cleveland. Good morning!' The man's voice rang out. 'Do forgive us for calling so unceremoniously, but one usually finds the womenfolk round at the back of the house these days, especially in the mornings.'

Womenfolk, thought Jane irrelevantly, how silly that sounded. And all this emphasis on the mornings.

'In the kitchen, doing the cooking,' went on the clergyman as if in explanation.

'Mrs. Glaze is doing that,' said Jane. It now occurred to her to wonder who her callers were and how they could know about the back gate, which was not immediately apparent. The clergyman, surely, was Canon Pritchard; therefore the woman must be his wife. They had thought to creep round the back and peer in at windows to surprise her in the kitchen, perhaps catch her in the very act of stubbing out a cigarette in the tea-leaves in the sink basket. She felt almost triumphant that they should have failed.

'Do come in,' she said, trying to sound gracious. 'My husband isn't in at the moment, but he should be coming back soon.'

They walked round to the front of the house and into the hall. From the drawing-room came the sound of somebody playing the piano in a rather florid Edwardian style. Mr. Mortlake was on his last lap. The arpeggios flowed; the chords rippled and modulated from major to minor and back again.

'This *is* like old times,' cried Mrs. Pritchard, 'to hear Mr. Mortlake playing again. His style is so very much his own.'

The door opened and Mr. Mortlake came out, emerged almost, a tall, dignified figure.

'Well, Daniel,' said Canon Pritchard, 'this is a pleasant surprise.'

Jane noticed that Mr. Mortlake's face really did light up. 'Why, it's the Canon,' he said. 'And Mrs. Pritchard. This is indeed a pleasant surprise. And how are you both keeping?'

'Very well, thank you, Daniel; and you're looking very fit too.'

Jane waited for Mr. Mortlake to say something about it not being like the old days with Canon Pritchard gone, but the

Canon, perhaps realising that something of the kind might come and wishing to spare Jane's feelings, had contrived to dismiss him in a very gracious kind of way that could not possibly give offence.

The party moved into the drawing-room. Jane wondered what time it was and what, if any, refreshment she could offer to her visitors. There was no sherry; she knew that. Presumably there could always be a cup of tea or even coffee, but were there any biscuits?

'Ah, you have your summer curtains up,' said Mrs. Pritchard, looking round the room. 'We always found this room so draughty even in summer that I often waited until May before I took down the velvet ones.'

'Yes, these are quite light ones. It has been a mild spring,' Jane observed. 'My husband likes air, of course.' In the daytime when the curtains were drawn back they looked better. Had the Pritchards called in the evening they would have noticed the shortness and skimpiness of the curtains, which did not even cover the windows in places.

'I find the curtains we had here a little too large for my new drawing-room,' went on Mrs. Pritchard.

'Really?' said Jane. This was not much of a conversation for the Canon, she thought, wishing that Nicholas would appear.

'Do you find your new position congenial?' she asked, trying to draw him into the conversation.

'Well,' he smiled, 'it could hardly be otherwise. The Bishop and I were at Rugby together, you know.'

'No, I didn't know. How nice. Arnold of Rugby,' Jane murmured.

'He was a *little* before my time, of course,' said the Canon.

'But the tradition still remains?' asked Jane. 'The lines on Rugby Chapel . . . I wish I could remember some of them now, but English Literature stopped at Wordsworth when I was up at Oxford, and somehow one doesn't remember things so well that one read since.'

Mrs. Pritchard stirred a little restlessly in her chair.

There was a knock at the door and Mrs. Glaze came in bearing a silver tray with a coffee-pot and cups upon it.

Jane turned to her gratefully. She would never have believed that Mrs. Glaze could show this treasure-like quality. No doubt it was for the Canon and his wife rather than for herself, but it had saved the situation. She had been feeling that things were pretty desperate if one found oneself talking about and almost quoting Matthew Arnold to comparative strangers, though anything was better than having to pretend you had winter and summer curtains when you had just curtains.

'Would you like me to pour out, madam?' Mrs. Glaze asked.

'Yes, please do, Mrs. Glaze,' said Jane, relaxing, and noticing with surprise that there was a plate of bourbon biscuits on the tray. Now wherever had Mrs. Glaze found those? she wondered.

'Black for you, madam?' asked Mrs. Glaze, turning to Mrs. Pritchard, 'and white for the Canon?'

It appeared that she had remembered correctly.

Conversation flowed more smoothly now. Various people in the village were asked after and discussed, though in not quite such an interesting way as Jane could have wished. Also she was very careful with her own comments, remembering how her tongue and curiosity were apt to run away with her.

'Has Fabian Driver married again?' Mrs. Pritchard asked.

'No, not yet,' said Jane.

'Not yet? Do you think he has anyone in mind?' Mrs. Pritchard leaned forward a little in her chair.

'Oh, I don't think so, but I suppose he will some time. After all, he is still a young man; barely forty, I believe.'

'Of course, there is nobody here for him,' went on Mrs. Pritchard. 'He would have to look further afield.'

'Yes, one does feel that he must be rather lonely here. . . .'

There was a pause and the Canon stood up. 'Well, my dear,' he turned to his wife. 'I think we shall have to be on our way.'

'We are to have luncheon with the Bishop,' Mrs. Pritchard explained. 'We left the motor outside.'

Going out to luncheon and in a motor, thought Jane, seeing a high Edwardian electric brougham and Mrs. Pritchard in a dust-coat and veiled motoring cap. But well-bred people talked like this even to-day, Jane believed. She hoped they would get a good meal at the Palace, but was prudent enough not to make any enquiries.

In the hall Canon Pritchard paused and held out his hands with a vague gesture. Jane thought for one wild moment that he was attempting to give her some kind of a blessing, but it appeared that he wanted to wash.

'Yes, of course,' said Jane, showing him into the little cloak-room. 'I wonder if there is a clean towel?' she added, knowing that there could not possibly be one.

'Yes, thank you, there is,' Canon Pritchard called out. Jane supposed that Mrs. Glaze must have put one there when she heard them arrive, and she now realised that had they been able to stay to lunch an adequate meal would have been provided. Mrs. Pritchard would have been able to say, 'We drove over to the Clevelands in the motor and stayed to luncheon.'

Mrs. Pritchard did not appear to want to wash. No doubt the Palace offered better amenities, Jane decided, as they stood rather uncertainly in the hall.

'You must come over to luncheon one day,' Mrs. Pritchard observed, 'and bring your husband.'

'Thank you. We should like to very much,' Jane said.

Canon Pritchard came out of the cloakroom and the three of them went out to the motor, which was not of an Edwardian type, rather to Jane's disappointment.

'Have the Clevelands a young child?' the Canon asked his wife as they drove away.

'I believe their daughter is about eighteen. She is at Oxford, I think.'

'A strange thing that,' said the Canon, changing gear. 'One

would have thought there was a child about the place. The soap in the wash-basin was modelled in the form of a rabbit, and there were other animals, too, a bear and an elephant.'

'And you washed your hands with a soap rabbit?' asked his wife seriously.

'Certainly. There was no other soap. I wonder if Mrs. Cleveland put them there; she seems rather an unusual woman.'

'Yes, there is something strange about her.'

'I think Cleveland is quite sound,' went on the Canon. 'None of this Modern Churchman's Union or any of that dangerous stuff . . .' He hesitated, perhaps meditating on the soap animals and what they could signify.

Jane and Mrs. Glaze were also talking about them. Jane had thanked her for bringing in the coffee and biscuits at such an opportune time and for providing the clean towel.

'Oh, madam,' said Mrs. Glaze, 'but I couldn't find a new tablet of soap.'

'Wasn't there any in the cloakroom?'

'Only the animals, madam.'

'Well, I believe it's quite good soap. I expect the Canon would enjoy using them. Men are such children in many ways.' Though perhaps not all in the same way, Jane thought. He may have regarded them as some dangerous form of idolatry.

'I was hoping he might think they belonged to Miss Flora,' said Mrs. Glaze.

'Yes, he might have thought that. After all she is still a child, really.' And yet even she was old enough to enjoy doing Milton with Lord Edgar Ravenswood and to fall in love with a young man called Paul who was reading Geography. Could children do these things?

Nicholas appeared just before lunch and Jane told him of her eventful morning. They had a good laugh about the soap animals.

'I wonder if he will tell the Bishop,' said Nicholas.

'It would be rather ominous if he kept it to himself,' said

Jane; 'it would seem as if he considered it rather important, not a matter for joking.'

'Oh, Pritchard has no sense of humour. I'm glad I managed to avoid him.'

'Yes, it was rather heavy going,' Jane agreed. 'I suppose he just came to have a look at things. Perhaps they would peep into the church when they were sure we weren't looking to see if they could detect any smell of incense or other Popish innovations.'

'I saw their car outside just as I was coming through the gate,' Nicholas admitted, 'so I slipped into the tool-shed till they'd gone. In any case, I had to see to my tobacco plants,' he added, looking a little ashamed.

'Well, really, Nicholas,' Jane protested, 'you might have come and helped me out.' But secretly she was rather pleased to have managed so well on her own.

## *Chapter Seventeen*

WHITSUNTIDE came and went, the weather grew warmer, and Prudence appeared at her office in elegant dark printed silk dresses; Miss Trapnell and Miss Clothier in cottons or rayons of rather dimmer patterns. The conversation began to be about holidays. Even Dr. Grampian raised the subject one morning when Prudence was in his room, and asked her when she would be taking hers.

'Not that it matters,' he added vaguely. 'I was wondering if it would coincide with mine. That is sometimes easier.'

A year ago Prudence would have seized on his words and twisted them into an 'Ah, if only we were really going on holiday together!' She had often imagined herself with him in the South of France or the Italian Lakes – she in the most elegant beach clothes and he wonderfully bronzed and mysteriously improved in looks and physique. But to-day, looking at him in his grey suit and dark tie, his shoulders hunched narrowly over his desk, it seemed quite fantastic to imagine him lying on a beach stripped to the waist.

'My wife wants to go to St. Tropez in September,' he said, as if reading her thoughts. 'We both feel the need for sun.'

'Oh yes, sun,' Prudence agreed. 'I haven't really fixed my holiday yet. I can go any time that suits you.'

'Well, the summer is a slack time,' he said, as if other times were busy, 'so please yourself.' Then he turned to a file of papers on his desk and Prudence felt that she had been dismissed.

She went into her own room, where she found Mr. Manifold talking to Miss Trapnell and Miss Clothier.

'. . . walking in the Pyrenees,' he was saying. 'In late September – otherwise it will be too hot.'

'It sounds fascinating,' said Prudence in what seemed to him a cold, scornful tone, 'but terribly energetic.'

'I don't like luxurious holidays,' he said rather fiercely. 'I haven't any use for that kind of thing. I like to be on the move, seeing different places.'

'My idea of a holiday is just to sit somewhere in the sun drinking,' retorted Prudence, aware as she said it that she was being rather ridiculous.

'Oh, I like drinking too,' said Mr. Manifold, 'but not in chromium-plated bars and hotels.'

Prudence felt anger rising within her, but could not think of anything to say.

'I'm very fond of Torquay myself,' said Miss Trapnell in an even tone. 'You always meet nice people and there's plenty to do if it rains.'

'I can't bear meeting people on holiday,' said Prudence childishly.

'Then you must be a lone wolf, like Mr. Manifold,' said Miss Clothier.

The idea of Mr. Manifold being any kind of a wolf made Prudence want to giggle, and she feared that he also had seized upon the vulgar meaning of the word, which was probably unknown to Miss Trapnell and Miss Clothier.

'I dare say that both Prudence and I have had our moments,' he said, leaving the two older ladies somewhat mystified.

*Prudence*! He had dared to call her by her Christian name! Had it just slipped out, she wondered, or was it deliberate?

'Really, he gets more insufferable every day,' she said, when he had gone out of the room.

'He's a nice young man, really,' said Miss Trapnell. 'And he's so good to his aunt. I happen to know that. I do think it's nice when a young man considers older people.'

'Good to his aunt?' Prudence asked, a little annoyed that Miss Trapnell should have this unlikely information about Mr. Manifold.

'He lives with his aunt,' Miss Trapnell explained. 'His parents are dead, you see.'

'Oh?' Prudence was curious in spite of herself.

'He is an orphan,' interposed Miss Clothier by way of explanation.

'The poor little poppet!' said Prudence in a light, offhand tone. Of course, lots of people of his age were orphans, she told herself. There was really nothing pathetic about it. She took out some work, determined to dismiss him from her mind, but Miss Trapnell seemed disinclined to return to her card index and would not leave the subject.

'Miss Manifold is a great one for church work,' she was saying. 'And she's very artistic. I've never seen the flowers looking so lovely as they did on Whit-Sunday. She'd put red and pink flowers on the pulpit, rhododendrons and peonies with some syringa and greenery. Red is the colour for Whitsuntide, of course.'

'But how did you see them?' Prudence asked. 'Do you live somewhere near?' She tried to imagine Miss Trapnell's North

London suburb, and Geoffrey Manifold and his aunt living somewhere near.

'Yes, quite near,' said Miss Trapnell. 'A threepenny bus ride away. I'm not actually in the same parish – St. Michael's, that is – but I'm on the electoral roll there. I'm afraid St. Jude's, that's the church whose parish I'm really in, is much too high for me. They have Asperges and all that kind of thing, and the vicar hears Confessions.' She lowered her voice.

'Does Mr. Manifold go to church?' Prudence asked.

'Well, no, Miss Bates, and that is a great grief to his aunt, I happen to know. But you know how these young men are, think they know the answer to all life's problems. But he is so good to her, so I suppose you can't have it all ways.'

'He's had a hard life too,' Miss Clothier interposed. 'You'd think he might have found consolation in going to church.'

'A hard life?' Prudence asked.

'Both his parents were killed in a motor accident when he was eighteen,' said Miss Trapnell, almost with a hint of triumph in her tone.

'Oh, *no* . . .' said Prudence in a strained voice. 'The poor boy . . .'

'Just when he was starting out on his University career,' said Miss Trapnell, piling it on.

'Well, I suppose he had scholarships and things,' said Prudence rather roughly. 'People usually do.'

'Yes, he was clever, of course. But it was a hard struggle.'

'Didn't his aunt help him?'

'Yes, I'm sure she did, but it was difficult for him.'

'He seems to have got over it now,' said Prudence, forcing herself to remember his rather bold manner and the fact that he had called her Prudence. But obviously he wasn't the kind of person to show his feelings . . . it was all over and done with, about ten years ago, she supposed; there was certainly nothing pathetic about him now. And no doubt he had had his moments – he had as good as told her so. All the same, the conversation

154

had left an uneasy feeling at the back of her mind. She felt that she might wake up in the middle of the night and remember it. She would see him in his raincoat with the collar turned up, going to have lunch in Lyons, standing in the queue reading the *New Statesman*.

'Have you fixed your holidays yet, Miss Bates?' asked Miss Trapnell.

'I expect I shall go somewhere with a friend,' Prudence answered rather evasively.

Naturally, her holiday plans now included Fabian, bronzed and handsome, lying on a beach or drinking on a terrace, and this required less of an effort of imagination than when her companion had been Arthur Grampian. But so far Fabian had said nothing definite about it. His last letter, indeed, had been unsatisfactory, perfunctory almost – it was difficult to describe exactly what was wrong. It had begun affectionately enough, but after that it had meandered on about nothing very much, the weather, even, and then come to an abrupt end, with half a sheet left blank. But then Fabian was not at his best as a letter-writer. Prudence had been uncomfortably conscious for some time that her letters were much better written and fuller of apt quotations than his were. She remembered one of his some weeks back in which he had started to quote Oscar Wilde and then evidently thought better of it and crossed it out. This seemed a little ominous, for Wilde had said so many things that one would hardly have wished said to oneself. Perhaps the truth was that Fabian was a man of deeds rather than words, though he was certainly very slow in coming to the point.

This next week-end she was to go and stay with Jane. Perhaps things would come to a head then. The country would be looking at its best; there would be the long evenings, the lanes with wild roses and meadowsweet, and above all Prudence herself, adorning Fabian's house and garden and looking so perfect there that he would surely wonder how he could ever imagine the place without her.

The guest-room at the vicarage was more attractive now than it had been in November; its very bareness gave it a cool, almost continental look. Prudence's summer housecoat, a white cotton patterned with roses and frilled at the neck and elbows, seemed less out of place than her turquoise blue wool or crimson velvet. Jane had put a vase of roses on the little table by the bed, but this time there was no photograph of Arthur Grampian to set it off. Prudence had as yet no photograph of Fabian and she felt that it would somehow have been in bad taste to flaunt him there at the vicarage, when he was to be seen in the flesh, walking about the village. So the table held only the roses, a book of poems that Fabian had given her and a novel of the kind that Prudence enjoyed, well written and tortuous, with a good dash of culture and the inevitable unhappy or indefinite ending, which was so like life.

It was the end of the Oxford term and Flora and her young friend Paul, who was to spend a few days with them, were expected in time for supper on the Friday evening. Jane, or rather Mrs. Glaze, had provided a boiled chicken, and Prudence offered to make a salad and see to the finishing touches.

'We mustn't treat this young man as if he were a curate,' Jane explained, 'but I don't want Flora to feel ashamed of her home.' She burst into a peal of laughter, 'Isn't that just the sort of thing they say in the answers to correspondents in a woman's magazine?'

'Have you some garlic?' Prudence asked.

'Garlic?' echoed Jane in astonishment. 'Certainly not! Imagine a clergyman and his wife going about the parish smelling of garlic!'

'But it does improve a salad.'

'Let the lettuce leaves be well washed,' said Jane airily; 'that's the main thing. I should have liked the kind of life where one ate food flavoured with garlic, but it was not to be. I don't suppose Flora's young man will mind. Geography and garlic don't seem to go together somehow. Of course Fabian may not

156

be satisfied, but it should be enough pleasure for him to see you, without bothering whether the salad bowl has been rubbed with garlic.'

'You've asked Fabian? You didn't tell me.'

'Yes; I thought it would make up the numbers,' said Jane rather grandly. 'And he promised to bring some wine – I hope he won't make too much fuss about it – the wine, I mean. We do happen to have a bottle of sherry, not the very best, but I have poured it into the decanter, so nobody will know. The decanter at least is a good one.'

When they had finished their preparations they went into the drawing-room, which in summer appeared to be a pleasant, airy room with french windows opening on to the lawn and the winter's draughts turned to cooling breezes most refreshing on a hot evening.

Fabian advanced over the lawn with the bottles in his arms, carrying them as carefully as if they had been new-born babies. He saw Jane and Prudence sitting inside the room before they saw him. Jane was in a kind of 'best' summer dress of indeterminate pattern and cut, the kind of thing worn by thousands of English women, but Prudence wore something black and filmy, chiffon perhaps, which looked deliciously cool and elegant.

'Why, there is Fabian!' exclaimed Jane. 'Now he will make his entrance just like a character in one of those domestic comedies that have french windows at the back of the stage. I wonder what his first words will be.'

'Good evening,' said Fabian, bowing slightly over his bottles.

Jane sprang up to take them from him, while Prudence raised her hand in a rather languid gesture and smiled up at him.

'Hullo, Fabian,' she said.

'Prudence, how nice to see you,' he replied. 'Now, do be careful of those bottles,' he said, turning to Jane. 'They don't want to be shaken up too much — and put them in a cool place, if you can.'

'Give him some sherry, Prue,' said Jane. 'I must take these away.'

'Well, darling,' said Fabian, bending down to kiss Prudence, but rather gingerly, as if afraid of disturbing her face and hair, 'you're looking very lovely tonight.'

He always says that, thought Prudence with a flash of irritation. But of course it might be that it was always true.

They sat a little awkwardly sipping their sherry until Nicholas came in, and then the sound of a car was heard and Jane's exuberant greeting to Flora and Paul.

The beginning of the meal was a little awkward, but Jane soon carried them forward on a rush of conversation.

'Paul is reading Geography,' she explained. 'It must be a fascinating subject. All those tables of rainfall and the other things – vegetation, climate, soil . . .' She waved her hands about, seeming unable to go any further into the delights of Geography.

Paul, who was a quiet, mousy-looking young man with very blue eyes – a typical undergraduate, Prudence thought – did not appear to be at all embarrassed at having attention drawn to himself. Geography was a fascinating subject to him and he was able to discourse at some length about what he was doing. Flora gazed at him with obvious devotion and occasionally made an intelligent comment as if to draw him out still further.

Oh, the strange and wonderful things that men could make women do! thought Jane. She remembered how once, long ago, she herself had started to learn Swedish – there was still a grammar now thick with dust lying in the attic; and when she had first met Nicholas she had tried Greek. And now here was her own daughter caught up in the higher flights of Geography! He seemed a nice young man, but that was only the least one could say. Was it also the most?

Prudence regarded the young couple with something like envy. To be eighteen again and starting out on a long series of love affairs of varying degrees of intensity seemed to her entirely enviable. She began to recall some of her own past triumphs, at Oxford and afterwards, and to compare them with her present state. Had there perhaps been a slight falling off lately? When Paul looked at her a kind of startled expression came into his eyes, so that she wondered whether she had overdone her make-up and the elegance of her dress and appeared formidable rather than feminine and desirable. Fabian and Nicholas, however, showed their appreciation by their glances and the wine soon put everybody into a more mellow mood.

'If only we could have wine at the Parochial Church Council meetings,' said Jane. 'We have tried tea and sandwiches and more comfortable chairs, but somehow it didn't make much difference. Wine is *really* what maketh glad the heart of man, isn't it?' She raised her glass to Fabian rather gaily.

Flora looked at her mother a little anxiously. Indeed, the younger members of the party seemed altogether more solemn than the older ones. It was difficult to keep Paul away from the higher flights of Geography, but eventually they were all recalling their Oxford days and Fabian his Cambridge ones, and it seemed that life had been much gayer then.

'Ah, we flung roses riotously!' said Jane. 'Nicholas, do you remember that evening when we serenaded the Principal from a punt on the river? Of course, when she came to the window we all moved on!'

Prudence smiled rather enigmatically as if she had subtler memories of the river, as indeed she had.

'Is there a strong revival of religion among the undergraduates to-day?' Nicholas asked, turning to Paul. 'One hears that there is.'

'I'm afraid I wouldn't know about that,' said Paul quite politely. 'Naturally, my interests lie in other fields.'

'But haven't you observed?' said Jane.

'People might like to keep it to themselves,' said Prudence.

'My friends are mostly geographers and anthropologists,' said Paul.

'Anthropologists,' echoed Fabian on a puzzled note. Prudence wondered if he were going to ask what they were and felt irritated with him for the small part he was playing in the conversation. If only Arthur Grampian had been there! she thought suddenly, hearing his rather flat, measured tones discoursing. Or even Geoffrey Manifold being rather aggressive about bars and holidays and his 'material.'

After dinner they had coffee, and then Flora said she would show Paul the village. Nicholas and Fabian began talking about gardening, so that Jane and Prudence somehow found themselves at the kitchen sink, faced with the washing-up for six people.

'Of course, I could leave it for Mrs. Glaze,' said Jane rather vaguely, scraping some bones from one plate to another. 'You certainly can't wash up in that pretty dress, Prudence. Wouldn't you like to go back and talk to the men?'

'No; I'll dry, if you can lend me an apron,' Prudence said. She watched Jane plunging dishes and glasses indiscriminately into the water without any attempt at a scientific arrangement or classification.

'Flora's young man might have done this quite well,' she said. 'Do you approve of him?'

'Well, I hardly know,' said Jane. 'One rather hopes that he will be the first of many. I have been trying to see how he could be described as "rather amusing," which was what Flora said about him in her letter.'

'He didn't really show it,' Prudence agreed, 'but perhaps he was shy and felt he had to go on talking about Geography. I dare say he is better when they're alone. Perhaps he is a wonderful lover.'

'Oh, dear!' Jane looked up from the sink anxiously. 'One doesn't want that kind of thing. Flora is only eighteen. What should be my attitude?'

'Flora is very sensible,' said Prudence. 'I shouldn't worry.'

'Yes, she isn't like me. Somehow Paul isn't quite what I'd

hoped for her. I know it's silly – but I'd hoped that Lord Edgar might fall in love with her – when they were at tutorials, you know.'

'But he hates women, surely?' Prudence asked.

'I know, that's the point. I'd imagined Flora breaking through all that.'

Prudence laughed and then looked a little apprehensively at Jane, who was swishing the wine-glasses about in an inch or two of brownish water at the bottom of the bowl. 'You really need clean water for the glasses,' she pointed out.

'And they should have been done first,' said Jane rather sadly. 'Look, the twilight is coming; we'd better have the light on.'

The light over the sink was a dim but unshaded bulb and added a kind of desolation to the whole scene, with its chicken bones and scattered crockery. Jane went on washing in an absent-minded way, looking out over the sink to the laurels outside.

'We have laurels outside Nicholas's study window and here,' she said thoughtfully. 'No doubt Nicholas and Mrs. Glaze deserve laurels, a whole wreath of them, but I don't. Oh, Prudence,' she said, turning to her friend with a little dripping mop in her hand, 'you and Fabian must make a fine thing of your married life, and I know you will. You'll be a splendid hostess and such a help to him in everything.'

'He hasn't asked me to marry him yet,' said Prudence.

'Why don't *you* ask *him*?' said Jane recklessly. 'Women are not in the same position as they were in Victorian times. They can do nearly everything that men can now. And they are getting so much bigger and taller and men are getting smaller, haven't you noticed?'

'Fabian is tall,' said Prudence rather complacently. 'I must say I like a man to be tall.'

'Ah, you like a rough tweed shoulder to cry on,' said Jane scornfully. 'Now, why don't you go and interrupt Fabian and

Nicholas in the rather dull conversation they must be having, and suggest a walk in the twilight?'

'You mean I should ask if *I* may see *him* home?' said Prudence derisively.

'Well, why not? Why shouldn't a woman take the initiative in a little thing like that?'

Prudence went on drying forks, and soon the sound of men's voices was heard in the passage.

'Can we help?' asked Nicholas in the tone of one who hopes he will be too late.

'Yes, we really should have offered sooner,' said Fabian, 'but I never feel I'm much good in a kitchen – not at the sink, any-way.'

'I never see why men should be good at cooking and yet not able to clear things up,' said Prudence rather acidly.

'Why don't you and Fabian leave the finishing touches to us,' said Jane. 'Husband and wife at the sink – that's very fitting.'

Fabian sighed. Jane wondered if he had bitter-sweet memories of washing-up with poor Constance.

'Good night, then,' he said. 'It has been such a pleasant evening.'

'Well, if you're sure I can't do any more,' said Prudence, hanging her damp drying-cloth on a line in the kitchen.

She walked into the hall with Fabian. The front door was open and she went out on to the steps.

'Perhaps I should be going now,' said Fabian. 'It seems rather a dismal end to the party, to leave them washing up.'

'Oh, I don't think Jane had anything else in mind. It was the meal that was the main thing.'

'I shall be seeing you to-morrow, darling,' said Fabian. 'You are all coming to tea with me. We shall have it in the garden under the walnut tree.'

'How nice,' said Prudence.

They had reached the gate by now and were standing rather

aimlessly by it. Some bats were wheeling about in the dusky air and Prudence put her hands up to her head and uttered a little cry.

'What is it, darling?' asked Fabian anxiously.

'All these bats! I loathe them.'

'Then you'd better go indoors,' he said sensibly. 'It would have been rather pleasant to go for a little walk, but I expect you are rather tired and it wouldn't really do.'

'Wouldn't it?'

'Well, you see the village people walk about at night, but we don't,' he declared.

'What a strange idea! Paul and Flora have gone for a walk, haven't they?'

'Ah, young love,' said Fabian fatuously. 'They make their own rules. It is quite probable that I may be elected to the Parochial Church Council next year,' he went on more seriously. 'You see what I mean.'

'Oh, yes,' Prudence laughed rather hysterically. 'Naturally you couldn't be seen walking in the dusk with a woman.'

'Well, it might look a little odd. Good night, darling,' he bent and kissed her hand. '*A domani!*'

Prudence walked back into the house and found Jane, her shoes off, lying on the drawing-room sofa.

'I didn't feel like going for a walk,' Prudence said. 'I'm rather tired, really.'

'How do you think it went – the evening?' Jane asked.

'Very well,' said Prudence politely. 'It was a lovely chicken.'

'A lovely chicken!' Jane laughed. 'Yes, it certainly was; and the wine and the conversation about Geography and then the washing up – you and Fabian, Flora and Paul, me and Nicholas.'

'Fabian isn't what you'd call a brilliant conversationalist,' said Prudence half to herself.

'Oh, who wants that!' said Jane. She yawned and got up from the sofa. 'Nicholas is out seeing to his tobacco plants – I shall fall asleep if I lie here any longer. Shall we go up before the "young people" get back? It might be rather daunting for them to be faced with me when they come in – of course, you would be different.'

'No; I think I'm quite ready for bed,' said Prudence. 'May I have a bath?'

'Yes, do!' said Jane enthusiastically.

Most of the hot water had been used for the great washing up, but it was a warm evening and Prudence lay for some time in the tepid water, contemplating the dingy ceiling of the vast room with its stained-glass window and the bath cowering in a corner. It was like having a bath in a chapel. I am drained of all emotion and nothing seems real, she thought, certainly not Fabian. Tea under the walnut tree to-morrow . . . and then what?

'Have you got something nice to read?' Jane asked, coming into Prudence's room.

'Yes, thank you; a novel.'

'And what could be better,' said Jane, 'particularly Mr. Green's latest, or is it Mr. Greene? I never know. Both are delightful in their different ways. And you have a book of poems too, if Mr. Green or Greene should fail to charm or soothe.'

'Yes. Fabian gave me that,' said Prudence rather quickly.

'A very nice anthology,' said Jane, turning the pages. Of course, it was the same as the one poor Constance had given to *him* which Jane had rescued when the 'things' were sorted out. Perhaps he did not know of any other. She turned back the pages quickly until she came to the fly-leaf. He had written, 'Prudence from Fabian,' with the date, and then,

*My Love is of a birth as rare*
*As 'tis for object strange and high;*

the same inscription as Constance had written for him fifteen years ago.

How strange that he should have remembered that, thought

Jane. Had it been somewhere in the back of his mind for all these years, to be brought out again, as a woman, searching through her piece-bag for a patch, might come upon a scrap of rare velvet or brocade?

She closed the book quickly. 'Does Fabian read much poetry?' she asked.

'No. I don't think so. He knows one or two tags,' said Prudence casually. 'Men don't really go in for that sort of thing like women do.'

'No,' Jane agreed; 'one has to accept that, together with their other limitations. Listen, I can hear Paul going up to his attic. I wonder if they had an amusing evening? One assumes that he has other conversation apart from Geography.'

'*O my America! My new-found-land,*' said Prudence. 'I wonder if he quoted that to her?'

'Oh, geographers don't read poetry,' said Jane confidently. 'Good night, Prue dear. Sleep well.'

## Chapter Eighteen

✖

THE NEXT day was Sunday, and Prudence was awakened early by Nicholas's voice calling from what seemed to be the depths of the linen cupboard on the landing.

'Jane, there's no clean shirt *here*! What did you do with the laundry?'

Then Jane seemed to come, there was a good deal of rushing up and down stairs and agitated conversation. It was not at all as Prudence had thought it would be. She had imagined that she might perhaps hear the quiet footsteps of Nicholas and Jane creeping out to Early Service. She might almost have wished that she could have joined them herself. Was every Sunday morning like this? she wondered. Looking back to the other occasions when she had stayed with them, she decided that it probably was. If *she* were married to a clergyman, she would see that everything was put out ready for him on the Saturday night. . . . She dozed off again and was woken by a knock at the door and Jane in her hat and coat coming in with a cup of tea in her hand.

'Good morning, Prue. I thought you'd like a cup of tea,' she said, standing by the bed. 'How interesting you look, even at this hour of the morning. The whole effect is very Regency.'

Prudence had bound up her hair in a kind of emerald green turban, a shade darker than her nightdress, which was of a very transparent material, a little shocking, Jane thought. It was perhaps a good thing that Nicholas had not brought in the tea.

'We are going to church, of course, but Flora will start getting the breakfast,' she said, thinking how wonderful it was that Prudence should have taken the trouble to curl up her hair after what had seemed to be rather an unsatisfactory evening with Fabian.

'Oh, then I'll get up and help her,' said Prudence without much enthusiasm.

'Well, thank you, Prue, but I dare say Paul will be doing that. I believe he is quite useful in the house.'

After Jane had gone, Prudence drank her tea and then turned over on to her side. She felt disinclined to get up and face penetrating glances from Paul's blue eyes. Did he talk about Geography at breakfast? she wondered. At the best of times it was not a meal she enjoyed, and the prospect of the company of a young man under twenty-five and Jane's bright conversation seemed altogether too much to be endured. However, when the time came, Paul and Flora seemed to be engrossed in their plans for the day and little notice was taken of her. She attended Matins out of politeness to her host and hostess and noticed with a kind of scornful interest that Fabian was in church. She determined to look her best when they met in the afternoon, and to behave rather coldly towards him.

Jessie Morrow knew that she could not hope to equal Prudence in elegance, so she made no special preparations for the tea party under the walnut tree to which she and Miss Doggett, perhaps because they were next-door neighbours and could not be left out, had been invited. Her strength would have to lie in the deepening intimacy that was growing up between her and Fabian on the evenings when Miss Doggett was out. Besides, did men really notice one's clothes as much as all that? She had certainly made an effort to appear more striking on the first evening when she had called on Fabian in Constance's old blue velvet dress, but at other times she had gone to him in whatever she happened to be wearing and he had not appeared to be any less affectionate towards her. She had almost welcomed Prudence's visit this week-end, for she felt that it might give Fabian a chance to straighten things out. Perhaps last night he had taken a walk with her in the dusk and they had talked about the situation. But then it occurred to her that perhaps it would be better if he waited until Sunday, which would be Prudence's last evening. She could then go back on Monday and it would be much less awkward. After that things would just take their course. But the first thing was to get rid of Prudence, Jessie thought ruthlessly.

'Just imagine how lucky!' Miss Doggett was saying. 'Mr. Driver has persuaded Mr. Lyall and his mother to come to tea.'

'However did he do that?' asked Jessie abstractedly. 'I suppose he just asked them and they had no excuse. He fancies himself dispensing hospitality to the great.'

'It should be a delightful party,' Miss Doggett purred. 'And such a fine day. I shall wear my navy and white and my new hat. I suppose you will wear your flowered crepe?'

'I had thought I would go in this,' said Jessie, pulling out a crumpled fold of her faded blue linen dress. 'I can't compete with Prudence Bates.'

'Compete with Miss Bates!' Miss Doggett's laugh rang out. 'I should think not, indeed. But you can at least wear a cleaner-looking dress. Our Member is going to be there, after all.'

'Well, I am not a supporter of his Party,' said Jessie.

'Now, now, Jessie; none of that nonsense. . . . Look.' They were standing by an upper window which overlooked Fabian's garden. 'Mrs. Arkright is putting out chairs under the walnut tree. She has been at it all morning, seeing to the food, Mr. Driver was to have only a light lunch – a salmon salad with cheese to follow. Not *tinned* salmon, of course,' she added hastily.

'No, one could hardly give a man tinned salmon,' said Jessie ironically.

'It is very popular among the working classes, of course, but that's another matter. I see no reason why we shouldn't be the first to arrive,' continued Miss Doggett on a different note. 'Somebody has got to be first after all.'

'Shall I watch out for a propitious moment?'

'Well, yes; we don't want to arrive too early, of course, not before the preparations are fully completed.'

Jessie waited at the window and saw Fabian, in a light grey suit of some thin material, step out on to the lawn. She drew back into the shelter of the curtain and observed him, moving a chair here and there, standing back and surveying the scene. He looked just a little common in the grey suit, she thought; perhaps the colour was too light or there was something not quite the thing about the way it was cut. She could almost imagine that he might be wearing brown-and-white shoes, like the hero of a musical comedy in the 'twenties, but that was hardly possible. Yet she felt, as we so often do with somebody we love, that any little defect could only make him more dear to her.

'I think we could perhaps go now,' she said aloud. 'Mr. Driver seems to be surveying the stage as if he expected somebody to make an entrance very shortly.'

At the gate they met Jane and Nicholas and Prudence, in a lilac cotton dress of deceptive simplicity.

'I'm glad we've met you,' said Jane. 'We were afraid we were too early.'

Fabian welcomed them and they lowered themselves cautiously into deck-chairs on the lawn.

'Your daughter isn't coming?' Miss Doggett asked.

'No; she has a friend staying and they have gone off somewhere for the day, to see a bit of the countryside.'

'I expect she has made some nice friends at Oxford,' said Miss Doggett.

'This is a young man,' said Jane obscurely.

'Oh?' Miss Doggett's eyes brightened.

'A geographer,' said Nicholas in a bluff kind of voice.

'Oh.' There was a slight falling-off of interest in Miss Doggett's tone. 'Of course, she will meet lots of young men,' she said reassuringly.

'I certainly hope so,' said Jane heartily. 'After all, she is only eighteen.'

'Ah, to be eighteen again!' said Fabian sentimentally.

'Is that a good age for a man?' Prudence asked, swinging her sun-glasses in her hand, like a picture in *Vogue*, Jessie thought, her eyes riveted on the crimson toe-nails that peeped out through the straps of her sandals.

'Yes, I think it is,' said Nicholas. 'You have your whole life before you, or so it seems.'

'All the things one was going to do, the books one was going to write,' said Jane dreamily, 'the brilliant marriages one was going to make.'

'Marriages?' said her husband. 'Well, well . . . Ah, here is Mrs. Lyall and her son.'

'Strange how different it sounds said like that,' said Jane. 'Usually one says Mr. Lyall and his mother.' He had timed his arrival well, she thought, but perhaps he had by now had enough practice, knowing that he must always be last.

The ladies almost rose from their deck-chairs at the sight of their beloved Member, who shook hands with them all. There were enquiries about his health, the word 'burden' was mentioned by Miss Doggett, Jane noticed, and Mrs. Arkright came hurrying out with the tea.

He will ask Prudence to pour out, thought Jessie, a sudden agony of fear breaking through her carefully schooled indifference, and indeed at the sight of the silver teapot Prudence had sat up a little in her deck-chair and taken off her sunglasses again.

'I have asked Mrs. Arkright if she will kindly pour out for us,' said Fabian. 'It is rather troublesome to have to do it oneself, and I am really no good at it.'

'A splendid idea. Then there will be no hard feelings among the ladies,' said Nicholas in his best vicar's manner.

'Would there be hard feelings?' asked Edward in an interested tone. 'Do people *like* pouring out tea?'

'I don't, dear,' said Mrs. Lyall. 'I get very flustered, as you know.'

'Well, it has a certain meaning, sometimes,' said Miss Doggett archly, with a glance at Prudence.

'Miss Bates shouldn't undertake it,' said Jessie brusquely. 'She might spill something on that pretty dress.'

'I'm sure Miss Bates would manage admirably,' said Edward.

'There is no need to spill anything, unless the teapot drips,' said Prudence.

'And we know that teapot,' said Miss Doggett in a warm, sentimental tone; 'it has never dripped in its life.'

Oh, we can't bring the dead into this, thought Jane, imagining Constance Driver presiding over the tea things. 'Our teapots always drip,' she said cheerfully. 'They are china ones with broken spouts.'

Mrs. Arkright handed round cups of tea and cucumber and tomato sandwiches, and then seemed to melt away. It was as if she had somehow changed into a bush or plant to efface herself from the company, and then miraculously become herself again just at the moment when cups needed refilling and plates were empty.

'What a fine walnut tree!' said Edward, looking up into its branches. 'It is so deliciously restful here. I can't think how long it is since I sat lazily in a garden, and it's really one of my favourite ways of spending time.'

'Don't you often have tea on the terrace at the House of Commons?' Jane asked. 'I've always thought that sounded very pleasant.'

Edward gave her one of his charming, weary smiles. 'One is usually entertaining constituents,' he said, 'and can't really relax.'

'Well, I do hope you will relax *here*,' said Miss Doggett vigorously.

'We are your constituents,' said Nicholas, 'but you need not feel that you must entertain us. Rather, *we* should entertain *you*.' He paused and a worried expression came on to his face. For how was it to be done? Country vicars are perhaps not used to entertaining Members of Parliament. Still, the women would see to it, he thought, relaxing again in his deck-chair.

'If only we knew how to,' said Fabian, with a smile only a shade less weary than Edward's.

'Edward just likes to sit quietly,' said his mother. 'That is really a change and a treat for him.'

'Yes, one does find it a great relief just to be able to relax in a garden,' said Fabian. 'I find the bustle of the City quite intolerable.'

'What is your work?' asked Mrs. Lyall.

'Oh, it is quite unspeakably dull,' said Fabian. 'I really couldn't discuss it here. I suppose it is the dullness of it all that makes me feel so exhausted.'

'Exhausted?' said Jessie rather sharply.

'Yes, exhausted.' Fabian closed his eyes for a moment.

'Life is certainly tiring these days,' Nicholas observed.

There was silence.

'A gloom seems to have fallen on the party,' said Jane. 'Perhaps it would be better if we all sat in silence. If the men find life so exhausting, our chatter might disturb them.'

The women made a gallant attempt to carry on the conversation among themselves. Mrs. Lyall talked all the time about her son and how she was hoping that he could be persuaded to take a real holiday. Miss Doggett listened sympathetically and recommended a guest-house in the Cotswolds which seemed to Jane hardly the kind of place for a Member of Parliament as exquisite as Edward, though, had he been of another party, perhaps, he might have considered it. Certainly he would be surrounded by doting middle-aged women, and perhaps that is not unpleasant to a member of any party or indeed to men in general, whether politicians or not.

The conversation about the guest-house became general among the women, for Prudence and Jessie had been unable to think of anything to say to each other, Prudence having no idea that they had anything at all in common and Jessie finding herself incapable of making any suitable use of her superior knowledge.

Fabian and Edward seemed to be trying to outdo each other in weariness, and even Nicholas was making some attempt to compete, detailing the number of services he had to take on Sundays and the many houses he had to visit during the week.

Suddenly there was a diversion. Jessie Morrow, getting up to pass a plate of cakes to Mrs. Lyall, knocked against the little table on which Prudence had put her cup of tea, so that the cup upset all over the skirt of her lilac cotton dress.

'Oh, Jessie, how could you be so clumsy!' stormed Miss Doggett. 'You have ruined Miss Bates's dress – that tea will stain it!'

'It doesn't matter,' said Prudence, stifling her first impulse of anger towards Miss Morrow's clumsiness. 'It's only cotton – it will wash.'

'You must take it off at once and soak it in cold water,' said Miss Doggett.

'Yes, come into the house,' said Fabian.

'She had better come into my house,' said Miss Doggett, 'and then I can lend her something to wear.'

'I have my car outside,' said Edward. 'We could easily drive to The Towers.'

'I think it would be more practical if she went back to the vicarage,' said Jane, 'and then she could change into one of her own dresses.'

Prudence felt foolish and irritated at being the centre of so much fuss. Edward and Fabian were perhaps a little annoyed at having attention diverted from their weariness, and it seemed inevitable now that the party should break up, especially as Nicholas began murmuring about it being time for Evensong.

'Yes, I suppose I should go,' said Jane.

'Well, we shall be meeting again in church,' said Miss Doggett.

'I am to read one of the Lessons, I believe,' said Edward with a touch of complacency. 'Thank you, Driver, for a most pleasant afternoon. An interlude for rest and refreshment.'

'I am worried about Miss Bates's dress,' said Miss Doggett to Jane. 'If you don't put it to soak in cold water at once that tea will stain. I'm very much afraid it may leave a mark.'

'It seems to be leaving a mark already,' said Jessie in an unsuitably detached tone for one who had been responsible for the disaster; 'rather the shape of Italy. I wonder if that can have any significance?'

'We shall consult *Enquire Within* about removing the stain,' said Jane. 'It is sure to have a good remedy – something to do with ox-gall or wormwood, so practical.'

'Well, Prudence,' said Fabian, rather at a loss, 'I expect I shall be seeing you soon in Town.'

'Oh, possibly,' said Prudence casually. 'Ring me up some time.'

Not a very satisfactory leave-taking, thought Jane. There

173

seemed to be some want of enthusiasm, some lack of proper sadness, unless their casual manner was merely a way of disguising their deeper feelings.

'That silly little woman,' said Prudence crossly as they walked home, 'upsetting my tea like that. And then everyone made such a fuss. I don't think I shall come to Evensong, Jane. I really don't feel in the mood.'

'Oh, don't you? What a pity,' said Jane. 'I love Evensong. There's something sad and essentially English about it, especially in the country, and so many of the old people are there. I always like that poem with the lines about gloved the hands that hold the hymnbook that this morning milked the cow. We have the old hymns here, you know. Ancient and Modern. *Sun of my Soul, thou Saviour dear* . . . the congregation love it and Nicholas wouldn't change it for the world.'

But Prudence did not want to be made to feel sad, and offered to stay at home and get the supper ready. After she had changed her dress she sat in the drawing-room, hoping that perhaps Fabian would telephone or call. But then she realised that of course he too would be at Evensong. A melancholy summer Sunday evening is a thing known to many women in love, she thought, seeing herself as rather ill-used, left alone in the big, untidy vicarage kitchen, opening a tin of soup and preparing things to go with spaghetti. Jane hadn't even any *long* spaghetti, she thought, the tears coming into her eyes, only horrid little broken-up bits. Oh, my Love, she said to herself, sitting down at the scrubbed kitchen table, thoughts of Fabian and Arthur Grampian and others, Philip, Henry and Laurence from the distant past, coming into her mind. Then she thought of Geoffrey Manifold and how good he was to his aunt, and a sense of the sadness of life in general came over her, so that she almost forgot about Fabian refusing to walk with her in the twilight in case it should prejudice his chances of being elected to the Parochial Church Council. When Jane and Nicholas came back from Evensong they found her crouching on the floor in the dining-room, delving in the dark sideboard cupboard among the empty biscuit barrels and tarnished cruets for the sherry decanter.

## Chapter Nineteen

✖

THE Tuesday following that week-end the weather broke, and on Wednesday it was still raining when Jessie Morrow set out for her afternoon off.

'I shall go to the pictures,' she said in answer to Miss Doggett's enquiries, 'and have a high tea at the Regal Café.'

'Why not call and see Canon and Mrs. Pritchard?' Miss Doggett suggested. 'You know we have an open invitation to visit her house any time.'

'The kind of invitation that includes everybody in the parish and means nobody,' said Jessie scornfully.

'I'm sure Mrs. Pritchard would give you a cup of tea.'

'But not plaice and chips, which is what I usually have after the pictures – plaice and chips, a fancy cake or two and a pot of good strong tea.'

'Mrs. Pritchard always had her own special blend, something between Earl Grey and Orange Pekoe,' said Miss Doggett rather wistfully. 'I suppose she still has it there, in those exquisitely thin cups. Poor Constance was fond of China tea, too.'

But Fabian likes Indian and a good strong cup, thought Jessie gleefully. Now that they had spent several of her half-days together he even enjoyed the fish tea which he had at first thought rather vulgar and had got over his anxiety lest anyone they knew might see them together. He still ate his plaice and chips a little furtively, though, and did not help himself to tomato ketchup as liberally as Jessie did.

'Well,' she said when she had poured out their second cups of tea, 'have you told her yet?'

'Told who?' asked Fabian nervously, glancing round the café. Perhaps it was not such a bad place to choose for a clandestine meeting after all. It was certainly not the kind of place where one was likely to meet Canon and Mrs. Pritchard or Edward Lyall and his mother.

'Why, Prudence, of course. You said you would break it to her this week-end.'

Fabian sighed heavily and plunged his fork into his cake with a dramatic gesture, so that a piece of it shot on to the floor.

'No, I'm afraid I didn't. What can I say to her? She'll be so hurt.'

'Hurt? And would it be the first time you'd ever hurt a woman?'

'Well, no; one has had to hurt people, I suppose,' said Fabian, tilting his head to one side. He had just realised that the distinguished-looking man sitting at that distant table was himself reflected in a mirror at the far end of the room. No wonder one had had to hurt people, he thought, resting his forehead on his hand.

'Now stop trying to look like Edward Lyall with his burden,' said Jessie sharply. 'Do you mean to tell me that you have said nothing at all to her?'

'We had very little conversation about anything. After dinner on Saturday we stood outside the vicarage gate, I remember, and she was frightened by a bat. I think she would have liked a walk in the twilight if it hadn't been for the bats. And then I felt I really couldn't suggest it. She would have expected me to kiss her, and one can't do that in the village.'

'Only behind locked doors,' said Jessie mockingly. 'It doesn't matter what you do in the privacy of your own home.'

'Oh, my dear . . . don't speak of that here. It isn't a worthy setting.' He pushed aside the vase of dusty pink paper artificial flowers and took hold of her hand.

'You had better not hold my hand,' said Jessie in a low voice. 'Flora Cleveland and that young man of hers have just come in.

176

I suppose they've been to the pictures too. *He* is not holding *her* hand. Perhaps middle-aged lovers are more sentimental – a beautiful thought.'

'I wonder if we could slip out another way without them seeing us?' asked Fabian anxiously. 'After all we don't want the news to get about too soon.'

'Not before you have finished with Prudence. Quickly, now, Flora has gone to the ladies' cloakroom and the young man will not recognise us, or certainly not me.'

'I will write to Prudence to-night,' said Fabian firmly as they hurried along the street. 'This deception is intolerable. Poor Prudence, she has always been loved. It will be a sad blow to her pride.'

'Look,' Jessie stopped outside an antique shop and looked in the window. 'I wonder if you would perhaps buy me some little token?' she said, feeling perhaps that Fabian was not likely to suggest it himself.

'This is rather an expensive shop, my dear,' he said cautiously. 'I have kept one or two of Constance's rings, and I was thinking . . .'

'Certainly, since I am to take her place I should have one of her rings,' said Jessie. 'Perhaps you have even kept her wedding ring with the inscription she told you to have engraved inside it?'

'Well, yes; I did not feel I could sell it. But I think you would probably prefer to have a new wedding ring,' said Fabian seriously. 'In any case, it might not fit you. But let me buy you some little trinket here. To-day seems to have been rather a special day, doesn't it? Look, there is a tray with an interesting assortment of things. Is there anything there you would like?'

'All on this tray, 15s.', Jessie read. Well, that was something, to have him spend fifteen shillings on a useless sentimental object for her. 'That little brooch with *Mizpah* on it. I think I should like that.'

'It's rather ugly, isn't it?' said Fabian doubtfully. '*Mizpah* has a depressing Biblical sound about it.'

'But it has a meaning. And it might be quite appropriate for us. It means "The Lord watch between me and thee when we are absent one from another." '

'Well, yes,' Fabian smiled.

They went into the shop and Fabian bought the brooch, which the shopkeeper wrapped in a piece of tissue paper, evidently not thinking it worthy of a box. When they had got outside, Jessie unwrapped it and pinned it on to her mackintosh.

'Thank you, dearest,' she said, taking his arm. 'Now I really feel somebody.'

It had always been their custom to leave and return to the village by different trains so that they should not be seen at the station together, but this time, perhaps because of *Mizpah*, they decided to return together and, if necessary, to pretend that they had met accidentally.

But now, although they were not to know it yet, it did not really matter what they did, for Miss Doggett, alone in the house, had come upon the truth about them. Stumbled on it, was how she put it to herself.

Ever since the week-end when Jessie had upset the tea on Prudence's dress, she had had a feeling that there was something different about Jessie. She had noticed her smiling to herself and had several times caught her at the window, looking down into Fabian's garden.

After Jessie had gone out for the afternoon, Miss Doggett felt restless and dissatisfied. She put her feet up as usual for her after luncheon rest and listened to a woman's programme on the wireless, but somehow its competent little talks about breast feeding, young children's questions, and a housewife's life in Nigeria did not seem to be planned for an elderly spinster. Her library book also failed to hold her attention, for although, according to the mystifying jargon of the publishers, its fourth large impression had been exhausted before publication, its effect on her was that of exhausting without granting the blessing of sleep. When at three o'clock, therefore, she had not managed to drop off, her thoughts turned to Jessie. Why had she deliberately upset a cup of tea over Miss Bates? For it seemed now as if the action had been deliberately calculated. What could she have hoped to gain by it? Miss Doggett pushed away her footstool, flung her book down on the floor and walked upstairs.

Jessie's room was without any definite character apart from that given to it by the miscellaneous pieces, unwanted in other rooms, with which it was furnished. In all the years that she had lived with Miss Doggett, Jessie had not succeeded in stamping it with her own personality. One would have imagined that a gentlewoman would have her 'things,' those objects – photographs, books, souvenirs collected on holiday – which can make a room furnished with other people's furniture into a kind of home. But Jessie seemed to have none of these. The only photograph was of her mother – Miss Doggett's Cousin Ella – a plain-looking woman with an unsuitably sardonic expression for a Victorian. She had married late and had made an unfortunate marriage – Miss Doggett's thoughts lingered with satisfaction on this theme for a few minutes, for Aubrey Morrow had left his wife and child after a few years – and then continued her examination of the room. The only books to be seen were the library book Jessie happened to be reading at that moment, a paper-backed detective novel that anybody might have and, rather oddly, an old *A.B.C.* There were no books of devotion, not even a Bible or a prayer-book, which one might certainly expect a spinster to possess. The 'objects' were even more unpromising – an ugly little china dog of some Scottish breed attached to an ash-tray, an old willow-pattern bowl with no apparent purpose, some dusty sea-shells in a box – it seemed almost as if Jessie had been at pains to suppress or conceal her personality. For there was no doubt that she had personality of an uncomfortable kind; she had inherited her mother's sardonic expression, and who could tell how much of her father there might be in her? These things always came out eventually. It was quite likely that she herself might make an unsuitable marriage. But who was there for her to make an unsuitable marriage with? That was the point. Miss Doggett's thoughts ranged rather wildly from the man who delivered the laundry and was rather free in his manner, to the Roman Catholic priest of the little tin church, whom Jessie had once admitted she thought handsome. Certainly the latter would be quite disgraceful. He would be unfrocked, no doubt. . . . Miss Doggett moved over to the wardrobe and opened it.

She knew all Jessie's clothes, the sage green jumper-suit, the grey tweed overcoat and the skirt that didn't quite match it, the blue marocain 'semi-evening' and the flowered crepe which had been her 'best' summer dress for some years now. It had a band of plain colour let into the skirt to lengthen it which dated it as having been new some time before 1947. Miss Doggett's hands moved idly among the fabrics, jersey, tweed, crepe, wool, cotton, until they suddenly touched velvet. Had Jessie a velvet dress? She tried to remember one, but failed, and so took down the hanger and brought the dress out. It was a blue velvet, long, with a square neck and tight-fitting sleeves. But when had she bought it? It was a good material, better than Jessie could have afforded. Constance Driver had once had one very like it, made specially for her at Marshall's. Surely it was this very dress! Jessie had shortened it and altered the neck in some way.

Miss Doggett stood with the dress in her hands, trying to think what this discovery could mean. Jessie must have hidden it away when they were sorting out poor Constance's things. Well, perhaps there was nothing much in that. She may have had a secret longing to possess a velvet dress, though she did not usually show any interest in clothes at all. Nevertheless, it gave Miss Doggett an uneasy feeling, which made her go over to the dressing-table and open the drawers. The bottom one was full of underclothes and stockings, quite unremarkable, nothing at all daring or unsuitable. There was a new pair of nylon stockings in a cellophane envelope, but everybody had those nowadays. The left-hand top drawer held handkerchiefs, gloves and one or two scarves. Miss Doggett lifted the pile of handkerchiefs and took out a larger one from the bottom. It was a man's handkerchief, the kind a woman might use when she had a cold. It was neatly marked with the initials, F.C.D. *Fabian Charlesworth Driver* . . . with an agitated movement Miss Doggett tugged at the handle of the right-hand drawer, but it would not open. It was locked.

She sat down rather heavily on the bed, still holding Fabian's handkerchief in her hand. The locked drawer, she thought, what could be in it? And why should Jessie have one of Fabian Driver's handkerchiefs? Had he dropped it accidentally when he was visiting them, or had it come into Jessie's possession in some other way? Could it be that there was something between him and Jessie?

Miss Doggett was now in a state of considerable agitation. She was angry at what seemed to be Jessie's deceit and yet excited at the same time. She went downstairs and made herself a pot of tea, hardly knowing that she did so. She longed to confide her discovery to somebody, to discuss, and brood over it, and began to consider the suitability of people she knew in the village. Most were married women too busy with their children and household cares; Mrs. Crampton and Mrs. Mayhew were stupid fluttering creatures; widows, she thought scornfully, with a silly, sentimental view of life. Mrs. Cleveland seemed to be the only person who might be at all suitable, and, who indeed, could be more so than the vicar's wife? One should always be able to take one's troubles, hopes and fears to the vicarage.

Miss Doggett finished her tea and took the tray into the kitchen, leaving it on the draining-board. Then she put on her mackintosh and a top-heavy-looking maroon felt hat, took her umbrella from the stand and set out.

It was raining heavily as she opened the vicarage gate and the laurels outside Nicholas's study window were dripping wet.

The garden wasn't what it used to be in the Pritchards' time, she thought. The grass was ragged and there was nothing in the front beds but a few straggling asters and nasturtiums.

Jane Cleveland herself came to the door. She was wearing an apron, and hastened to explain this unusual circumstance by telling Miss Doggett that she was bottling plums.

'Or, rather, trying to,' she added. 'Nicholas is doing most of the work. The jars are just due to come out of the oven and have the boiling syrup poured into them. Then the tops must be put on – it's all very nerve-racking.'

Miss Doggett, who knew all about bottling plums, was hardly listening to what Jane said. It was most disconcerting to find her doing anything at all, and she wondered whether it might not be better to postpone the real object of her visit and come back at a more propitious time.

'I really wanted to ask your advice about something,' she began.

'Ask *my* advice?' Jane's face brightened. 'But how splendid! Do come in. Perhaps you wouldn't mind sitting with us in the kitchen while we finish these bottles? They won't take long!'

Miss Doggett followed Jane rather unwillingly down the long stone passage that led to the kitchen.

'It's Miss Doggett, dear,' said Jane, flinging open the door. 'She wants to ask my advice about something.'

Really, thought Miss Doggett irritably, this is most unsuitable. For not only was the table covered with all the paraphernalia of bottling – jars, metal caps, rubber rings, plums, jugs, kettles, and sheets of newspaper – but the kitchen itself seemed to be festooned with enormous green leaves which hung down from everywhere that things could hang down from, the mantelpiece, the dresser, the clothes airer and the hooks in the ceiling which had once held hams and sides of bacon. Miss Doggett held her hands up to her hat, feeling as if she were in some Amazonian jungle and that poisonous snakes and insects might drop on to her from the great hanging leaves. To make matters worse, the vicar now emerged from behind a screen of leaves, his usual mild expression betraying that there was nothing at all extraordinary about the situation. He too was wearing a flowered apron which somehow took away from the dignity of his clerical collar, Miss Doggett felt.

'Ah, Miss Doggett, how nice to see you.' He advanced towards her with his hand outstretched. 'My wife has probably told you that we are bottling plums. And I am trying to dry some of my tobacco leaves – ideally it should be done outside, in the sun, of course.'

Miss Doggett was quite unable to think of anything suitable to say. There did not even seem to be anywhere to sit down until Jane had removed a plate of plum stones from one of the kitchen chairs, and she found herself forced to chatter about trivialities, while the jars were being taken from the oven, filled up with boiling syrup and sealed.

'There now,' said Jane, screwing up the last cap. 'I wonder if I shall have the courage to test these to-morrow. It seems to require such a very great deal of faith to lift them up just by their glass tops. I suppose it is like going over to Rome – once you see that it works you wonder how you could ever have doubted it.'

'Really, Jane . . .' protested her husband, 'I hardly think . . .'

'But of course they don't always work,' Jane went on. 'Sometimes the top comes away in your hand.'

'Personally, I find the other method more satisfactory,' said Miss Doggett. 'I don't think I have ever had a failure.'

'Well, well. We must try that next year,' said Nicholas. 'But it seemed rather more complicated.'

'I always think it's worth taking that little extra bit of trouble,' said Miss Doggett complacently.

'Oh, my leaves,' said Nicholas anxiously, putting up a hand to touch them. 'I wonder how dry they are or how dry they should be?'

Neither of the ladies seemed able to answer his question, and Jane suddenly turned to Miss Doggett and reminded her that she had wanted her advice on some matter. 'I think you said you wanted to ask *me*?' she added.

'Well, there is no objection to the vicar hearing what I have to say,' said Miss Doggett.

'I feel I can almost count as another woman,' said Nicholas, perhaps rather too lightly, for he was still thinking more of his tobacco leaves than of Miss Doggett's mission.

'The matter concerns a man and a woman,' said Miss Doggett obscurely, for she hardly knew how to begin. The plums and tobacco leaves and the general scene of disorder in the vicarage kitchen had taken words away from her. She had imagined herself coming out with it on the doorstep, almost. It was to have been the spontaneous overflow of powerful feelings rather than emotion recollected in tranquillity.

'Has there been some trouble in the village?' Jane asked. 'Some girl in the family way?'

Miss Doggett shuddered. She had certainly not thought of *that*. And yet who could tell where Jessie's behaviour might have led her?

'No; it isn't that,' she said firmly. 'I may as well say quite plainly what it is.'

'Yes, it doesn't really help to know what it is *not*,' said Jane seriously.

There was a short pause, and then Miss Doggett said in a kind of burst, 'I think there may be something between Jessie and Mr. Driver.'

'Between Fabian and Miss Morrow?' repeated Jane, not quite echoing her words. 'But what could there be?'

'An understanding, a friendship, something more than that, perhaps. I hardly know – I feel I hardly *wish* to know.' This last sentence was not strictly true. There was nothing Miss Doggett wished to know more.

'Well, I suppose they could be friends,' said Jane doubtfully.

'But he is engaged to Miss Bates – unofficially, of course, but I think it is generally understood.'

'My dear, I don't think so,' interposed Nicholas. 'I think that was an arrangement you and Prudence made between yourselves. I don't think it is in Driver's mind at all.'

'But how do you know what is in his mind?' Jane asked indignantly. 'How can you?'

'We had some conversation the other evening when he was here to dinner. I understood then that he was not thinking of marrying again.'

'So that is what men talk about when they're alone together,' said Jane angrily. 'While Prue and I were struggling with the washing-up for six people you and Fabian were planning that he should not marry again!'

'Well, dear, hardly that. . . .'

'I suppose he decided that once was enough and you encouraged him by pointing out that the Church frowns on the remarriage of widowers?'

'My dear Jane, I could hardly have done that. You know quite well that there can be no objection to a widower remarrying. In any case, I feel we are getting off the point. After all, Miss Doggett hasn't yet told us her reasons for supposing that there is an – er – understanding between Driver and Miss Morrow.'

Miss Doggett was in a difficulty here, for she did not feel that she could admit to having found one of Fabian's handkerchiefs among Jessie's. So she had to content herself with vague hints, indicating that she had had a 'feeling' for some time, that she had 'noticed things,' which were not really very convincing.

Nobody could quite see what was to be done at the moment. Jane was concerned only with Prudence, and the effect the news – if it was news – might have on her. Nicholas, perhaps unconsciously taking the part of men against women, felt that it was hardly anybody's business to interfere at this stage. In any case there was nothing that *he* could do.

'After all, I'm not an intimate friend of Driver's,' he pointed out. 'Jane really knows him better than I do. I could, of course, say something if it appeared to be necessary, though I hardly know what. . . .'

'Don't you worry about that!' said Jane vigorously. 'I shall have no hesitation in facing him with it, if I feel that he has been trifling with Prue in any way. And why shouldn't we go now?' she turned to Miss Doggett. 'The sooner the better, *I* think. Perhaps you would come with me, Miss Doggett?'

'I should be very careful what you say, dear,' said Nicholas in a warning tone. 'After all, it isn't really any of our business, . . .' But the women were out of earshot by this time, and he turned back to his tobacco leaves with a feeling of relief. The whole thing seemed to be of very little importance, the kind of mountain women were apt to make out of what was hardly even a molehill. He went to the window and saw that it was still raining. He wondered whether Jane had remembered to take a mackintosh.

She had snatched up the first one she saw hanging in the hall, which happened to be Nicholas's black clerical one and came nearly down to her ankles. She wore nothing on her head, but having naturally curly hair she seldom did, and brushed aside Miss Doggett's offer of a share of her tartan umbrella. Miss Doggett could have wished that she did not look quite so odd, almost ridiculous. There must be nothing comic about the scene that was about to be enacted. It was altogether a most serious business, she had not until now stopped to consider its possible implications. 'Something between Jessie and Mr. Driver . . .' something disgraceful, that possibility immediately sprang to mind when remembering Jessie's strange personality and her mother's unsuitable marriage. On the other hand, it might be something depressingly respectable and above-board, no more than a friendship. . . .

'Prue will be *so* upset,' murmured Jane, tramping through the rain in the long black mackintosh. 'Miss Doggett, I'm sure you must be mistaken. Is Miss Morrow at home? Couldn't we ask her? Though,' she went on, 'it might be better to ask Fabian right out. Women do occasionally get the wrong idea – imagine that there is more in a man's feelings for them than there really is.' As perhaps poor Prudence had done. But then she remembered 'Miss Bates and her love affairs'. . . . Surely *she* could not have been mistaken?

'Jessie has had her half-day to-day,' said Miss Doggett. 'She usually goes to the cinema. I doubt whether she will be back yet.'

'Then perhaps we had better call on Fabian,' said Jane, faltering a little, for even her courage was beginning to ebb. What were they going to say to him? Wouldn't he regard them as a couple of interfering busybodies and be perfectly justified in so doing?

Fabian's house looked very quiet and unoccupied as they approached it. Mrs. Arkright would have gone by now, leaving him a cold supper, with perhaps some soup that he could heat up himself. Jane and Miss Doggett were not to know that Fabian and Jessie were in the drawing-room having an argument about how Prudence should be told and who should do it. It was almost a relief to Fabian when the front-door bell rang and he saw Jane and Miss Doggett standing on the doorstep in the rain.

'Ah, come in,' he said, almost in a welcoming tone. 'It's a horrid evening to be out.'

He showed them into the drawing-room. Miss Doggett let out a kind of cry on seeing Jessie there.

'So it's true,' she said, sinking down into a chair. 'There *is* something between you!'

Jessie did not answer, and Fabian, who had his back to them, was busy with glasses and bottles which he took out of a corner cupboard. He supposed that the occasion was one which called for a drink; indeed, in his life there was hardly any occasion which did not.

'Sherry or gin?' he asked in a rather neutral voice, ignoring Miss Doggett's question.

'Oh, gin, thank you,' said Jane indignantly.

Miss Doggett did not answer, so he placed a glass of sherry near her.

Jane took a great gulp of her colourless drink and then gasped and coughed. She had forgotten how unpleasant it was.

'Fabian and I are going to be married,' said Jessie calmly. 'We were going to tell you, but you seem to have forestalled us.'

'Yes, we are to be married,' said Fabian. 'It seems to have come to that.'

For an instant Jane bridled indignantly on Jessie's behalf. It seems to have come to that! What a way to announce that you loved a woman and were going to marry her! Could men do no better than that these days? Then she remembered Prudence in her red velvet housecoat and her evasive answers to the questions Jane had put to her about her relationship with Fabian.

'And what about Prudence?' she asked. 'You seem to have forgotten her.'

Fabian clasped his hands together in a despairing gesture. 'Oh, what am I to do,' he moaned, pacing about the room. 'I haven't had the courage to tell her yet. I blame myself for this.'

'Yes, I think you should probably shoulder *this* burden,' said Jane. 'It is better to finish with one thing before you start another.' And yet, she thought, how hopeless to say a thing like that; it was like telling a child to put away one toy before he took out a new one to play with.

'It was not much really between Prudence and me,' said Fabian lamely; 'perhaps less than you thought. We had dinner together once or twice and went to a few theatres. I certainly thought her very attractive and charming, but she could never take Constance's place.'

'So Jessie has done that?' asked Miss Doggett in an interested tone. 'And yet in many ways they are so unlike. Who would ever have thought. . . ?'

'Prudence would have wanted so much,' Fabian went on, pacing about the room and giving the impression that he was talking to himself. 'Her letters, wonderful letters in a way, but so difficult to answer. And then she would have wanted to change everything here. She used to go to Heal's and look at curtain materials – she even chose a new wallpaper for Constance's old room.'

Poor darling Prue, thought Jane, how sure she must have been. 'I suppose *I* could tell her what has happened,' she said. 'I could write to her.'

Fabian stopped his pacing and stood in front of Jane.

'*Could* you?' he said gratefully. 'That would be such a help. I shall of course write as well. I feel that I must do that.'

'Yes, Fabian, you must,' said Jane firmly. 'Men can't expect women to do quite everything for them.'

'Poor Miss Bates,' said Miss Doggett perfunctorily.

'Oh, she has plenty of admirers,' said Jane brusquely.

'Then she will soon get over this,' went on Miss Doggett, for she had now lost interest in Prudence and was already planning Jessie's wedding from her house. There could be no possible objection to a church wedding, for although Fabian had not always behaved very well when poor Constance was alive, there had been no question of divorce or anything disgraceful like that. Obviously, Edward Lyall and his mother would expect an invitation to the wedding. It would be quite an event in the neighbourhood.

'Well, Jessie,' she said in a satisfied tone, 'I think Constance would have been pleased at this news.'

'Yes, wouldn't she,' said Fabian, also with some satisfaction. 'I think it would have been just what she would have wished. Perhaps she does know and is giving us her blessing in some way. I feel very strongly that perhaps, in some way . . .' His sentence petered out rather feebly. Perhaps he was conscious of Jane's eyes upon him, and she now stood up, pushing aside her unfinished glass of gin with an impatient gesture. She had no sympathy with Fabian's sentimental theology, and indeed felt that her part in the proceedings was over. Nobody took much notice of her as she said goodbye and let herself out of the house.

When she reached home she found that Flora and Paul had returned and were in the kitchen getting supper. Nicholas was wandering about among his tobacco leaves, occasionally fingering one to see if it was drying well.

'How did it go?' he asked anxiously.

'We found them both at Fabian's house. Miss Doggett seems to have been right. Fabian and Jessie are to be married, apparently.' Jane sat down wearily, still wearing Nicholas's black mackintosh.

'Are you talking about Mr. Driver and Miss Morrow?' called Flora from the gas stove. 'We saw them having tea at the Regal Café, didn't we, Paul?'

'Did we? I remember your saying something about a man and a woman sitting there. Wasn't it that man who came to dinner the other evening who didn't seem to know what an anthropologist was?'

So that was how Fabian was to be known to Paul, thought Jane with a flash of amusement. He would hardly have been very pleased.

Supper was rather a gloomy meal. Nicholas and Jane did not say much, for Jane was brooding about what she should say to Prudence, and the young people spoke in low whispers, as if there were a death in the house. After the meal was over Jane retired to write her letter and Nicholas to his study for some unspecified purpose.

Paul and Flora settled themselves to the washing-up and could be heard singing in the back kitchen.

'Poor Prudence,' said Flora. 'We did hope that *this* time . . . what did you think of her?'

'Rather attractive in a way, but she looks about thirty, you know,' said Paul solemnly.

'I wonder if I shall get like that,' Flora mused.

'How do you mean?'

'Oh, falling in love with people and casting them off and then being cast off myself in the end.'

'But need it be the end for her?'

'Well, the supply of suitable men isn't inexhaustible when one reaches her age – not like it is at Oxford.'

Paul, who was nineteen and had already had several romances, made no comment. 'Do you think this Fabian man attractive?' he asked at length.

'Yes; I suppose so, in a rather used-up, Byronic sort of way. But he's rather middle-aged, really.' Flora squeezed out the dish cloth and draped it neatly over the papier-mâché washing-up bowl.

'Let's go into the garden,' said Paul; 'it's stopped raining now.'

Looking through her bedroom window, biting the end of her pen, Jane saw them walking hand-in-hand down the path between the clumps of Michaelmas daisies. She remembered noticing the title of a play on the wireless, *Love and Geography*. She had wondered at the time what possible connection there could be between the two. Well, it was a nice evening now that the rain had stopped, she thought absently, turning back to the blank sheet of paper before her.

In the damp, earwig-infested summer-house, which was an old-fashioned wooden structure with diamond-paned windows of crimson, orange and royal blue stained-glass, Paul put his arms around Flora and began quoting Donne,

*O my America! My new-found-land . . .*

as Prudence had suggested that he might. But Jane, the anxious mother, was now deep in her letter and the sentences were flowing quite easily.

# Chapter Twenty

✖

So Prudence had not been Fabian's mistress, after all. This was the thought that seemed uppermost in Jane's mind as she sat trying to think of what she could say to Prudence, and she was displeased with herself that it should be so. But thinking over Prudence's guarded answer when she had put the question to her plainly and Fabian's remarks of a few hours ago, it did seem as if the worst – which was what Jane called it in her own mind – had not happened. This should certainly make the situation easier. Prudence's feelings would be less deeply involved and there could be no chance that she might be going to have a baby. Though it seemed, Jane thought, as if that kind of thing didn't happen nowadays. It would have been a help if she could have known what Fabian was going to say in his letter, but he had given no indication, beyond promising that he 'would write a line'. Yet his whole bearing, hand clasped to brow, tragic eyes and ruffled hair, pointed to his taking the attitude that this would hurt him more than it hurt Prudence. Jane felt that he would write from the depths of a wretchedness that would not necessarily be insincere because its outward signs were so theatrical. Presumably attractive men and probably women too must always be suffering in this way; they must so often have to reject and cast aside love, and perhaps even practice did not always make them ruthless and cold-blooded enough to do it without feeling any qualms.

Of course, Jane told herself, in an effort to relieve her own misery and her feeling of guilt for the part she had played in bringing them together, Prue hadn't really been in love with Fabian. Indeed, it was obvious that at times she found him both boring and irritating. But wasn't that what so many marriages were – finding a person boring and irritating and yet loving him? Who could imagine a man who was *never* boring or irritating? It had all seemed so very suitable, so very much the thing for a woman of twenty-nine, and there was no doubt that Prudence's pride would be seriously wounded when she realised that it was plain, mousy Jessie Morrow who had taken Fabian away from her. Perhaps this was after all what men liked to come home to, someone restful and neutral, who had no thought of changing the curtains or wallpapers? Jessie, who, for all her dim appearance, was very shrewd, had no doubt realised this. A beautiful wife would have been too much for Fabian, for one handsome person is enough in a marriage, if there is to be any beauty at all. And so often there isn't, Jane thought, drawing little houses on the blotting-paper, remembering the grey and fawn couples one saw so often in hotel lounges, hardly distinguishable, men from women, in their dimness.

> *Difference of sex no more we knew,*
> *Than our Guardian Angels do . . .*

she thought, suddenly smiling to herself at the way a not quite appropriate quotation would come into her mind on nearly every occasion.

Then she returned resolutely to the matter in hand, and after marshalling her confused thoughts succeeded in writing a loving and sympathetic letter which brought the tears to Prudence's eyes more readily than Fabian's scrawl, stressing *his* wretchedness and how much better off she would be without him.

Both letters had arrived by the same post, when Prudence, in her rose-patterned, frilled summer housecoat, was preparing breakfast in her neat little kitchen.

The blow was none the less shattering for being not entirely unexpected, for although Prudence had noticed a falling off in Fabian's affection the last time she had seen him, she had attributed it to his preoccupation with the Parochial Church

Council and what people would think if he were seen walking in the village with her at night. She had not really doubted that they would meet again in London and that all would then be well.

She stood holding Jane's letter in one hand, while the other automatically moved the toaster from under the grill.

'You know so much more than I do about the making and breaking of love affairs,' Jane had written, 'so I hope you will not long be unhappy over this, or not *too* long. But on the morning when you get this letter you will be alone, darling Prue, so be sure and give yourself a *good breakfast*, if you possibly can. . . .'

Dear Jane, Prudence smiled; it was really unlike her to be so practical. Well, the toast was not burnt and the coffee was just starting to bubble up into the top of the percolator, there was no reason why she should snatch it off the gas before it had had a chance to get as strong as she liked it. She would have some orange-juice, too, and perhaps even a boiled egg. Later she might not feel like eating.

It was a hot day. Prudence dressed with her usual elegance and painted her face and eyes with almost more than her usual care. It was at once force of habit and a kind of defiance. But as she stood waiting to cross the road to the bus she felt curiously detached, as one sometimes does in a time of great happiness or misery, and began to wonder whether she would even be able to negotiate the traffic safely.

She arrived at the office without mishap, however. Miss Clothier was on holiday, and although Miss Trapnell seemed in some way incomplete without her, the conversation was exactly the same as if they had both been there.

'Such a lovely day!' said Miss Trapnell. 'I always find I wake earlier on these fine mornings. In fact, I was here and had started work at a quarter-past nine this morning.'

'Then you will be able to go at a quarter-past five,' said Prudence absently.

She turned to her work almost with relief, hoping to lose herself in it. She even began to type out some tables of figures, work which she normally considered beneath her, and found it very soothing. Occasionally, however, other thoughts broke through the careful barrier she had put up. What was she going to say to Fabian when she answered his letter? Who would go with her on her summer holiday now?

At about a quarter to eleven Miss Trapnell looked at her watch and remarked, 'I hope Dr. Grampian hasn't called Marilyn in for dictation this morning.'

'Why? What difference can it make to us?'

'Well, don't you see, Miss Bates, with Gloria on holiday there is only Marilyn to make the tea, and if Dr. Grampian is dictating to her it may be delayed. He would not realise that it was getting to be time to put the kettle on.'

'No. I suppose he would consider that he had a mind above such things,' said Prudence.

'Well, Miss Bates, it's hardly a question of being *above* them. They are very important, vital, you might say. Somebody must be thinking about them or we should soon notice it, and men would be the first to complain.'

'I'll go and make the tea if Marilyn is with Dr. Grampian,' said Prudence apathetically.

'*You*, Miss Bates? Well, I hardly think you could, you know. It isn't your place to, or mine, for that matter. It's rather difficult, really.'

'It seems impossible,' said Prudence.

They went on with their work in silence for a few minutes and then Miss Trapnell said, 'I think I'll just go and see what's happening. I might perhaps put the kettle on.'

When she had gone out of the room Prudence's control seemed to give way. She leaned her forehead down on her typewriter and felt the cold metal against her brow.

The door opened and Geoffrey Manifold came in.

'Well, and how is Prudence to-day?' he asked in a rather jaunty tone.

Prudence did not answer, but began to cry.

Perhaps she was hardly conscious of him standing there by her table and would have cried anyway, but if she had expected to find his arms around her, consoling her, she was disappointed. He just stood by awkwardly, embarrassed as men often are at the sight of a woman in tears.

'You'll spoil your make-up,' he said in what seemed a callous tone. 'Gramp will probably summon you in any minute now, and it will be rather difficult to repair the damage, won't it? Doesn't that stuff come off your eyelashes when you cry?'

'It's supposed not to,' sniffed Prudence, taking out her handkerchief and mopping her eyes very gingerly. 'But I believe you're right; it *has* run.' She looked up at him and noticed with a slight shock that the expression of his eyes did not match the indifference of his tone.

'Is there anything I can do?' he asked.

*Do?* thought Prudence, rather wildly, contemplating his plaid shirt and tie. 'Well, you might help me with these tables. I don't seem able to get them right somehow.'

They sat quietly side by side, until Miss Trapnell, rather flustered, came in carrying a tray with three cups on it.

'Marilyn is still in there with him,' she said, 'so I had to make the tea myself, there was nothing else for it. *Most* inconsiderate of him, I think. I went in with his cup and he didn't even look up to say thank you.'

'Well, we'll say thank you,' said Mr. Manifold, putting on a certain amount of charm. '*We're* most grateful, aren't we, Miss Bates?'

'Yes, we certainly are.'

'I don't know whether I've made your Nescafé as you like it, Mr. Manifold,' said Miss Trapnell fussily. 'I wasn't sure how much milk you liked, so I brought it separately in a jug.'

'Thank you. That's very kind of you, but I usually have it black.'

Miss Trapnell sat down in her chair and sighed, exhausted with the exertions of tea-making.

'Dr. Grampian did say that he wanted to see you, Miss Bates, when you were free.'

'When *I* was free?' asked Prudence. 'It isn't like him to be so considerate.'

She went upstairs and paused outside his door. His voice droned on, dictating endless sentences without verbs.

Prudence tapped on the door.

'Come in, come in,' he said crossly, for he was not feeling very well this morning. Lucy had given a party the evening before which had gone on rather too long; the company had been boring and the drink strong and abundant. They could not really afford to give parties on such a scale. . . . 'Go away now,' he said, dismissing Marilyn, 'and bring that back to me when you've typed it. Now, Miss Bates, what is it?'

'I thought you wanted me,' said Prudence, feeling utterly forlorn. She was too much wrapped up in her own desolation to realise that he had a hangover. A year ago, she would have thought: Ah, one of Lucy's parties. Poor darling, I must humour him. But to-day it was she who must be humoured.

'Well, I don't think I did,' he said brusquely. 'Unless you've got anything to show me?'

'No, I haven't. But you told Miss Trapnell . . .'

'Oh, whatever it was, I've forgotten now.' Her heavy expensive scent, totally unsuitable for the office, reminded him of the party last night. He was only very slightly gratified to notice, when he looked up to dismiss her, that her eyes seemed to be full of tears. But over lunch at his club, the high, querulous voice of a Bishop complaining because there was no more Camembert left made him smile. And all because the tears in Miss Bates's eyes proved that he still retained his old power over women.

Prudence had hurried into the lavatory, where she had cried noiselessly for a few moments and then gone out to what she felt must be a solitary lunch. She chose a restaurant which was rather expensive, but frequented mainly by women, so that she felt no embarrassment at being alone. Here, she knew, she could get the kind of food she deserved, for she must be more than usually kind to herself to-day. A dry Martini and then a little smoked salmon; she felt she could manage that. There was a certain consolation in the crowds of fashionably dressed women, especially as Prudence felt that she could equal and even excel some of them. Had they too suffered in love? she wondered. Were some of them suffering even at this moment? Or had they passed through suffering to something worse, the blankness and boredom of indifference? It was impossible to tell from their smooth, well-groomed faces, and Prudence wondered whether she too looked as indifferent. Or might somebody ask, 'Who is that interesting-looking young woman, with the traces of tears on her cheeks, eating smoked salmon?'

'And what would you like to follow, madam?' asked the waitress. 'I can recommend the chicken.'

'Well,' Prudence hesitated, 'perhaps just a slice of the breast, and a very few vegetables.' No sweet, of course, unless there was some fresh fruit, a really ripe yellow-fleshed peach, perhaps? And afterwards, the blackest of black coffee.

There was Saturday to come and Sunday, she thought. Jane had offered to come up and spend the week-end with her if it would be any help, but she felt that having to cope with Jane might be too much for her. She would have to face her loving questions; she might even be asked again whether she had been Fabian's mistress.

Fabian had not been so much to Prudence's flat as to have left behind any particularly poignant memories. He had admired the rose-coloured curtains, they had sat together on the rather uncomfortable little Regency sofa and he had kissed her there, but he had never stayed for a night, pottered about in the

198

kitchen, put up a shelf or mended a flex. Indeed, with his own elegance, he had seemed to fit into the general scheme of furnishing rather too well, like a turbaned blackamoor holding a lamp, so that he might have been no more than just another 'amusing' object.

In the evening Prudence wrote to him, a sad, resigned letter, a little masterpiece in its way, which he was to shed tears over as he stood in his garden reading it, with the first leaves beginning to drop down from the walnut tree.

Life with Jessie suddenly seemed a frightening prospect, unless it could be like life with Constance all over again, with little romantic episodes here and there. But Jessie was too sharp to allow that. It was as if a net had closed round him. He went into the house and put Prudence's letter away in a secret drawer of his desk, where, years later, he might come upon it, and either wonder which of all his many loves she had been, or brood regretfully over it as a wonderful thing that had come into his life too late.

## Chapter Twenty-One

✠

SATURDAY passed somehow for Prudence in a rather fanatical tidying of her flat, in much polishing and dusting, and in buying herself all the nicest things she could think of to eat and drink. In the evening she had asked her contemporary, Eleanor Hitchens, to dinner, and quite enjoyed herself, hinting at tragedy, while Eleanor, her good-natured face beaming, said with a kind of rough sympathy, 'Oh, Prue, you and your men and all these emotional upsets! Doesn't it make life very wearing? Still, you were just the same at Oxford, I remember. Whoever was it then – Peter or Philip or Henry or somebody?'

Prudence smiled. It had been Peter and Philip and Henry

at one time or another. Not to mention Laurence and Giles.

'You ought to get married,' said Eleanor sensibly. 'That would settle you.' She hitched up her tweed skirt and stretched out her legs, clad in lisle stockings, to the warmth of the gas-fire, which Prudence, who wore only a thin dress, had thought necessary on this warm evening. 'Look at my awful stockings. I didn't have time to change after golf. I suppose I'll never get a man if I don't take more trouble with myself,' Eleanor went on, but she spoke comfortably and without regret, thinking of her flat in Westminster, so convenient for the Ministry, her week-end golf, concerts and theatres with women friends, in the best seats and with a good supper afterwards. Prue could have this kind of life if she wanted it; one couldn't go on having romantic love affairs indefinitely. One had to settle down sooner or later into the comfortable spinster or the contented or bored wife.

'We were going on holiday together,' said Prudence, perhaps not very truthfully. 'Now I suppose I shan't go anywhere.'

'Come to Spain with me, end of September,' said Eleanor brisk and practical. 'Even if you got bored with my company, you'd get some decent food and sunbathing. It would do you good – you must have a holiday, you know. Besides, you might meet some handsome Señor.'

Prudence smiled and thanked her, saying she would think about it and let her know. People were being so kind to her. Dear Jane and dear Eleanor, what would one do without the sympathy of other women?

The next day was Sunday, and Prudence woke up in tears. She supposed that she must have been crying in her sleep, before the consciousness of what had happened came beating down upon her. Her life was blank and the summer seemed to have gone. She lay listening to a church bell ringing and the rain pattering on the leaves in the square, wishing that she had the consolations of religion to help her. Now, at ten minutes to eight, she thought, Anglo-Catholic women with unpowdered faces and pale lips would be hurrying out to Early Service, without even the comfort of a cup of tea inside them. And at about nine o'clock or a little before, they would come back, happy and serene, to enjoy a larger breakfast than usual and the Sunday papers. The Romans, too, would slip into a convenient Mass at nine-thirty or some late and sensible time, and feel that they had done their duty for the day. Perhaps that would be the best kind of faith to have. Prudence imagined herself on holiday in Spain, a black lace mantilla draped over her hair, hurrying into some dark Cathedral. Perhaps she could do something about it even now. She remembered a poster by the Church she passed every day on her way to the bus. TALKS ON THE CATHOLIC FAITH FOR NON-CATHOLICS, BY FATHER KEOGH. Tuesday evenings, at 8. But then she imagined herself sitting on a hard, uncomfortable chair after a day's work, listening to a lecture by a raw Irish peasant that was phrased for people less intelligent than herself. Better, surely, to go along to Farm Street and be instructed by a calm pale Jesuit who would know the answers to all one's doubts. Then, in the street where she did her shopping there was the Chapel, with a notice outside which said: ALL WELCOME. The minister, the Rev. Bernard Tabb, had the letters B.D., B.SC. after his name. The fact that he was a Bachelor of Science might give a particular authority to his sermons, Prudence always felt; he might quite possibly know *all* the answers, grapple boldly with doubt and overcome it because he knew the best and worst of both worlds. He might even tackle evolution and the atomic bomb and make sense of it all. But of course, she thought, echoing Fabian's sentiments as he walked in the village, one just couldn't go to Chapel; one just didn't. Nor even to those exotic religious meetings advertised on the back of the *New Statesman*, which always seemed to take place in Bayswater.

These thoughts gave her strength enough to get up from her bed and make herself a pot of tea and some toast. As she lay back against her pale green pillows she could see her reflection in the looking-glass on the wall opposite. She was not quite at her best at this hour, but rather appealing in her plainness, sipping her favourite Lapsang Souchong, at ten and sixpence a pound, out of a fragile white-and-gold cup.

When she had finished her breakfast and read the Sunday papers, she took up a volume of George Herbert's poems which Jane had once given to her. The book opened at a poem called *Hope*, and she read:

> *I gave to Hope a watch of mine; but he*
> *    An anchor gave to me.*
> *Then an old Prayer-book I did present;*
> *    And he an optic sent.*
> *With that I gave a vial full of tears;*
> *    But he, a few green ears.*
> *Ah, loiterer! I'll no more, no more I'll bring;*
> *    I did expect a ring.*

It puzzled and disturbed her and she lay quietly for some time, trying to think out what it meant. Yet she was comforted too and it reminded her of Jane and Nicholas, Morning Prayer and Matins and Evensong in a damp country church with pews, and dusty red hassocks. No light oak chairs, incense or neat leather kneelers. Perhaps the Anglican way was the best after all. It was the way she had been brought up in. Should she perhaps go up to see her mother in Herefordshire and revisit the scenes of her childhood? The idea was attractive, but then she saw how it would be: the wet green garden, her mother and her friends all looking sadly older, playing their afternoon bridge, their eager eyes full of the questions they did not quite like to ask. Why didn't she come and see her mother more often? What did she do in London? What was her work with Dr. Grampian? Why wasn't she married yet?

Lunch was a rather sad meal, hardly up to Prudence's usual standard. She had not the heart even to cook the small chicken she had bought for herself. Afterwards she tried to read a novel and fell asleep for a while, but at three o'clock she woke and there seemed to be nothing to do but to lie brooding in her chair, looking at the few letters Fabian had written to her, until it was time to make a cup of tea. Now the Lapsang Souchong tasted smoky and bitter, rather like disinfectant, she thought. As if she were putting an end to herself with Lysol.

At five o'clock the telephone rang. Prudence supposed it might be Jane, anxious to know how she was getting through the day, but when she picked up the receiver and a man's voice answered the thought leapt into her mind that of course it was Fabian. The whole thing had been a terrible mistake, a bad dream.

Her illusion was shattered in a second and the voice announced that it was Geoffrey Manifold, and asked how she was.

'Oh, all right, thank you,' said Prudence, very much taken aback.

'After tea on Sunday is always such a depressing time,' he went on. 'I was just wondering if you were free and would like to come out to dinner and perhaps see a film?'

'That's very sweet of you. I think perhaps I should.'

'Good. Then I'll call for you at half-past six.'

How kind of him! It gave Prudence a warm feeling to realise that perhaps he had been thinking of her to-day when she had been so unhappy. 'Mr. Manifold is so good to his aunt.' For the first time that day she felt like laughing, and went quickly to change and decorate her face and finger-nails. Then she set out drinks on a tray and waited for him to come.

They were both a little shy at first. They had not met out of working hours before, and his neat dark suit looked less familiar than the plaid shirt and corduroy trousers which Prudence had expected.

He looked round the Regency elegance of Prudence's sitting-room with a half-nervous, half-scornful expression on his face.

'Just the sort of place you ought to live in,' he said at

last. 'Very *Vogue* and all that. Not quite my cup of tea, I'm afraid.'

I'm not asking you to live with me, thought Prudence angrily; merely to have a drink. 'What would you like?' she asked, indicating her collection of bottles. 'And don't say you prefer beer, because I haven't any.'

He smiled. 'I'm sorry,' he said. 'I'm afraid I was rather rude about your flat. After all, I'm supposed to be here to comfort you, aren't I?'

'To comfort me?' asked Prudence rather indignantly. 'How do you know that?'

'I thought your heart was broken,' he said looking into his glass of gin. 'Never mind; it will pass.'

'How do *you* know it will?'

'Oh, I'm always having trouble with my girl-friends,' he said lightly.

Prudence felt a little stab of jealousy. How ridiculous this was! She wanted to ask in a formal tone 'And have you many girl-friends at the moment?' but pride held her back. How dared anyone be unkind to him! she thought fiercely.

'Where would you like to have dinner?' he asked rather stiffly.

As usual on the occasions when this question was put to her Prudence was unable to think of anywhere except Claridge's or Lyons, neither of which seemed really suitable. But in the end it seemed that Geoffrey knew of a quiet place in Soho where the food wasn't bad.

They were sitting studying the menu when a man at the next table came up to them and gazing intently at them with his bright beady eyes, said in a low voice, 'I do *not* recommend the *pâté* here to-night, but the *bouillabaisse* is excellent. An odd thing that – I felt I couldn't bear you to order the *pâté*.'

Prudence and Geoffrey thanked him in a rather embarrassed way.

'Oh, it is such an *anxious* moment,' he said, 'that first glance at the menu, will there be *anything at all* that one can eat? *Then felt I like some watcher of the skies,* on first looking into Chapman's Homer, you know. . . . I always feel that if I can do *anything* for my fellow diners. . . .'

'Mr. Caldicote,' said a waiter, approaching with a bottle, 'I think you will find this sufficiently *chambré* now, sir.'

'Ah, Henry, you naughty man! You've just plunged it into a bowl of hot water, *I* know. . . .'

'Oh, Mr. Caldicote, *sir* . . .' They both laughed.

'A not entirely unworthy little Beaujolais,' said the strange man, and, waving his hand in a friendly manner, he returned to his table.

'Well, now,' said Geoffrey, 'I wonder if we dare eat anything after that?'

'Is there *anything at all* that we can eat?' laughed Prudence.

She was surprised to find that she was quite hungry, and enjoyed her roast duck and red wine. 'You know,' she said, after a while, 'I'm not sure that I really want to go to a film. Would you mind if we didn't?'

'Not at all. I only suggested it because one can't expect a girl to be satisfied with nothing more than one's company as an evening's entertainment.'

'That was nice of you,' said Prudence. 'So many men think one should be delighted with just that.' But perhaps the girl-friends expected more?

'There is a new film at the Academy,' said Geoffrey.

'Le something de Monsieur something,' said Prudence.

'I expect it begins in a fog on a quay and a ship is hooting somewhere.'

'And a girl in a mackintosh and a beret is standing in a door-way.'

'And then she and a man who emerges out of the fog go into a café full of that tinny French music.'

'And a little later on there's the room with the iron bedstead and the girl in her petticoat. . . .'

'So we've really seen the film,' said Geoffrey.

'Talking of France, have you planned your holiday yet?' she asked. 'All that grim walking and no lazing in the sun drinking?'

'Yes. I've arranged it all. What about yours?'

'I'm probably going to Spain with a friend,' said Prudence rather mysteriously. Again she saw herself slipping into Mass with a black lace mantilla arranged becomingly over her hair.

'I shall be very near Spain. Perhaps we may even meet? I may see you sitting drinking on the terrace of a luxury hotel while I walk by with my rucksack.'

'And I'll invite you to share a bottle of wine with me!' Prudence laughed. It was all most unsuitable, she told herself. Fabian barely cold in his grave, and here she was laughing with Geoffrey Manifold, of all people. Whatever would Jane say?

Jane would hardly have known what to say, but when she rang Prudence's flat at about nine o'clock, she was rather disturbed to get no reply.

'Whatever happens, one always imagines that people will listen to the nine o'clock news,' she said. 'I do hope Prue is all right.' A dreadful picture came to her of gas-ovens and overdoses of drugs, and of how she had always thought the block of flats where Prudence lived the kind of place one might be found dead in. 'Oh, Nicholas, you don't think she would do anything *foolish*, do you?'

'Oh, but she is always doing foolish things,' he said mildly.

'Yes, but you don't think she would do anything *to herself*, do you?'

'Certainly not, darling. Prudence is much too fond of herself for there to be any danger of that.'

'I know. I expect she's having dinner with Dr. Grampian!' said Jane suddenly. 'That's why she wasn't in. What a terrible week this has been, everything going wrong like this. Thank goodness we are to have our holiday soon. I only hope your *locum* doesn't fail.'

'Well, I shan't know if he does, and we shall certainly be too far away to be able to do anything about it,' said Nicholas comfortably.

'They'll all be waiting there,' said Jane, warming to the subject. 'Eleven o'clock will strike. There will be agitated whisperings among the congregation and then a hurried consultation between the churchwardens. I suppose Mr. Mortlake and Mr. Whiting would be able to take some kind of a service?'

'Certainly. It is the ancient right and duty of the churchwardens to recite the Divine Office of Morning Prayer,' said Nicholas. 'I suppose they would be perfectly justified in exercising it.'

'But wouldn't the Bishop have to be consulted first?'

'My dear Jane,' said Nicholas, now with a tinge of exasperation in his tone, 'I'm sure Mr. Boultbee of the Church Missionary Society will be perfectly reliable. There is no need to worry about it.'

## Chapter Twenty-Two

✖

THE CHURCH in the Cornish village where the Clevelands were spending their holiday was a little Higher than either Jane or Nicholas had been used to.

'What a good thing you aren't having to assist in any way,' said Jane after they had attended the Sung Mass on their last Sunday morning.

'There's nothing to it, really,' said Nicholas rather touchily. 'One soon gets into the way of ritual.'

'But supposing it had been sprung on you unexpectedly,' Jane persisted, 'would you really have known what to do?'

'A clergyman of the Church of England should be ready for every emergency, from Asperges and Incense to North End Position and Evening Communion.'

'Ah, yes; our weakness and our glory,' said Jane. 'Was that what St. Paul meant about being all things to all men?' she mused. 'Of course, if we had had Mowbray's *Church Guide* we could have seen that this was not quite on our level. I wonder if anybody has ever thought of compiling a guide of *Low* churches – putting "N" for North End Position and "E" for Evening Communion against them?'

'People who want a Low church don't usually have to search so hard as those who want Catholic Privileges,' Nicholas pointed out.

'I do wish Prue had decided to join us,' said Jane. 'I'm rather worried about her being in Spain. She says she's never seen so many priests in her life.'

'Well, there could hardly be much danger from them.'

'No, perhaps not. But think of all those shops full of rosaries and statues. You know how impressionable she is. She also says that she has visited the birthplace of St. Ignatius Loyola, and that she had an English-speaking Jesuit all to herself to show her round.'

'I think that a Jesuit would be even less likely than an ordinary priest to fall for Prudence's charms,' said Nicholas reassuringly.

'But don't you see, it's Prue falling for the charms of Rome that I'm afraid of,' said Jane. 'And that's not the worst. Listen to this! "Geoffrey and I went to see a bullfight at Pamplona. We had to get up at four a.m., but it was well worth it." Now who on earth is Geoffrey? I've never heard her mention him before. I quite understood that she was going with Eleanor Hitchens, and she's such a very sensible, solid sort of person.'

'She may have met this Geoffrey in Spain,' suggested Nicholas. 'Perhaps she and Eleanor quarrelled and separated, as people quite often do on holiday.'

'Well, I do hope it really *is* all right. I shall be quite glad to be home and back to normal again.'

They arrived home on a Saturday evening to find the garden like a jungle and Mrs. Glaze welcoming them almost as if they had been Canon and Mrs. Pritchard, Jane felt.

'Well, I *am* glad to see you back, madam, and the vicar too,' she said warmly. 'It'll be a nice change, we all feel.'

'A change?' said Jane. 'But Mr. Boultbee was only here for three Sundays. You can hardly have got tired of him in so short a time.'

'It's tired of Africa, *we* are,' said Mrs. Glaze firmly. 'Six sermons about Africa, we've had. It's more than flesh and blood can stand, madam. I was really shocked at some of their customs.' She paused, and then added in a brighter tone, 'I've got some nice chops for your supper. I expect you'll be ready for it. Mr. Driver is having chops too. Mrs. Arkright was going to braise them for him with some vegetables. It was a pity about him and Miss Bates.'

'Oh, yes,' said Jane hurriedly. 'I suppose it was. But of course there was nothing official, no engagement, you know.'

'Well, they both tried hard in their different ways, Miss Bates and Miss Morrow, and Miss Morrow won. What Miss Morrow *had*, we shall never know. She may have stooped to ways that Miss Bates wouldn't have dreamed of.' Mrs. Glaze looked at Jane hopefully, but Jane was unable to throw any light on the matter. She felt she did not quite like to think of what Jessie might have done to get what she wanted. Perhaps *she* had been Fabian's mistress? Well, they would never know that now.

'It *is* nice to be home, just the three of us,' she said, as they sat down to their dish of chops with tomatoes, runner beans and mashed potatoes.

'Oh, Mother, you *always* say that after a holiday,' said Flora impatiently.

'Do I, darling? Yes, I suppose I'm getting to the age when

one doesn't realise how often one says the same thing and doesn't really care,' said Jane complacently. 'I suppose it's one of the compensations of growing older.'

'I can hear somebody coming to the door,' said Flora. 'I suppose I'd better go and see who it is. Mrs. Glaze will have gone by now.'

The bell rang and she opened the door to find Mr. Oliver on the doorstep.

'Good evening, Miss Cleveland,' he said. 'I wonder if I could see the vicar for a moment?'

However could I have thought him interesting? Flora asked herself, ashamed at her lack of taste rather than her fickleness. That thin face, like some underfed animal, the fair hair with a curly bit in front . . . forgotten were the exquisite Evensongs when his face had appeared so spiritual in the dim light. Oh, Paul, *darling* Paul, she thought, as she showed Mr. Oliver into the study, how was she going to bear the weeks until Oxford term began and she would meet him again after a lecture outside the School of Geography?

'I hope things are going well at the Bank?' she asked formally.

'Yes, thank you, Miss Cleveland. I shall be taking my holiday soon.'

'In October? That seems rather late. I do hope you will get some good weather. I'll tell my father you're here.'

'I suppose you put him in the study,' said Jane as Flora came back into the room. 'What a pity we can't all hear what he has to say.'

Nicholas left the room and Jane and Flora began to clear the table.

'I can't hear raised angry voices,' said Jane regretfully. 'Mr. Oliver seems to be very subdued to-night. I wonder what he can have called about? It must be something rather important if it has to be discussed when we have been back from our holiday barely an hour.'

'They seem to be coming out of the study now,' said Flora. 'It hasn't taken long, whatever it was.'

Jane hurried out into the hall. 'Good evening, Mr. Oliver,' she said. 'I hope you are well?'

'Very well, thank you, Mrs. Cleveland; and I hope you have had a good holiday.'

Jane thanked him and waited hopefully.

'I have just been telling the vicar that I am afraid I shan't be seeing so much of you in the future.'

'I'm sorry to hear that. Are you leaving the district?'

'Well, not exactly that, Mrs. Cleveland. Not to put too fine a point on it, I have joined Father Lomax's congregation.'

'Oh.' Jane hardly knew whether to express regret or to congratulate him. One got the idea that he had somehow been promoted. Friend, go up higher, she thought.

'I have been going to the services there for some months, off and on, you know,' declared Mr. Oliver. 'And I find the form of the service, the ritual, you know, really more to my liking, with all due respect to you and the vicar.'

'Oh, I *quite* see,' said Jane sympathetically.

'And then there has been a certain amount of friction on some matters, as you may well be aware,' he continued.

'Yes, of course. That evening I found you all in the choir vestry . . .'

'Of course, Mr. Mortlake has his point of view, but things can't stand still. Life isn't what it was fifty years ago.'

'No, of course not,' said Jane in a rather puzzled tone. 'But you will miss reading the Lessons, won't you?'

Mr. Oliver smiled in a rather superior way. 'Well, Mrs. Cleveland, I am fortunate enough to have found a little niche waiting for me at St. Stephen's. The post of thurifer has fallen vacant and I have been asked to fill it. The gentleman who used to do it has embraced the Roman Faith.'

'Well I never,' said Jane. 'You will be quite busy, then.'

'Yes, Mrs. Cleveland. There will be the Sung Mass at eleven

and Solemn Evensong at half-past six, and sometimes a Sung Mass during the week, on Days of Obligation, you know.'

'We must all come and see you swinging the censer,' Jane began before she realised that it would hardly be practicable. 'Good night,' she said quickly and hurried back into the dining-room, where Nicholas stood rather disconsolate, looking down at the chop-bones now congealed in their fat.

'Oh, dear, I feel I have failed there,' he said.

'Darling, you have done no such thing,' said Jane warmly. 'You can't help it if he quarrelled with Mr. Mortlake and Mr. Whiting and likes incense and all that sort of thing.'

'What was that you said about finding them all in the choir vestry one evening?' Nicholas asked.

'I just happened to be passing and heard them all squabbling in there. So I went in to see if there was anything I could do.'

'My poor Jane,' – he put his arm around her shoulders and they gazed down together at the remains of their supper – 'what can any of us do with these people?'

'We can only go blundering along in that state of life unto which it shall please God to call us,' said Jane. 'I was going to be such a splendid clergyman's wife when I married you, but somehow it hasn't turned out like *The Daisy Chain* or *The Last Chronicles of Barset*.'

'How you would have stood by me if I had been accused of stealing a cheque,' said Nicholas. 'I can just imagine you! Oh, now who is this coming to the door? Quite a crowd of people. Do you remember our first evening here and how you thought a crowd of parishioners ought to be coming up to the door to welcome us?'

'And nobody came except Mrs. Glaze with a parcel of liver for our supper!' Jane laughed. 'Well, now I can't complain. It seems to be Miss Doggett with Jessie and Fabian. I will go and ask Flora to make some coffee.'

'Ah, how nice it is to have you back,' said Miss Doggett, advancing into the room with her hand outstretched in welcome.

'Mr. Boultbee seems to have done us a good turn,' said Nicholas. 'I gather his sermons were not much liked.'

'No; we got very tired of Africa and I didn't feel that what he told us rang quite true. He said that one African chief had had a thousand wives. I found that a little difficult to believe.'

'Well, we know what men are,' said Jane casually, surprised that Miss Doggett, with her insistence on men only wanting one thing, should have found it difficult to believe.

'Oh, come now,' protested Fabian, for she seemed to have glanced in his direction. 'And in any case, it was in the olden days, before Mr. Boultbee got to work there.'

At this point Flora brought in the coffee, and Jane began to pour it out rather carelessly.

'Jessie and I were thinking that we might as well get married as soon as conveniently possible,' said Fabian. 'After all, we are neither of us very young.'

'I can arrange that for you at any time,' said Nicholas. 'You know about banns and licences and that kind of thing, I imagine?'

'Nicholas usually gives a talk to young couples before they marry,' said Jane hopefully. 'But perhaps it will hardly be necessary in this case.'

'He might just take Fabian aside,' said Jessie.

Nicholas began to talk to them about arrangements, and Miss Doggett said to Jane in a low voice, 'He has at last decided to do something about a stone for poor Constance's grave.'

'I'm very glad to hear it! What is it to be like?'

'Something quite plain and dignified. He thought Cornish granite, with a suitable inscription. They spent their honeymoon in Cornwall, you know.'

> 'Stay for me there; I will not fail
> To meet thee in that hollow vale.
> And think not much of my delay;
> I am already on the way . . .'

quoted Jane softly. 'What a good thing there is no marriage or giving in marriage in the after-life; it will certainly help to smooth things out. Is Jessie to wear a white dress?'

'No; we thought white would hardly be suitable. Something in a soft blue or dove grey, we thought, with a small hat; and a spray of flowers, not a bouquet.'

'Brides over thirty shouldn't wear white,' said Jessie, who had now joined them.

'Well, they may have a perfect right to,' said Jane.

'A woman over thirty might not like you to think that,' said Jessie quickly. 'There can be something shameful about flaunting one's lack of experience.'

Jane, as a clergyman's wife, hardly knew how to answer this. Also, she was remembering Mrs. Glaze's hint that Jessie might have 'stooped to ways Miss Bates wouldn't have dreamed of'. It was a subject best left alone, especially with Flora in the room.

Before they went, Fabian managed to manœuvre Jane into the conservatory leading out of the drawing-room.

'I had to have a word with you,' he said. 'How is she, my poor Prudence?'

'Well, at the moment she seems to be on holiday in Spain with somebody called Geoffrey,' said Jane sharply.

'Oh, really?' Fabian looked decidedly crestfallen. 'Can she have forgotten so soon?'

'I expect so. Haven't you?'

'I – forget? My dear Jane . . .' He put one hand up to his brow with a characteristic gesture, while his other hand seemed to wander along the slatted wooden shelves of the conservatory, with the flower-pots full of old used earth and dried-up bulbs with withered leaves, until it came to rest on what felt like a piece of statuary. He looked down in surprise at feeling his hand touch stone, and started at seeing the headless body of a dwarf which had once stood in the rockery in the front garden.

'I can't understand Mrs. Pritchard having that thing in her garden,' said Jane. 'She always struck me as being a person of taste, if nothing else. The head is here,' she said rather brightly, lifting it up by its little beard and holding it out towards Fabian.

'Don't.' He shuddered as if she had indeed offered it to him and he were rejecting it. 'Life's such a muddle, isn't it? How can we ever hope to do the right thing?'

Jane wanted to agree and to offer him the broken dwarf, perhaps for Constance's grave, as a kind of comment on the futility of earthly love, but instead she said gently, 'You must make Jessie happy. That will be the right thing for you now.'

'Yes, I suppose so,' he sighed.

'What plot are you two hatching?' said Miss Doggett's voice. 'Come, it's nearly dark, and we shall need Fabian to escort us home.'

'Rather a sad little procession,' said Jane, hearing the last scrunching of their footsteps on the gravel. 'Fabian being led away captive by the women.'

'Like *Samson Agonistes*,' observed Flora.

'*Oh, dark, dark . . .*' said Jane, laughing rather wildly. 'I told him that Prudence had forgotten him. I wonder if she has?'

## *Chapter Twenty-Three*

IT APPEARED that Prudence had forgotten Fabian to the same extent as she had forgotten Philip, Henry, Laurence and the others. That is to say, he had been given a place in the shrine of her past loves; the urn containing his ashes had been ceremonially deposited in the niche where it would always remain.

Philip, Henry, Laurence, Peter, Fabian and who could tell how many others there might be?

'I feel really that it *may* have happened for the best,' she said to Jane as they lunched again at the vegetarian restaurant.

'Well, yes; things do turn out that way really,' said Jane, glancing round the room, and seeing what looked like the same people eating the same food as before. She remembered rather sadly that she had not lunched here with Prudence since she had first had the idea of bringing her and Fabian together. Here were the same bearded and foreign gentlemen, and the same woman, dressed in orange and wearing heavy silver jewellery, who looked as if she might have been somebody's mistress in the nineteen-twenties. At the idea of being somebody's mistress, Jane became embarrassed, and began scrabbling about rather violently in her shredded cabbage salad.

'I wonder if one ever finds a caterpillar or anything like that,' she said in a loud, nervous tone.

Prudence did not answer, so Jane went on, still in the same tone, 'Now tell me, who is this Geoffrey? You mentioned him in your letter, but I'd never heard of him before.'

'Hush, Jane. Don't talk so *loud*. He's a young man who works for Arthur Grampian. I've known him for quite a long time. He was very kind to me when Fabian . . . you know . . . and then we happened to meet on holiday.'

'And do you like him?' asked Jane, lowering her voice and trying not to sound at all eager or interested.

'Well, yes, in a way,' Prudence hesitated. 'We get on quite well together. It was pleasant in Spain. I suppose it's the attraction of opposites really. But of course it wouldn't *do* at all.'

'Why wouldn't it?' asked Jane bluntly.

'Everything would be spoilt if anything came of it,' said Prudence seriously. 'Don't you see what I mean? That's almost the best thing about it.'

Jane felt very humble and inexperienced before such subtleties.

'Do you mean it's a kind of negative relationship like you once had with Arthur Grampian?' she asked, trying hard to appear intelligent and understanding.

'Oh, there's nothing *negative* about it. Quite the reverse! We shall probably hurt each other very much before it's finished, but we're doomed really.' There was a smile on Prudence's face as she said these words, for the experience of being in love with such an ordinary young man as Geoffrey Manifold was altogether new and delightful to her.

> '*Therefore the Love which us doth join*
> *But Fate so enviously debars,*
> *Is the Conjunction of the Mind,*
> *And Opposition of the Stars,*'

said Jane. 'Is that it, perhaps?' How much easier it was when one could find a quotation to light up the way; even Prudence seemed satisfied with Marvell's summing-up of the situation.

As they approached the building where Prudence's office was, Jane noticed a thin, dark young man wearing a raincoat standing in the doorway, and Prudence introduced him. And so Jane shook hands with Geoffrey as she had shaken hands with Arthur some months ago, and was amazed as she had been then at the wonder of love. What object could Fate possibly have in enviously debarring love between Prudence and such an ordinary and colourless young man as this appeared to be? But of course, she remembered, that was why women were so wonderful; it was their love and imagination that transformed these unremarkable beings. For most men, when one came to think of it, were undistinguished to look at, if not postively ugly. Fabian was an exception, and perhaps love affairs with handsome men tended to be less stable because so much less sympathy and imagination were needed on the woman's part?

But there was no opportunity to say any of this to Prudence, and soon she had left her turning to Geoffrey with every appearance of pleasure. Must it not be rather depressing to embark on a love affair that one knew to be doomed from the start? And yet, Jane supposed, people were doing it all the time, plunging boldly in with no thought of future misery.

She stood by a bus-stop, wondering what she should do. Then she remembered that there was a religious bookshop nearby, and it seemed very suitable that she should go into it and choose presents for the Confirmation candidates. Little holy books, she thought vaguely, stopping by a table and taking up what appeared to be a manual of questions and answers about points of ceremonial.

'Why do the Psalms end with a pneuma?' she read, wondering what it could mean and pondering on the answer. Her hands moved over to another pile and she found herself among books about Confession, the Answer to Rome and the mysteries of the Alcuin Society.

'Can I help you, madam?' asked an assistant, a kindly, grey-haired woman.

One's life followed a kind of pattern, with the same things cropping up again and again, but it seemed to Jane, floundering about among the books, that the question was not one that could be lightly dismissed now. 'No; thank you. I was just looking round,' was what one usually said. Just looking round the Anglican Church, from one extreme to the other, perhaps climbing higher and higher, peeping over the top to have a look at Rome on the other side, and then quickly drawing back.

'Thank you. I wanted some little books suitable for Confirmation candidates,' said Jane in a surprisingly firm and thoughtful tone. 'Not too High, you know.'

'I understand, madam,' said the assistant. 'I think you will probably find what you want on *this* table.'

Jane set to work with concentration and in ten minutes had chosen a number of little books and even a few early Christmas cards.

By now it was almost tea-time, but Jane, in her newly-acquired virtue, did not feel disposed to linger in Town, listening to the music at a Corner House or eating expensive cakes in the restaurant of one of the big stores. She would go without tea, as a kind of penance for all the times she had failed as a vicar's wife. Also, by catching a train now, she would avoid the rush-hour.

But at the junction where she had to change she found that she had some minutes to wait for a train, and decided that she had perhaps earned a cup of railway station tea and a bun.

She stood waiting in the orderly little queue, contemplating the window at the back of the counter, which had stained-glass panels showing a design of grapes. They imagined us drinking wine here, she thought, and longed to share her thought with somebody. She turned away to carry her cup to a table and there behind her in the queue was Edward Lyall.

'They imagined us drinking wine here,' she said, pointing to the grapes on the window. 'I was thinking of that when I saw you and wondered if anybody else had ever noticed it.'

'No, I can't say that I had,' Edward admitted.

'I don't suppose you often drink tea here,' said Jane. 'It seems unsuitable for you to be here now.'

'I often have a cup of tea while I'm waiting for a train.'

'You don't always drive down from London in your car, then?'

'Oh, no. I feel I ought to travel by train sometimes.'

'You mean you want to know what your constituents have to endure? The tea too weak or too strong, the stale sandwich, the grimy upholstery, the window that won't open, the waiting on the draughty platform . . .' Jane could have gone on indefinitely, feeling like one of our great modern poets, had not Edward interrupted her with an embarrassed laugh.

'You want to carry our burden as well as your own?' went on Jane relentlessly.

'Now you're making fun of me,' he said with a very sweet

smile. 'But at least let me carry your parcel. Look, here's the train.'

'I wasn't really making fun of you,' said Jane as they settled themselves in the carriage. 'I was seeing you as a human being for the first time.'

'Do I appear so unlike one, then?'

'It isn't your fault if you do. As Our Beloved Member you are naturally put on a pedestal, and when you come down it's a bit like a clergyman going into a pub wearing his clerical collar. You see what I mean?'

'One does want to get to know people,' said Edward. 'There is little opportunity for the sort of friendly conversation we are having now. It was very pleasant that Sunday afternoon at Fabian Driver's, wasn't it?'

'Ah, yes; tea under the walnut tree. How long ago it seems!'

'Your friend Miss Bates lives somewhere near Regent's Park, doesn't she?' Edward asked. 'I was wondering if I might run across her one day.'

'She has been on holiday,' said Jane, a sudden hope rising within her. 'But I expect she will be coming to stay with us again quite soon.'

'Then I shall look forward to meeting her again.'

They parted at the station, but Jane was a little absent-minded in her leave-taking, for she was full of a wonderful new idea. Edward and Prudence. . . . Why hadn't it occurred to her before? Prudence living at the Towers, a much more worthy setting for her than Fabian Driver's house. The sound of footsteps hurrying behind her and Edward's voice calling that she had forgotten her parcel broke into her dream.

'My parcel?' she said in a dazed voice. 'Why, of course! Thank you so much.' Her parcel, the proof of the good work she had done in the bookshop, nearly left behind, and all because she had been matchmaking again!

'Well, dear,' said Nicholas, appearing at the front door, 'how was Prudence?'

'Oh, *very* well,' said Jane enthusiastically. 'And look, I've remembered to get books for the Confirmation candidates. The assistant was so helpful.'

'Splendid, dear,' said Nicholas. 'And I'm glad Prudence isn't taking this business too much to heart.'

Jane looked at the clock in the hall. It said five-past six.

'Dear Prue,' she said. 'I suppose she will be waiting in the bus queue now, or going out somewhere with Conjunction of the Mind and Opposition of the Stars.'

But in this she was wrong, for at five minutes to six Prudence had received a summons to Arthur Grampian's room.

'Well, really, Miss Bates,' said Miss Clothier. 'I call that *most* inconsiderate. Whatever can he want at this time?'

'I should be inclined to go in wearing your hat and coat,' said Miss Trapnell. 'Then he will see that you are not to be trifled with.'

'I shall be quite firm,' said Prudence. 'In any case, I have an engagement this evening.'

'She and Mr. Manifold are going to the cinema,' said Miss Clothier to Miss Trapnell. 'I happen to know that.'

'I wonder if she has met his aunt yet?' asked Miss Trapnell in a tone full of meaning.

Prudence went to Arthur Grampian's room and looked in through the open door. He was sitting at his desk wearing an overcoat, although the gas-fire was full on and all the windows shut.

'Did you want me for something?' Prudence asked.

'Ah, Prudence' – he came towards her and took her hand – 'the melancholy mood is upon me this evening.'

'Is something the matter, then?'

'Not more than usual, but I have a desire for charming company. I hoped that you might be able to dine with me.' He looked at her intently, but could not see if there were tears in her eyes.

'I'm afraid I have an engagement this evening,' said Prudence firmly. 'You had better go and have dinner at your club. Perhaps we could go out some other time?'

She stooped to turn out the gas-fire and then began tidying his desk. Let him go among the bishops to-night, she thought, suddenly overwhelmed by the richness of her life. We have many more evenings before us if we want them.